Books by S

Historical Western Romance Series

MacLarens of Fire Mountain

Tougher than the Rest, Book One
Faster than the Rest, Book Two
Harder than the Rest, Book Three
Stronger than the Rest, Book Four
Deadlier than the Rest, Book Five
Wilder than the Rest, Book Six

Redemption Mountain

Redemption's Edge, Book One
Wildfire Creek, Book Two
Sunrise Ridge, Book Three
Dixie Moon, Book Four
Survivor Pass, Book Five
Promise Trail, Book Six
Deep River, Book Seven
Courage Canyon, Book Eight
Forsaken Falls, Book Nine, Coming next in the series!

MacLarens of Boundary Mountain

Colin's Quest, Book One,
Brodie's Gamble, Book Two
Quinn's Honor, Book Three
Sam's Legacy, Book Four
Heather's Choice, Book Five
Nate's Destiny, Book Six, Coming next in the series!

Contemporary Romance Series

MacLarens of Fire Mountain

Second Summer, Book One
Hard Landing, Book Two
One More Day, Book Three
All Your Nights, Book Four
Always Love You, Book Five
Hearts Don't Lie, Book Six
No Getting Over You, Book Seven
'Til the Sun Comes Up, Book Eight
Foolish Heart, Book Nine
Forever Love, Book Ten, Coming next in the series!

Peregrine Bay

Reclaiming Love, Book One, A Novella
Our Kind of Love, Book Two

Burnt River

Shane's Burden, Book One by Peggy Henderson
Thorn's Journey, Book Two by Shirleen Davies
Aqua's Achilles, Book Three by Kate Cambridge
Ashley's Hope, Book Four by Amelia Adams
Harpur's Secret, Book Five by Kay P. Dawson
Mason's Rescue, Book Six by Peggy L. Henderson
Del's Choice, Book Seven by Shirleen Davies
Watch for more books in this series!

Find all of my books at:
https://www.shirleendavies.com/books.html

The best way to stay in touch is to subscribe to my newsletter. Go to *www.shirleendavies.com* and subscribe in the box at the top of the right column that asks for your email. You'll be notified of new books before they are released, have chances to win great prizes, and receive other subscriber-only specials.

Heather's Choice

**MacLarens of Boundary Mountain
Historical Western Romance Series**

SHIRLEEN DAVIES

**Book Five in the MacLarens of
Boundary Mountain**

Historical Western Romance Series

For permission requests, contact the publisher.

Avalanche Ranch Press, LLC
PO Box 12618
Prescott, AZ 86304

Heather's Choice is a work of fiction. Names, characters, places, and incidents are either products of the author's imagination or used fictitiously. Any resemblance to actual events, locales, or persons, living or dead, is wholly coincidental.

Book conversions by Joseph Murray at 3rdplanetpublishing.com

Cover design by Kim Killion

ISBN: 978-1-941786-56-7

I care about quality, so if you find something in error, please contact me via email at
shirleen@shirleendavies.com

Description

Heather's Choice, Book Five, MacLarens of Boundary Mountain Historical Western Romance Series

What is a man to do when the woman he loves refuses to acknowledge his existence?

Caleb Stewart never forgot the girl he met on the wagon train west. When his family continued to Oregon, hers to California, he never expected to see her again. Years later, an unexpected invitation takes him south, to the Circle M ranch and right into the path of the girl he'd watched ride off in the back of a wagon years before.

Heather MacLaren loves nothing more than working on the family ranch. Men, emotions, and relationships hold little appeal, even when a young man from her past drifts back into her life, messing up her ordered existence and causing Heather to doubt everything she believes.

Caleb's work on the Circle M ranch is better than he'd ever allowed himself to dream. As a valued ranch hand, he's become the rare outsider the MacLarens have claimed as their own. His only disappointment is the young woman who's made it clear she'll never drop her defenses enough to share his feelings.

Facing a hard truth, Caleb is forced to make a tough decision.

First, he must help his adopted family eliminate a danger threatening to destroy not only Circle M but the entire MacLaren clan.

Heather has faced many challenges as the oldest female MacLaren cousin. But nothing prepares her for the savagery of the attacks against her family. Although they all stand together, there's one person she knows will always remain by her side. He's also the one man who has the ability to crush her spirit...and her heart.

Will fighting side-by-side to save the Circle M strengthen their bond? Or will it tear their tenuous relationship apart?

Heather's Choice, book five in the MacLarens of Boundary Mountain Historical Western Romance Series, is a stand-alone, full-length novel with an HEA and no cliffhanger.

Visit my website for a list of characters for each series.
https://www.shirleendavies.com/character-list.html

Acknowledgements

Many thanks to my husband, Richard, for always being by my side during this wonderful adventure. Your support, insights, and suggestions are greatly appreciated.

As always, many thanks to my editor, Kim Young, proofreader, Alicia Carmical, Joseph Murray, who is superb at formatting my books for print and electronic versions, my cover designer, Kim Killion.

Heather's Choice

Prologue

Wagon Train Heading West, 1859

Caleb Stewart kept his thoughts to himself as he walked beside his family's wagon, keeping the oxen moving. It wouldn't be long before the train split into two groups—one heading north to Oregon and Washington, the other continuing to California.

The Stewarts and MacGregors were part of the first group. The large MacLaren family and a few other wagons made up the second. How he wished he could be a part of those heading to California. Not because he dreamed of a life in the rapidly expanding state bordering the Pacific Ocean. His interest was more basic. Caleb fantasized about a life with a certain MacLaren girl, a union he knew his father would never allow.

At fifteen, Heather MacLaren was already a beauty with light brown hair, moss green eyes, and an attitude that warned most people off. Not Caleb. At seventeen, he'd known the moment he saw her he'd never find a better match.

His father, William, would think him delusional for even considering a marriage with Heather. Unlike the MacGregors and MacLarens, whose history of feuds was founded back in the old country, the Stewarts and MacLarens had been allies. It had been the Stewarts who'd come to their aid when the rivalry with the MacGregors had been at its height. Several generations later, his father didn't care about the alliance with the MacLarens.

William's ire had been focused on a newer rivalry, one emerging during the wagon train's journey west. It encompassed the four oldest MacLaren brothers—Angus, Gillis, Ewan, and Ian—with a particular loathing of Gillis, Heather's father.

Worse, Caleb knew it had nothing to do with anything except jealousy and greed. William hated the fact the MacLarens had been more successful than the Stewarts since both clans' arrival in the new world. It was ridiculous, petty, and malicious, but still a reality for his father, as tangible as the oxen who pulled their wagon.

"Caleb, you must keep the animals moving. You'll not be daydreaming today as you have every day since we left Independence." William sat atop the only horse the family owned, doing his best to appear more important than the other men. If only he knew how the others laughed behind his back. Not the MacLarens, though. From what Caleb could tell, they never spoke a word of derision about William. Instead, they ignored him, a fate worse than any spoken ridicule.

"Aye, Da." Caleb cringed at the brogue in his voice. He wasn't ashamed of his Scottish heritage. Instead, he held a particular pride in being an

American and all the opportunities available in their new country. He vowed to concentrate harder on removing the speech patterns of his father, the brogue that set him apart.

Although they'd spent almost no time together, Caleb had once confessed to Heather his desire to rid himself of the deeply ingrained burr. She'd laughed at him, calling him daft. Her ridicule had only served to intensify his resolve.

Glancing up, he looked into the wagon ahead of them in the line. Heather sat at the back, her legs dangling outside, unaware of him watching her. If she noticed, he had no doubt she'd shout at him to stop staring, alerting all the MacLarens to his interest.

"Caleb, I need you to help with the baby?"

His mother's voice pulled his gaze away from Heather before she noticed him. "Da wants me out here."

"Aye, I understand, but I'm needing you to hold the wee bairn for a bit while I check on your brother."

Caleb let out a frustrated breath as he climbed up to take his mother's seat in front, holding out his arms for his nine-month-old brother. He oftentimes felt more like a father to his two younger siblings than an older brother. The baby needed constant attention, and at six, his other brother carried little of the load. Caleb knew his work would increase once they reached Oregon.

"You'll not be letting your interest in the MacLaren girl show, Caleb." His mother glanced over her shoulder, her words startling him. Seeing the shock on his face, she smiled. "You didn't think anyone knew of your feelings, did you?"

"Nae, Ma."

"Does the lass know?"

"Nae, she doesn't."

"It is wise you haven't let her know. Your da won't be approving a union. You saw what happened when Colin MacLaren asked Dougal MacGregor for approval to wed Sarah. I'll not be watching the same happen to you."

Caleb nodded. Most of the camp had seen what transpired when Colin and his father, Angus, approached Dougal. The lad hadn't been able to hide his anger or his heartbreak at being rejected.

"I'll not be asking for anyone's hand, Ma. The lass is much too young."

"Your day will come, Caleb. Tomorrow, we will reach Fort Hall. The following morning, the MacLarens will depart for California while we take the trail to Oregon. It's best to put any thoughts of the lass out of your mind."

Holding the wagon lines in one hand, cradling his brother in the other, Caleb glanced at the back of the MacLaren wagon. Heather had disappeared, the flap now closed and tied.

His dreams would not be fulfilled this day, nor tomorrow, nor next year. It didn't mean he could never achieve them.

Caleb already knew the MacLarens purchased land in California, not far from the small town of Conviction. When his brothers were older, his commitment to his father fulfilled, he'd leave. His future wouldn't be determined by the prejudices of his father nor the dictates of others. Caleb's future, his dreams, were his to fulfill, even if they included a certain beautiful, young, and prickly MacLaren.

Chapter One

Music wafted into the still evening from the large community building in front of Heather MacLaren. Sucking in a shaky breath, she smoothed her hands down the dress her cousin, Jinny, had altered for her. She'd been a fool to attend the dance. It had been years since she'd made an appearance at the event celebrating the approaching summer, and months since she'd worn a dress in public.

"Don't just stand there, Heather. Let's get inside where everyone can get a look at you."

Heather's throat constricted. A week ago, she'd thought it a good idea to accompany Mildred Evanston, a widow and the owner of the ranch where she worked. Jinny, along with Heather's sister-in-law, Emma, had selected and altered a dress, made certain she remembered the dance lessons learned as a child, and showed her how to fix her hair.

They'd been excited to have her join them, and Heather had allowed their enthusiasm to shift to her. It was a mistake. She didn't belong here, had no business pretending she did.

"Nae, Mrs. Evanston. I'll not be going inside quite yet."

Mildred walked up to her, slipping an arm through Heather's. "Nonsense. You are a vision. Remaining outside a little longer won't change the impact you'll have on the men when you enter. Might as well get it over with, girl."

Arguing with her boss would serve no purpose except delaying the inevitable. Straightening, Heather accepted the fact she couldn't change the course of tonight's events. At this point, she could only hope not to humiliate herself more than necessary.

Walking up the steps, Heather pushed open the door of the building Conviction had built for dances, wedding celebrations, and town meetings. Following Mildred inside, she stopped, pushing aside the anxiety threatening to overwhelm her. She'd never seen the large room so crowded. Her gaze moved about, landing on Jinny and Emma, then moving to her brother, Quinn. Relief washed over Heather—an instant before she spotted Caleb Stewart next to them, his intense stare focused on her.

"Oh my. Look who's here." Emma's gaze focused on Heather and Mildred as they walked forward. Standing, she motioned them over.

Caleb's jaw slackened at the beauty coming toward him. Heather MacLaren turned heads as she strolled across the dance floor, unaware of the stir her presence caused. He'd never seen her in such a fashionable dress, light brown hair twisted into an intricate knot and highlighted with flowers, curled strands falling to her shoulders. He exhaled, the slow breath calming his racing heart. Without thought, his steps led him to meet her.

"Good evening, Heather." The slight catch in his voice surprised him. He'd been around Heather a good deal since following Colin and Sarah back to California from Oregon. She was still the most beautiful woman he'd ever met, and still the most frustrating. At twenty-one, she hadn't changed much from the feisty fifteen-year-old who'd first attracted him.

"Good evening, Caleb."

He noticed a slight blush creep up her face, briefly wondering at the cause before Heather continued.

"I believe you've met Mrs. Evanston."

"Of course. Good evening, Mrs. Evanston. You look beautiful tonight." He bowed at the waist, eliciting a chuckle from the older woman.

"Enough of that, young man. It's Heather who's beautiful."

Caleb swallowed the knot in his throat. "Yes, ma'am." He glanced at Heather, who averted her eyes, looking toward Emma and Jinny. "Please, let me escort you to our table." Standing between them, he placed his hands on his waist, waiting as they slipped their arms through his for the short walk to the table.

Caleb stood aside as Emma and Jinny greeted the women, hugging Heather. When they sat down, he turned, moving across the room toward a petite redhead.

"Good evening. I'm Caleb Stewart."

The young woman looked up at him, her lips turning up at the corners. "Miranda Harris."

"I don't believe I've seen you in town before tonight." He glanced at Heather, who leaned close to Jinny, deep in some private conversation.

"I'm visiting a family friend. August Fielder."

His eyes widened a little.

"Ah, I see you know him."

Caleb nodded. "Not well, but he is a prominent citizen in Conviction and a partner with the MacLarens."

She cocked her head. "You know the MacLarens?"

"I do. Would you like me to introduce you to them?" He inclined his head in the direction of their tables.

Miranda followed his gaze before shaking her head. "Not right now. I'm enjoying the music too much." Again, she looked up at him, this time with unconcealed interest.

"Would you care to dance?"

"I'd love to, Mr. Stewart."

Leading her onto the dance floor, Caleb did his best to keep his mind off Heather, knowing the attempt was futile. He concentrated on the attractive woman in front of him. Looking down, he caught a glimpse of her pretty blue eyes, noticing the sprinkling of freckles across her nose.

"You said Mr. Fielder is a family friend."

"Well, he and my father have known each other since they were boys. They attended law school together. I've actually only met him a few times."

Caleb lifted a brow. "Yet you traveled out here alone, to stay with him."

"Oh, I didn't travel alone. I came out with my aunt and uncle, who are also friends with August." She nodded toward a table where Fielder sat with a couple he didn't recognize. "They're over there."

"How long will you be staying?"

"Not long. Perhaps another two weeks, then we'll go back. Now, tell me about yourself, Mr. Stewart."

Heather tried to keep her attention on Jinny and their conversation, finding it hard as she watched Caleb on the dance floor. She knew her cousin still hurt from the abrupt departure of Sam Covington, one of Conviction's deputies and the man Jinny had fallen in love with. She felt a stab of guilt for not being a better friend.

At first, Heather had found a sense of peace at being away from the boisterous MacLaren clan. After her time away, it surprised her how much she missed her family and those they'd accepted into their family, such as Caleb.

To her surprise, she missed his superior attitude, the way he'd let her make mistakes without teasing her, unlike her brothers and male cousins. Most of all, she missed the smoldering glances he tried to hide.

Jinny's voice drew her attention. "I wish you'd come home more, Heather. Everyone misses you."

She gave little protest. "I do come for Sunday supper." Her gaze wandered to Caleb again, who hadn't left the dance floor. By her count, this was his third dance with the redhead. "Who is Caleb dancing with?"

Jinny looked around. "From what I've heard, she's visiting August Fielder with her aunt and uncle. I can't remember her name, but I'm sure Caleb can tell you once he comes back to the table." Jinny's voice held enough humor to let Heather know she wasn't fooling her cousin. "The lad's been an eejit about you since traveling here from Oregon, Heather. Sarah thinks he fancied you on the wagon trip west."

Heather's eyes widened. "I doubt that's so."

"Aye, that's what Sarah believes. You'll be dancing with him if he asks, won't you?"

Heather hesitated, insecurity clear on her face as she bit her lower lip. "I'd hoped *no one* would ask me."

"Nae, you'll be on the dance floor before long." Jinny hid a smile, getting the attention of a man a couple tables away.

"What are you doing?" Heather hissed out before standing.

"Shhh." Jinny stood, ignoring her cousin's glaring stare as Deke approached. "Heather, I'd like to introduce Deke Arrington, Mr. Ferguson's nephew. Mr. Arrington, this is my cousin, Miss Heather MacLaren."

"It's a pleasure, Miss MacLaren. Would you care to dance?"

Heather turned to Jinny, giving her a scalding look before looking back at Deke. "Aye, Mr. Arrington. I'd love to dance with you."

Caleb returned Miranda to her table, noting her aunt and uncle were no longer seated with Fielder.

"Caleb, I see you've met Miss Harris."

"Yes, sir." He glanced at Miranda. "She's endured my presence for several dances."

12

Miranda smiled. "Oh, it was my pleasure, Mr. Stewart."

"If you'll excuse me, I'll leave you to enjoy the festivities." Caleb nodded, then turned away, walking toward Brodie and Quinn MacLaren across the room. "Gentlemen."

"I see you've met the lovely Miss Harris." Brodie, Conviction's sheriff and Jinny's older brother, lifted his glass, tilting it toward Fielder's table.

Caleb nodded. "She seems a nice enough young lady."

Quinn scratched his chin, ignoring the discussion of Miranda. "Do either of you recognize the man talking with Uncle Ian?"

Brodie and Caleb looked across the room, seeing a man of medium height, dressed all in black, talking with the younger of the two surviving MacLaren elders. His clothes were made of fine cloth, the vest of black brocade with silver threads, his boots polished to a high gloss. The deep red handkerchief in his pocket matched the color of his hair and beard.

Caleb shook his head. "I've never seen him before."

"Nae," Brodie chuckled. "I believe I'd remember a man with such a striking appearance."

Quinn shook his head, his gaze narrowing on the man. "There's something about him that's familiar."

Brodie looked between Quinn and Caleb. "I'm thinking it's time we introduce ourselves to him."

Making their way across the room, Caleb let his gaze return to Heather, who danced with a man he didn't recognize. "Who's Heather dancing with?"

"Deke Arrington. He works for his uncle, Rube Ferguson, who owns the saddlery," Brodie explained. "Why don't you ask her to dance?"

Caleb choked out a laugh. "You know as well as I do she'd turn me down."

Brodie clasped him on the shoulder as they joined Ian. "Perhaps. But you'll never know until you ask."

"Good evening, lads." Ian shook each of their hands before turning to the man next to him. "I don't believe you've met Mr. Giles Delacroix. Giles, these are my nephews, Brodie and Quinn, and a family friend, Caleb Stewart."

Brodie stuck out his hand. "Mr. Delacroix. What brings you to Conviction?"

Ian chuckled. "You'll have to excuse my nephew, Giles. Brodie is our sheriff, and quite a good one."

Accepting Brodie's hand, Giles studied him for an instant. "It's the job of the sheriff to know who comes and goes from his town. To answer your question, I have business in Conviction. I'm on the board of the San Francisco Merchant Bank. We opened an office here a few months ago."

Quinn stiffened at the words. He still couldn't remember meeting the man, but he certainly recognized the name of the bank. Its manager had disappeared several months before, under strange circumstances, after denying loan extensions to several ranchers. It had happened before he married Emma, when Quinn had been working as foreman on her parents' ranch.

Brodie nodded. "Aye. Your employee, Chester Bailey, left town suddenly. Then your manager, Deegan James, quit."

Giles shook his head. "A tragedy took him away."

"He'll not be returning?"

"It's quite doubtful, Sheriff. We sent another fellow from San Francisco to manage the office. He may be a little inexperienced, but I'm sure he'll serve the bank, and your town, well."

Quinn shifted his stance, his gut telling him something didn't feel right. "Do you intend to continue supporting the ranchers in the area, Mr. Delacroix?"

"Quinn MacLaren, is it?" Giles asked as he studied the young cowboy.

"Aye, sir."

"Well, it's understandable you'd be concerned about the way my bank deals with ranchers. From what Ian has said, your family's ranch is quite solvent, not at all in need of additional funds."

"Aye...for now. The cattle and horse businesses are dependent on orders from our buyers. I'll not be lying to you about the uncertainty in ranching. Small changes in price make a big difference to a spread our size."

Giles studied Quinn, wondering if all the MacLarens were as astute at the business side of ranching. Most meant only to get by, feed their families, pass along their ranch when they died. The MacLarens were a different breed. He made a mental note to learn as much about the family, and their operation, as possible.

"I must say, I'm not as familiar with the running of a ranch as I am with merchants and the shipping business. I'll need to make certain our manager understands your needs. Even better, I'd suggest we plan to meet before I leave for San Francisco." He looked at Ian. "Let me know how many you'd like to have at the meeting and I'll make all the arrangements."

"Aye. It's a good idea for you and your managers to meet with us. I'll not be giving you false hope, though. The MacLarens have done business with the Bank of Conviction for years."

Giles nodded. "Ah, yes. The small bank controlled by August Fielder."

Delacroix's stance and demeaning tone had more than one of the men bristling.

Ian gritted his teeth, forcing out a smooth reply. "He may control the shares, but the man is more than fair in his dealings. My brother, Ewan, and I sit on the board, along with several others. No matter the shares, each member has an equal vote on bank matters."

Giles stroked his chin, considering this information. His bank worked in a different fashion. Although the board voted, the two prominent families who held the majority ownership ran the bank like their personal money machine. Out of twelve board seats, four were held by members of the families. The other eight were held by close personal friends and the bank's attorney. There was little room for dissenting views as there seemed to be at the local bank.

Ian set his glass down, crossing his arms. "We're a small community, Mr. Delacroix. We know the people, their hardships, and their needs. Unlike many big city banks, our goal is to help our neighbors through hard times."

"Not jump on any chance to foreclose on the properties," Quinn interjected, recalling the difficult times faced by his wife's parents. Much of it due to the way the San Francisco bank dealt with them.

Ian glanced at his nephew, then back at Delacroix. "As you can see, Giles, our family has been raised to speak their minds. Quinn makes a good point. There are some who will never deal with your bank due to some unfortunate circumstances when Chester Bailey disappeared."

"I'd like a chance to turn the town's opinion around, Ian. Don't you agree a meeting will give us a chance to start the process?"

Ian nodded. "Aye. It will be a start."

Brodie held out his hand to Giles. "If you'll excuse me, I believe my wife has been waiting long enough for the dance I promised her. I'll look forward to the meeting."

"As will I, Sheriff." Giles glanced at Ian. "About how many people do you expect to bring?"

"At least fourteen." Ian nodded at Caleb, letting him know he'd be included.

Giles chuckled. "Well, that is a goodly number."

"Aye, and I'll be warning you. We'll be bringing some of the MacLaren women. You best be prepared."

"I'm sorry, Heather. I'd hoped Caleb would ask you to dance." Jinny slipped her arm through her cousin's as they walked outside.

"Nae. It's best he didn't." Heather took one more glance across the room, seeing Caleb speaking with the young woman from back east. The one he'd danced with several times, while ignoring her. She didn't realize her disappointment would be so acute.

"Aye. You probably would've turned him down."

Heather nodded, although she wasn't so certain. "Well, I've done my duty and accompanied Mrs. Evanston to the dance. I won't be doing this again for a long time."

Jinny shook her head. "Just because Caleb is an eejit doesn't mean you should go back into hiding."

Heather chuckled, the sound falling flat. "Aye, the lad is an eejit and always has been. Obnoxious and condescending, as are most of the MacLaren men."

Jinny looked at her. "But he's not a MacLaren."

"Aye, he is in spirit, if not name." They walked to the wagon, seeing Mildred waiting for them. "I've more than enough work at the Evanston ranch to keep me busy. If I never see Caleb Stewart again, I'll consider myself blessed."

Jinny bit her lip. Someday, Heather and Caleb would come to their senses, confronting the feelings between them. It could be weeks or months, but the reckoning would come. Jinny was certain of it.

Chapter Two

Circle M Ranch
Several months later

"You've been a wonderful help, Heather. I don't know what I would've done without you." Mildred Evanston stood next to the wagon loaded with what remained of her personal belongings. Health and age had forced her to make the hard decision to sell her ranch. The bright spot in the difficult process had been August Fielder and the MacLarens buying the property. She knew they'd continue to make a success of the ranch she and her late husband had started.

Heather's eyes teared, the strong emotions catching her off guard. She'd come to love the widow, and although she understood the reasons for her leaving, hated to see her go. "Are you sure you want to live in San Francisco? Wouldn't you rather find a place in town where you'd be close?"

Mildred raised her chin, taking another look at the home her husband had built. "No. I've made up my mind. My sister-in-law and her husband live there and have plenty of room for me. Remember, San Francisco isn't so far away. I'm still fit enough to ride or take the stagecoach, so you won't be getting rid of me completely. Besides, it's time for new blood.

I think Ewan and Ian made the right decision, making Caleb foreman." She patted Heather's arm. "I know you wanted it, but you've still got much to learn. Working with Colin and Quinn at Circle M is the perfect solution."

Heather shook her head. "Nae. I'm fine with their decision. Caleb will be a fine foreman, and it's time I returned to my family, although working under Quinn will be a challenge."

Throwing back her head, Mildred laughed. "You're a strong woman, Heather. You'll set your brother straight in no time. Just watch your temper and lace your words with honey...not vinegar."

Heather drew in a slow breath. She'd heard the widow say the same so many times, it finally seemed to take a place in her mind. At least she hoped it had. "Aye. I'll remember."

"When do you go back to Circle M?" Mildred climbed aboard the wagon, waving a dismissive hand at Heather when she tried to help.

"Today. Caleb and Blaine will be here this afternoon. I'll leave soon after they arrive."

Picking up the wagon lines, Mildred glanced around, her gaze landing on Heather. "It would do well for you to stay until tomorrow. Show Caleb and Blaine around. Introduce them to the two ranch hands who are staying."

Heather clasped her hands together, staring down at her muddy boots. "I do wish Levi had stayed."

"I know you do, girl. Ewan and Ian wanted him to stay. They even offered him a higher wage and the choice of working anywhere on their land." Mildred leaned back, letting the lines rest in her hands. "Levi needed time away."

"He told me he planned to travel south, along the ocean, until the point where California touches Mexico." Heather thought of the Evanston's longtime foreman. Levi had been hired by Mildred's husband as a young man in his twenties. He stayed for more than twenty years, through good times and bad, taken less pay while doing more work, and became a good friend of the couple.

When Heather arrived at the ranch, Levi ignored her initial antagonism, was amused at her combative nature, and allowed her to voice the pain she'd held close inside. Levi encouraged her to speak of her father, Gillis, and how much she missed him after he and her uncle, Angus, had been murdered. In some ways, he became the father she'd lost. His departure had cut deeply.

Straightening her back, Mildred once again held the lines in a firm grip. "He may return someday, Heather. Levi still has many friends in Conviction. Perhaps he'll change his mind and accept a job with your family."

"Aye, perhaps you are right." A slight smile touched Heather's lips. "I'll be doing my best to think good thoughts, even as I try to keep my temper under control when working with Quinn."

"You do that and you'll be fine. It's time for me to start for town and leave you to the rest of today's chores."

Heather stepped up to the wagon. "Send me an address once you get settled in San Francisco."

Mildred nodded. "And you'll write back about what's going on here?"

"I promise." Ignoring the lump in her throat, Heather did her best to hide the tears threatening to spill. The widow had become dear to her in a short time and she'd be missed.

Without another word, Mildred nodded, slapping the lines to get the wagon moving.

"Are you ready?" Blaine held his horse steady as Caleb mounted Jupiter.

"I am."

Colin walked up, stroking a hand down the neck of Caleb's horse. "Make a list of what is needed at the new place. If we don't have enough here, we'll send men into town."

Blaine nodded at his older brother. "Aye, Colin. We'll need a few days to see what's needed and learn the property."

Stepping away from Jupiter, Colin looked between his brother and Caleb. "Ask Heather to stay a few days longer. She knows the condition of the ranch."

"Not necessary. Blaine and I can handle it without her. The sooner she leaves, the sooner she'll be here to help you and Quinn."

Colin shook his head. As the oldest MacLaren cousin, he'd known Caleb since they'd traveled west in the wagon train, watched as the sparks flew between him and Heather, and saw Caleb's feelings for her fade as she continued to treat him as no more than a friend.

"If the lass is a distraction, send her back this afternoon."

Blaine laughed. "Ach. The lass is always a distraction, Colin."

"Aye. Most times I would agree with you." Colin glanced at Caleb, seeing his features still.

Caleb couldn't find it in him to join their bantering. He knew they loved their cousin and wanted only the best for her, but his chest still constricted whenever she entered his mind. A sudden urge to leave gripped him.

Reining Jupiter around, he looked at the brothers. "If you two are finished, it's time Blaine and

I got moving." He didn't wait for Blaine before kicking his horse into a lope, preparing his mind to see Heather after months of keeping his distance.

The last time he'd been in the same place with her for more than a few minutes was at the community dance. She'd walked into the room a vision, taking his breath away. Twice he'd tried to get close, wanting to ask her for a dance. Each time, she'd turned away, feigning interest in a conversation with whoever stood close. He'd known her actions were not by accident.

His evening had been saved by meeting Miranda Harris. She wasn't Heather, but her eager attention, easy laugh, and enchanting banter kept his mind off the woman he wanted. A few days after the dance, Miranda returned home. The evening was a turning point for him.

Caleb had loved Heather for a long time, having no indication she felt the same. At least he'd never declared his feelings aloud, humiliating himself in front of the family he now regarded as his own. It had taken a while, but after the dance, he'd made the hard decision to let her go.

Since then, he'd worked the northern lands purchased from Juan Estrada, returning to the main house only when summoned, and avoiding Sunday suppers. He'd heard from her brothers and cousins that Heather began returning to see her mother, Audrey, more often, sometimes riding over on

Sunday morning and staying until Tuesday before returning to the Evanston ranch. It was during this time Mildred had spoken with August Fielder and the MacLarens about selling. It hadn't taken long to reach an agreement.

"It still surprises me Heather made no issue of you being made foreman."

Caleb startled, so lost in his own thoughts he'd forgotten Blaine rode beside him. "She handled it well when Ewan announced it."

"Aye, in front of the family. We'll see how the lass does today when it's just the three of us."

Caleb had already considered how she'd act when she saw him ride up. "She's been coming back to the ranch for a while now. Has she ever mentioned any displeasure at the decision?"

Blaine rubbed the back of his neck, then shook his head. "Nae. Other than asking a few questions of Colin and Quinn about what she'll be doing, the lass has remained silent on it. You know, lad, it hasn't gone unnoticed you've been making yourself absent from family suppers."

"Ian and Ewan know my reasons. There's been much work at the northern property and few extra men to help."

"So it has nothing to do with a certain lass?"

Caleb narrowed his gaze at him. "Even if I had an interest in one, when would I have time for a woman?"

Blaine grinned. "I'm believing you'd have time if she were close by."

Nostrils flaring as his irritation grew, Caleb reined to a stop. "If you've something to say, Blaine, say it plainly."

Studying his friend's face, Blaine shook his head. "I mean nothing by my jesting. The constant arguing between you and Heather had us all believing there were feelings between you two."

Caleb snorted. "There aren't."

Blaine nodded. "Aye. I can see the lack of it on your face."

"We'll be there in another mile. I want to send Heather back to Circle M today. Are we agreed?"

"Aye, Caleb, we are."

His shoulders relaxing in relief, Caleb nodded before guiding Jupiter along the trail.

Heather set down the pitchfork, swiping an arm across her forehead. The cool breeze of fall did nothing to stop the heat of cleaning the stalls. Looking around, she felt a slight thrill at one more chore completed.

For some strange reason, surprising Caleb with the sound condition of the ranch meant something. After all these months of not being around him, she hated to think his approval meant anything, yet it did.

It had been Levi Abrams who'd broken through her defenses, convincing Heather her hidden feelings for Caleb weren't something to be ashamed of or tuck away in some private place. Neither would they hinder her ability to ride beside him. She'd always seen Caleb as a rival, someone who would take away a position on the ranch she'd earned by competing against her brothers and cousins. Levi had turned her thinking around. Him and Mildred Evanston.

Heather had never known the older woman's husband beyond a mere greeting in town. She knew nothing of the couple's life together, or how they'd ridden side by side as they built their ranch into a success. Learning of their shared history had come after many nights of sitting on the porch next to Mildred, sharing stories about their families.

To Heather's surprise, Mildred had been able to combine her love of riding and the ranch with her role as a wife, never seeing any conflict between the two. She'd helped Heather see the MacLaren women, including her mother, Audrey, differently. They all had a role, a place in the family where their talents were needed and appreciated. Over time, she'd convinced Heather she could be both—an accomplished ranch hand and a wife—if she ever chose to take on both roles.

Levi helped her with the first and Mildred with the second, something Heather never allowed her family to do. Instead of feeling trapped, it freed her to consider a life she'd never considered. One including Caleb, if it wasn't too late.

The revelation had come a few weeks before the community dance. She'd almost reneged several times about accompanying Mildred. In the end, she'd sought help from Jinny and Emma, determined to take a step toward bringing Caleb back into her life. She'd pushed him away for far too long. The time had come to discover if they could build anything together.

Instead of achieving her goal, she'd watched, her heart sinking, as he gave all his attention to a woman Heather didn't know. Pretty, petite, with a bright smile, she'd sparked something in Caleb even Heather could detect from across the room.

Learning the young woman had returned home a few days after the dance, Heather had allowed herself to hope Caleb would once again notice her. She'd returned to the ranch more often, hoping for time with him after Sunday suppers. Instead, he'd stayed away, choosing to eat his meals alone rather than share a table with her.

The sale of the Evanston ranch gave Heather hope Caleb would see her for what she'd become, not what she was when she'd continued to spurn him.

The sound of horses drew her attention to the trail from the north—the one used by the MacLarens when they rode onto Evanston lands. Her heart sputtered and her chest tightened seeing Caleb ride up with Blaine.

Caleb drew in a shaky breath at the sight of Heather standing outside the barn—dirty, sweaty, and still the most beautiful woman he'd ever seen. Reining Jupiter to a stop, he slid to the ground.

"Good morning, Heather." Walking toward her, he noticed a slight twitch to her lips before she nodded.

"And to you, Caleb. You're here earlier than I expected."

Looking from the barn to the house, he nodded. "Blaine and I decided to get an early start. Is Mrs. Evanston around?"

"No. She left just after sunrise." She glanced over her shoulder to see her cousin walk up.

"Morning, lass. Did Widow Evanston leave you alone with the chores?"

"We've two other men. They rode off after loading the wagon for her trip to town."

"Where to?" Caleb asked, continuing his scrutiny of the ranch.

"They're checking the herd in the farthest pasture south of here. That left me to do what was needed here." She glanced down at her dirty pants and winced. Caleb had seen her a hundred times in pants and a man's shirt. It didn't seem to matter. His gaze hadn't spent more than two seconds on her since he arrived.

Caleb finished his perusal of the surrounding area, focusing his attention on her. "How much more until you've finished?"

She tilted her head to the side. "Finished?"

"Your chores."

"Oh, well...I suppose I'm finished for now. I usually help Mildred start the midday meal about now, but I can show you two around, if you're ready."

Caleb glanced at Blaine, who looked away, offering no support. Crossing his arms, he looked at her. "No need. We can take care of our own food and seeing the ranch." He saw her face fall, bright eyes pale, and felt a pang of guilt. It had been his decision to send her back so soon. His request had obviously been a surprise. "Fact is, Colin asked us to send you back right away."

Her gaze shifted to Blaine, who ignored the disappointed look. "I'll, uh...be watering the horses."

"No, I'll do it. You help Heather get her belongings together."

Her jaw tightened at the clear dismissal. "I'll be needing neither of your help. It won't take long, then

I'll be off the ranch." She lifted her chin, refusing to look at either one as she turned toward the house.

When she'd disappeared inside, the door slamming shut behind her, Blaine walked up to Caleb, shoving his shoulder.

"There was no need to treat the lass so poorly. I'll not be ignoring your rude behavior a second time. Do you understand?"

Caleb wrenched off his hat, threading fingers through his overly long, dark hair. Blaine was tall and strong, with a reputation for being a jokester, unless provoked. At just over six feet tall with broad shoulders and muscles from years of working on ranches, Caleb knew a fight with Blaine would be a mistake. Slamming his hat back on his head, he fisted his hands at his sides.

"Yes, I understand."

Blaine's eyes still held a hard glint as he held out the reins. "You take care of the horses. I'll see to Heather." Storming off, he glanced over his shoulder. "And if you're knowing what's best for you, you'll stay away until she leaves."

Caleb nodded. He'd been a horse's arse with no good reason for his behavior. Heather had done nothing except explain her chores and offer to make them dinner, not once showing the attitude he'd come to expect. His only excuse had been the way her green eyes sparkled with unguarded warmth when he'd walked up. Her reaction had caught him by surprise, making him wish for things she'd never willingly give. All he could think about was calming his raging desire by driving her away.

Stalking toward the barn, he turned at the sound of the door slamming a second time. Blaine would take care of smoothing over the tension Caleb had caused. He'd help her pack and see her off while Caleb hid in the silence of the barn, waiting for a sense of peace.

Chapter Three

"He's such an arse, Blaine." Heather threw some clothes at a satchel, ignoring the fact they slid to the floor.

"Aye, he can be, lass." Picking them up, Blaine rolled them before placing them into the satchel. "He's a lot on his mind."

Rounding on him, she crossed her arms. "Well, he'll not be taking his temper out on me. I'm glad to be leaving."

Blaine nodded, his lips in a grim smile. "Being back home will do you good. Aunt Audrey misses you." He picked up another piece of clothing, adding it to those already packed.

"Aye. Anywhere will be better than here."

He shook his head, wanting her to continue until her anger had all been spent. "Colin and Quinn have a good list of work for you to do. You might be wanting to prepare yourself."

"I'll not be needing to prepare. I'm used to hard work and lots of it. When Levi left a few weeks ago, I took on most of his chores while Mildred worked with the men." She thought again of the widow and the ex-foreman, her anger beginning to wane. She looked at Blaine. "Levi and Mrs. Evanston were good to me."

Blaine pursed his lips, nodding. "I'm certain they were, lass."

She pulled three dresses from the wardrobe, glancing up in time to see Blaine's eyes widen. "What is it?"

Not wanting to restore her anger, he shrugged. "I've not seen those before. Did Widow Evanston make them for you?"

Walking to the bed, she carefully laid each down. "Jinny altered this one for the community dance. I made the others."

Blaine caught himself before he blurted out something that would reignite her temper. "I'd not heard you'd learned to sew. Aunt Audrey said you hated making your own clothes."

Focusing on folding each dress and slipping them carefully into the satchel, she kept her gaze averted. "Mrs. Evanston taught me. She said I could be the best ranch hand around during the day, but in the evening, I needed to show everyone I was also a lady." Settling her hands on the rim of the satchel, she looked at him. "Do you think I can be a lady, Blaine?"

His mouth opened for a quick response, then closed as he thought through his answer. She'd already been cast off by Caleb this morning. Blaine had no desire to build upon what he'd done.

"Of course you can, lass. You've many MacLaren women to learn from, and if the community dance was an example, you've already shown yourself a lady."

Walking to the window, she pulled back the curtains, looking down at the barn. "No matter how hard I try, some will never see me as a lady."

Understanding gripped Blaine. Stepping beside her, he rested a hand on her shoulder. "Then whoever the lad is, he's daft. You'll not be wasting your time on lads such as that."

A self-deprecating laugh escaped. "It seems I'll not be wasting my time on *any* lad. I'm twenty-one and have never even been kissed."

Blaine held up his hands, stepping away. "You'll not be saying any more to me, Heather."

Settling her hands on her hips, she glared at him. "We all know the MacLaren men visit the *ladies* of Buckie's Castle when they want to be schooled."

Blaine took another step away. "Heather..."

"Don't you be trying to correct me. It's no secret each one of the lads has spent time with Gwen—"

Blaine cut her off. "That's enough, lass. We'll not be speaking of such things. Gwen is a fine woman with a hard past. Besides, she left the saloon months ago to help Doc Vickery."

Dropping her arms to her sides, she turned away, her gaze returning to the barn. Letting out a breath, she looked back at Blaine, her voice low but strong. "Did he ever visit Gwen?"

Blaine shook his head, knowing who she asked about. "I'll not be answering such a question, lass. What Caleb does is his business, not mine...or yours."

Studying the firm set of his jaw, the way his gaze didn't meet hers, she shrugged. "Which means he's been with her."

Blaine didn't answer this time, knowing she'd only continue with her questions.

"Women have no such tutor," she said, almost to herself.

Scrubbing a hand down his face, he looked at the satchel. "Do you have more?"

Shaking her head, she looked down at the dirty clothes. It didn't matter if she wore them back to Circle M or not. No one there would expect her to arrive in anything else.

"Nae. I've no more."

"I'll be meeting you downstairs then. Do you need me to saddle Shamrock?"

"Nae. I'll be saddling her myself. I'd be grateful if Caleb was out of the barn when I come down."

"Aye. I'll be letting him know."

Heather stayed in the room a few minutes longer, accepting this was the last time she'd find comfort within these four walls. The decision had been made and she'd abide by it. After Caleb's words this morning, she no longer wanted to stay. He'd made his thoughts clear. No longer did he feel anything for her, other than perhaps a small measure of friendship. It truly was time to turn away and move on.

Circle M

"Did you hear we have a new schoolteacher?" Sarah kept watch on little Grant as she helped the other women prepare Sunday supper.

Heather looked at Sarah from her spot at the stove. "Nae. What do you know of her?"

"Little, I'm afraid. Jinny said she came from somewhere back east at the recommendation of August Fielder. I think her name is Miranda."

Sucking in a slow breath, Heather pushed aside the unease at a name she'd heard months before. Rocking back on her heels, she looked down at Grant, who sat at Sarah's feet. Soon, he'd be walking, then they'd all need to keep watch of his actions.

"When Jinny arrives, we'll ask her what else she knows of the new teacher." Sarah bent down next to Grant, wiping his face with a damp cloth.

Heather didn't need to learn more about the woman Caleb had paid considerable attention to at the community dance. She wondered if he'd already learned of her return to Conviction.

Sarah looked over at Heather. "And there is other news. August Fielder has accepted a partner into his

38

law firm. I believe Ma and Aunt Audrey invited them both to supper tonight."

"Are you thinking Mr. Fielder will be bringing the new schoolteacher?" Heather continued her work at the stove, doing her best to feign indifference.

Sarah shrugged, ignorant as to the real purpose of Heather's question. "Perhaps. Either way, we have plenty of food."

Chuckling, Heather nodded. "Aye. We've always plenty."

"Ach. The weather is turning colder with each passing hour." Jinny came through the kitchen doorway, setting a bowl on the table. Her mother, Lorna, and Emma followed right behind, placing bowls of their own alongside Jinny's. "Heather, did Sarah mention August Fielder and his guest will be joining us for supper?"

"Aye, just now. She also talked of a new schoolteacher. Do you know her?"

Jinny retied her apron, taking stock of the food on the table. "Aye. I met her at the community dance last spring. Her name is Miranda Harris."

Lorna moved next to Sarah, then bent to lift Grant into her arms. "I heard she is staying at the boardinghouse until the house provided by the town is ready."

Sarah looked at Lorna. "Then she'll be joining us tonight?"

"Aye, I would expect it."

Emma filled a pot with water, glancing over her shoulder. "As I recall, Caleb spent considerable time with her at the dance."

No one noticed the way Heather's shoulders slumped at the comment. She'd been back a couple weeks. In that time, she'd stayed busy working with Colin and Quinn, doing all they asked without complaint. When the work had been completed, she'd joined her mother in the house, helping to prepare supper, the same as she'd done with Mildred.

Caleb hadn't appeared during her time back. No one expected him tonight, for which she was grateful. It would give her a chance to study the woman who'd held his interest and changed the direction of Heather's life.

"We're so glad you could join us tonight, Mr. Fielder." Colin's mother, Kyla, held the front door open, gesturing for August and his guests to enter.

Bending, he placed a chaste kiss on her cheek. "We've known each other a good deal of time. I believe it is time you called me August."

"Aye, as long as you call me Kyla."

"Done." Turning, he nodded toward the two people behind him. "I don't believe you had a chance to meet Miss Harris at the dance last spring. Kyla, this is Miranda Harris, our newest schoolteacher.

Next to her is my new partner, Bayard Donahue. Miranda and Bay, Mrs. Kyla MacLaren."

After greetings were exchanged, Kyla stood aside, ushering them into the large front room. "Everyone, August Fielder has arrived with his guests, Miranda Harris and Bayard Donahue. Please make them feel welcome."

Heather watched from the dining room, unable to pull her gaze from Miranda. To her disappointment, the young woman was every bit as stunning as she'd been at the dance. Walking toward her, Heather noticed how petite she was, with silky red hair and clear blue eyes. At the dance, she hadn't seen the sprinkling of freckles across the young woman's nose.

"Miss Harris?"

Miranda turned, offering a broad smile. "Yes?"

"I'm Heather MacLaren."

"It's such a pleasure to meet you." Miranda didn't make eye contact, instead focusing her gaze around the room. "There are so many MacLarens. It will be difficult to keep you all straight."

She still hadn't acknowledged Heather with more than words.

"Is there someone in particular you're looking for, Miss Harris? Perhaps I can help."

Miranda's startled gaze whipped to Heather, a slight blush creeping up her face. "Well, I am looking for a gentleman I met at the dance when I was here last spring."

Heather steeled her features, knowing the name Miranda would speak.

"Caleb Stewart. Do you know him?"

"Aye. He's our foreman at the ranch we purchased south of here." Heather should've continued, telling Miranda not to expect him. Instead, she let the young woman continue her hopeful search. "He's not appeared for Sunday supper in quite a while."

"Oh. I'd so hoped to see him again."

Heather felt a tinge of guilt at Miranda's obvious disappointment. It wasn't her fault Heather hadn't come to her senses about Caleb sooner. "You're welcome to sit next to me at supper. I'd love to hear of your life back east."

Miranda fidgeted with the sleeve of her dress, then let out a breath. "Thank you, Miss MacLaren. That would be lovely."

"I don't believe we've met." Bay walked up, nodding at Miranda while focusing his attention on the woman beside her.

Heather glanced at the man who'd arrived with Miranda and August, taking a good look at him for the first time.

"Nae, we haven't."

"Bayard Donahue." He made a slight bow, his eyes never leaving hers.

"Heather MacLaren, Mr. Donahue."

"It's a pleasure, Miss MacLaren. I hope it isn't rude of me to ask, but are you married to a MacLaren?"

Heather laughed, her eyes dancing. "Nae, Mr. Donahue. I'm afraid I was born into this unruly clan. Quinn is my brother."

Bay looked around the room. "Only one sibling, Miss MacLaren?"

"Nae. I've four others. Bram is over there talking with our cousin, Camden."

Bay nodded. "Yes, I've met both of them."

"Thane will be staying in the barn with one of the heifers who's ready to calve. The two youngest, Lara and Bryce, are playing with their cousins. They'll be having supper at Aunt Lorna and Uncle Ewan's home."

"I see. Colin mentioned your aunt and uncle would be arriving a little late. So, do you live on the ranch or in town, Miss MacLaren?"

She bit her lip, clasping her hands together. "At the ranch. I work with Colin and Quinn."

A smile split Bay's face. "You appear to be the kind of woman who enjoys being outside. Do you work with the cattle or horses?"

His quick acceptance of her role at the ranch surprised her. "The cattle. Emma, Quinn's wife, works with the horses."

Miranda snickered. "It must be challenging working with your family all day, then coming in to have supper with them."

"Aye, some days are more difficult than others. I'd be wishing it no other way, though."

Patting her hair, Miranda's mouth tilted up at the corners. "My family would never be able to do it. We love each other, but we're constantly at odds. My parents expect little of me, except to marry and have children."

Bay shifted a little toward her. "Yet they allowed you to come west to teach."

Chuckling, Miranda shook her head. "They grew tired of my badgering them, Mr. Donahue. I assure you, it was no easy task getting them to agree with my decision. In the end, they gave up rather than continue to fight me on it."

"Do you have siblings, Miss Harris?"

Any sign of humor left her face, her eyes clouding. "I have an older brother, Mr. Donahue. Many years ago, he and our father had a horrible fight one night. The next morning, he was gone and never returned."

"My apologies, Miss Harris. I didn't mean to bring up such a distressful topic."

She blinked, doing her best to ignore the moisture in her eyes. "It's quite all right, Mr. Donahue. I was only six when it happened, so I've

44

grown used to him being gone. Although I'll never forget him."

Heather's heart sank at the story, knowing how hard it was to lose someone you loved. Her father and her uncle, Angus, had been gunned down, leaving a devastated family behind. She didn't believe she'd ever get used to them being gone.

"And you, Mr. Donahue. Have you family?" Heather asked.

"I have two older brothers. Although if you asked them, I'm certain they'd find it easy to disavow their association with me."

"Surely you're joking."

"Unfortunately, Miss Harris, I'm not. They couldn't wait for me to leave home and come west." He glanced around, massaging the back of his neck. "My parents and brothers consider me the black sheep of the family, and for good reason."

"And what reason is that?" Heather asked.

The answer died on his lips at the sound of the front door opening and closing. Heather watched as Ewan and Lorna entered, greeting the family, then walking up to August, who'd been speaking with Ian.

A few seconds later, Brodie and his wife, Maggie, arrived, making their way straight to Heather's group. Leaning over to kiss his cousin's cheek, Brodie looked at Miranda.

"Miss Harris. It's good to see you again. This is my wife, Maggie. Maggie, this is the new teacher I spoke of, Miranda Harris."

Miranda spoke up first. "It's a pleasure to meet the wife of our town sheriff. I'm certain you'll have many interesting stories to tell."

Maggie smiled, slipping her arm through her husband's. "Brodie is quite good at keeping the most interesting stories to himself."

As Brodie was about to introduce himself to the man standing with Heather and Miranda, Ewan walked up, extending his hand toward Bay. "Apologies for being late. You must be August's new partner. I'm Ewan MacLaren."

Taking his hand, Bay grinned at the elder MacLaren. "No apology needed, Mr. MacLaren. It's a pleasure to meet you. I'm Bayard Donahue."

Ewan stared at him a moment before his brows lifted. "Bayard Donahue?"

Bay's smile faded. "Yes, sir."

"The gunfighter?"

Chapter Four

Bay's body stilled as his hand moved to where his gun normally rested on his right hip. August Fielder insisted he didn't need one around the MacLarens, so he'd tucked it away in his saddlebag a few feet from the front porch. Still, old habits die hard. The lack of his old friend at his side made him feel exposed, vulnerable.

The sound of boots scuffing along the wooden floor alerted him to the silence Ewan's question had caused. Bay had hoped to avoid this discussion today, knowing his wish was futile.

Glancing around, he found himself surrounded by questioning looks. The absence of fear surprised him. These people were used to standing up for themselves, refusing to cower to any man or the label given him. Gunfighter, gunman, shootist—he'd been called all these titles at one time or another. He'd never relished any of them.

"I've been called a gunfighter, Mr. MacLaren."

Ewan studied him, noting the absence of a gun. In contrast, Brodie, Quinn, and Colin still had theirs strapped around their waists. If Sam Covington, Jinny's husband, weren't still in town, he'd be here wearing his.

"What do you call yourself now, Mr. Donahue?"

Bay shot a look at August. The man's face showed more amusement than concern. "A lawyer, sir. The same as Mr. Fielder."

Ewan nodded, glancing at Bay's empty glass. "Then that's what you are. May I get you another drink?"

A simple question, yet tensions dissolved, shoulders relaxed, conversations resumed, and Bay's hand calmed at his side.

"Yes, sir. I'd appreciate it." Bay ventured a look at Brodie. "Are you all right with this, Sheriff?"

A warning appeared in Brodie's eyes as his lips twisted into a grim smile. "I've been looking into your background, Mr. Donahue. There are no wanted posters for the work you've done."

Ewan walked up, extending the glass of whiskey to Bay, not intruding on the discussion.

Bay nodded, accepting the drink. "Work. An apt name for the type of assignments I used to take."

"As long as your past stays behind you, I'm seeing no problem with you living in Conviction."

"Then we are in agreement, Sheriff."

"Aye, we are."

"Who would like more pie?" Kyla glanced around the table, her gaze landing on Bay. "Mr. Donahue?"

"No, thank you, ma'am. I couldn't fit another bite in here." He patted his stomach, leaning back in his chair.

"Brodie?"

"Nae, Aunt Kyla. I've had more than I should." Brodie sat next to Bay, deciding he wanted the time to learn more about the ex-gunfighter turned lawyer.

"Well now, if the younger men aren't interested, I suppose it's up to me to have another slice of your wonderful berry pie, Kyla." August picked up his plate, passing it down the table to her. When it came back, he took a huge bite, following it with a sip of his second cup of coffee. "We could use cooking like this in Conviction."

Kyla laughed. "And what about the Gold Dust restaurant? They offer some very bonny food."

Ewan nodded. "Aye, Kyla, but not as good as you and the other lasses make."

She sat back in her chair, crossing her arms. "You lads will not be charming any of us into opening a new restaurant in town. We've more than our share of work here."

August finished the last bite of his pie, clearing his throat. "A restaurant is opening in the new hotel. Bay finished the contracts last week."

"What hotel?" Heather asked.

As they'd agreed, she'd taken a seat next to Miranda. Bay sat on her other side. Between the two of them, they'd kept Heather occupied with stories of

49

growing up on the other end of the country. Education, family expectations, social circles—they discussed them all over roast beef, smoked ham, potatoes, squash, cabbage, carrots, and endless cups of coffee. The one topic off limits was Bay's past as a gunfighter.

Bay leaned toward her. "The Feather River Hotel, Heather."

"It will be the finest establishment in California. Outside of San Francisco, of course."

Ian chuckled. "Aye, August, it will."

"Who are the owners?" Colin sat with his arm on the back of Sarah's chair.

August leaned forward. "The Fleming and Barrow families from San Francisco are the major investors. There are some minority owners here in Conviction."

Colin's eyes narrowed, his gaze moving to his uncles. "Are the MacLarens one of them?"

"Aye, lad," Ewan answered.

"A wee amount, lad." Ian looked at those around the table, knowing what they were thinking. The MacLarens never made major decisions without discussing them within the family. This time, Ian and Ewan had gone outside the usual routine, making the decision alone.

The eldest cousins glanced around, a thread of unease building between them.

Ewan held up a hand, getting their attention. "We'll be speaking of this later tonight, lads. Ian and I will explain it all."

He'd set the boundaries. They wouldn't be talking of family business in front of their guests, even if August already partnered with them in several investments.

Before anyone else could respond, the front door burst open. Sam rushed inside, glanced at his wife, Jinny, then at Brodie.

"We have a problem in town."

Standing, Brodie walked up to him, both turning their backs to those at the table. "What is it?"

Sam ignored the worry he saw in Jinny's eyes, lowering his voice. "A group of people have taken it upon themselves to cleanse the town."

Brodie frowned. "Cleanse the town?"

Sam shook his head, his lips curled in disgust. "Rid Conviction of the Chinese."

"Where's Jack?" Brodie mentioned the only other deputy. Nate Hollis, a valued member of his group, had left Conviction on personal business a couple weeks before. Until Nate returned, if he returned, protecting the town was left to three men.

"Right now, people are meeting in the community building. Jack and I watched for an hour, seeing the crowd swell and the voices get louder. Jack stayed, but there isn't much one man can do if they decide to turn into a mob."

Brodie nodded, his fists clenching at his sides.

"What is it?" Colin walked up beside him, followed by Quinn.

"There's a mob forming in town."

"For what purpose?" Quinn asked.

Brodie nodded at Sam, who explained. "There are people who believe the Chinese are taking jobs that should belong to citizens. In particular, men who served in the war and have come west to start over. The docks, Gold Dust, and saloons have all hired Chinese workers. Jack is keeping watch, but the rhetoric is building. I'm afraid it won't be long before they turn into a mob and march into Chinatown."

"Sam and I need to return to town in case that happens."

Colin looked at his cousin. "I'll be going with you, Brodie."

"Aye. I'll be going, too," Quinn added.

Sam nodded toward the table. "We need to let our wives know."

He and Jinny had been married a short time. She'd planned to ride back into town after supper. Sam had to convince her to ride back with him now, going straight to the house they shared with his son and father. It was far enough from Chinatown his family would be safe from the actions of the mob.

Brodie nodded. "I'll let Ian and Ewan know after I let Maggie know we're leaving. We've no time to waste."

Fifteen minutes later, the four men, their wives, plus Camden, Sean, Bram, and Fletcher MacLaren rode their horses to Conviction. Brodie hadn't put up much of a fight when they insisted on going, knowing his brother, Fletcher, and their cousins would only follow. It had been Bay who needed to be talked out of helping. The last person Brodie needed controlling an unruly crowd was an ex-gunfighter, a man who planned to make Conviction his home.

Heather stood on the front porch, watching them ride off, wishing she was with them.

"You wish you were going?"

She turned at Bay's deep voice, wrapping her arms around her waist. "Aye. It's hard to stay behind."

Bay leaned against a post, his arms crossed over his chest. "I know the feeling. If Brodie hadn't stopped me, I'd be riding with them."

Heather glanced at him, her lips twitching. "It's best you didn't. The lads have worked together a long time, can read each other's thoughts. They'd have no time to be looking out for you."

Dropping his arms to his sides, he straightened, lifting a brow at her. "Look out for me?"

"Aye, Mr. Donahue. They've minds of their own. They'd not be wanting you in their way."

Bay leaned closer. "May I tell you a secret, Miss MacLaren?"

She stilled, a shiver running through her as his warm breath washed over her cheek. "Aye."

"I'd rather be here, talking with you."

She drew back, seeing the twinkle in his eyes, and laughed. "Ach, you'll not be fooling me, Mr. Donahue. You'd rather be in town with the lads."

Scratching his head, Bay let out a breath. "You've found me out, Miss MacLaren. Still, I'm not complaining."

"Here you two are." Miranda stepped outside, moving next to Bay. "It's such a shame the men had to leave so early."

"Aye. It's the way of it out here."

Miranda looked at her. "Surely these types of things don't happen often."

Heather eyed the young woman who had to be close to her own age of twenty-one. She couldn't imagine living where each day was predictable.

"More often than we'd like." Heather looked up at the evening sky, wondering what Caleb was doing.

"It's too bad Mr. Stewart couldn't join us. I so looked forward to seeing him again."

She winced at Miranda's comment. In truth, Heather knew Caleb would have wanted to see her, too. "I'll let him know you've come to Conviction."

"That would be lovely. Let him know I'll be at the schoolhouse if he wants to come by and see me."

Heather forced a smile. "Aye. I'll be sure to do that."

"It's time we started back to town." August walked outside, Kyla beside him.

Miranda stepped up to her, taking Kyla's hands. "Thank you so much for your hospitality, Mrs. MacLaren. I had a wonderful time."

"Aye, so did we, Miss Harris."

August looked at Kyla. "We'll have to do this again soon. Perhaps supper at my house."

Grinning, she shook her head. "You've no room for a clan our size, August."

"Then we'll have a more intimate group."

Heather's jaw dropped. She had no idea August had an interest in her aunt, and judging by the look on Kyla's face, neither did she.

Bay slipped past Heather. "Thank you for including me, Mrs. MacLaren. It's been a while since I've had such a wonderful Sunday afternoon." He glanced over his shoulder at Heather. "I hope you'll consider including me again."

"Aye. You're welcome anytime, Mr. Donahue."

Within minutes, August and Miranda drove away in the wagon, Bay beside them on his horse.

Heather followed their retreating forms until they'd taken the trail to town, then shifted her gaze south toward the Evanston ranch. Caleb and Blaine would be eating their own supper, probably the stew Aunt Kyla sent over the day before. Or they'd be with the other two men, playing cards, learning more about the ranch. It wouldn't take Caleb long to start improving the operation. The thought tugged at her heart.

All the teaching from Mildred and Levi had helped her grow from a spoiled, selfish girl into what she now considered a woman who knew more of what she wanted. Too bad it had come too late.

Caleb sat on the hill separating Circle M from the Evanston ranch. A couple miles north and he'd be able to see the ranch house, the MacLarens mulling about after a hearty supper. Every Sunday, the meal took place at a different house. He didn't even know where they would've eaten today. It caused him a pang of regret. The meals were where everyone caught up with what happened each week, announcements were made, and plans for the future were discussed. Unless he chose otherwise, they'd always included him. Now he learned of decisions days later, if someone rode over to tell them.

Blaine hadn't even gone today, which came as a surprise. They both expected to hear about it from his mother, Kyla. She might even ride over herself to chastise her son, and possibly Caleb, about being absent. He chuckled at the image of Kyla, fisted hands on her hips, glaring up at the taller men, scolding them as if they were still young boys. *Mothers and their children,* he thought. Even when grown, they still felt a huge responsibility for keeping them on the right path.

Caleb thought of his own mother. Considerate, caring, and completely subservient to his overbearing father. Unlike his mother, the MacLaren women didn't hesitate to express their views. There wasn't a shy woman in the family, and certainly not Heather. It had been what drew him to her and what ultimately pushed him away. A man could only take so much before the message got through. He'd been wrong to ever believe he had a future with her.

At twenty-three, he had many years to consider marriage. The only other woman who'd held his attention for more than a few minutes was Miranda Harris. She'd left as abruptly as she'd arrived, returning to her home back east.

Preparing to rein Jupiter back toward the ranch, Caleb looked west, his gaze halting on what appeared to be smoke coming from the direction of town. He stilled in the saddle, blinking a few times to clear his eyes, believing it had to be an illusion. It wasn't.

Reining his horse around, Caleb rode straight back to the ranch. If he could see smoke from this far away, the fire had to be huge, and most likely out of control. Brodie and Sam would need all available men, and Caleb had no intention of watching from the safety of the hill.

Galloping to the barn, he yelled for Blaine, explaining what he'd seen. After saddling his horse and leaving quick instructions for the ranch hands, Blaine followed Caleb to town. Smoke led them to the scene of the fire, the mob, and the men trying to control both.

"Brodie!" Blaine barely reined to a stop before jumping off and running to his cousin. "What is happening?"

"I'll be explaining later. Right now, I need you and Caleb to help Sam and Jack with the crowd." Reaching into his pocket, he pulled out two badges. "Wear these."

Blaine saw the two shouting at a mob of men, who shouted back. Close by were his brother, Camden, and several cousins. "Aye. We'll be taking care of those miscreants, then be back to help you lads with the fire."

Three hours later, twenty men filled the cells in the jail, and the fire had been reduced to cinders. Too late to ride back to their homes, the MacLarens and Caleb took beds at the Gold Dust with plans to meet for breakfast and talk about what happened.

Waking after four hours of sleep, Caleb scrubbed both hands down his face. He wanted to see the damage to the shops in Chinatown before meeting the others for breakfast and the discussion of how to deal with mobs in the future. The bitterness of the crowd had surprised most in Conviction. There had been talk, mainly behind closed doors, of the resentment building against the Chinese. The town council thought they had time to deal with those most vocal, come to an understanding of how to work together. They'd been wrong.

A number of those upset exploded into violence before anyone could stop them. It had taken several of the townsfolk, as well as a good number of MacLarens, to curtail the brutality and put out the fires in Chinatown.

Dressing, Caleb secured his gunbelt, then grabbed his hat. If he hurried, he'd have time to see the damage in daylight and return to the Gold Dust by the time the others arrived.

The sun had risen over the eastern hills when he stepped onto the boardwalk. Jupiter was boarded at the livery down the street. Walking would be quicker. Caleb didn't know what to expect as he walked north toward the docks.

Chinatown had started away from the original main street, far enough so the inhabitants could keep to themselves when not working in the restaurants, saloons, or at the docks. From what he knew, the fire had started at the corner of one building, an odd-shaped structure not attached to any others. The fact an open space existed between it and the next building had saved an entire block from going up in flames.

The smell of smoke still hung in the air, reaching him before he made it more than a block. Caleb heard at least one person had died. He didn't know if it was a member of the mob or one of the Chinese. Either way, it was one death too many.

Picking up his pace, he traveled the next block in a couple minutes before coming to an abrupt stop. The building had all but collapsed, charred wood still smoldering. He didn't attempt to walk through the rubble. Instead, he studied the damage, relieved it hadn't been worse.

A few Chinese picked through the contents. Fires were common. Those set intentionally were not.

"Caleb Stewart."

He turned at the sound of the familiar voice. August's driver pulled the carriage to a stop. "Mr. Fielder. I didn't expect to see you here this early." He walked up to the door, peering inside. A sense of recognition gripped him when he saw another person inside the carriage, head bowed.

"I'm going to the Gold Dust to meet with the sheriff. I assume you'll be heading there soon."

"Uh...yes, sir."

"I need to take my guest to the boardinghouse, then I'll be along. Because of the violence last night, I had Miss Harris stay with me."

Caleb swallowed as Miranda raised her head, her gaze meeting his as she smiled. "Good morning, Mr. Stewart. I'd hoped to see you again."

Chapter Five

Caleb checked the last of the herd, his thoughts on the outcome of the meeting a few days before and the fact Miranda had returned to Conviction.

Breakfast had expanded to include most of the town council. It hadn't taken long for an agreement to be reached. Brodie would do whatever it took to hire more deputies, including sending telegrams to every major city across the country if needed.

The men who'd set the fire had been identified and would be judged for their actions. The rest, after a stern warning from Brodie, were sent home to their families.

Reining his horse around, he took another look at the cattle grazing in the southern pasture, thinking of the pretty schoolteacher. He didn't know how he felt about Miranda accepting a teaching job in town.

She hadn't tried to hide her interest in him. Even August seemed to notice the way she flirted in the few minutes he'd talked to them through the carriage window. Caleb hadn't refused when August offered him a ride to the Gold Dust. One stipulation was they needed to stop at the boardinghouse first. The second was a request for Caleb to escort Miranda inside.

Caleb had no intention of refusing August's request, even if it might appear to Miranda he held more interest in her than he did. He shouldn't have worried. She thanked him for his courtesy, then hurried up the stairs to her room without a backward glance.

"Are you thinking about the lass in town?" Blaine reined to a stop next to him. Caleb wished he'd never mentioned Miranda or her apparent interest in him.

Dismounting, he checked Jupiter's hooves, dislodging a rock from one. "Thinking about what Brodie's going to do about needing more deputies. He's in a tough situation."

"Aye, he is. When Colin rode over here yesterday to see if we needed more help, he talked of one or two of the Circle M men working as temporary deputies until Brodie hires more."

"We're shorthanded enough, Blaine."

Taking off his hat, Blaine shook his head, then ran a hand through his hair. "Aye. We sometimes forget we have lasses willing to help us. Emma is as good a cattle woman as most men. Geneen rides as if she were born on a horse. The same with Jinny. Heather...well, we all know she has as much experience as any of us."

A wry grin twisted Caleb's lips. "And believes she's better than all of us combined."

"Aye. The lass is not lacking in her high opinion of herself." Settling the hat back on his head, his brows furrowed. "It's a strange thing, though. Colin said she's been doing well working with him and Quinn. No complaints, does all they ask."

Swinging back into the saddle, Caleb shook his head. "What about when she disagrees with them?"

"Colin says the lass still speaks her mind when she's thinking they're wrong. But there's been no sign of her anger, lashing out at the lads with the least provocation." Resting his hands on the saddle horn, Blaine leaned forward. "Maybe the lass has changed, Caleb."

"The boys are fools if they think she's lost her temper or arrogant ways. She'll return to them once life settles back to normal at the ranch and she doesn't have Widow Evanston to fall back on." Caleb winced at the trace of bitterness in his voice.

A part of him always thought if Heather had stayed at Circle M, they might have been able to settle their differences, maybe explore what they had together. In his opinion, she'd taken the coward's route by riding south to live for close to a year.

"I've been thinking it may have been the widow and her foreman, Levi, who might have set Heather straight. Most of the lads disagree with me on this, but maybe the lass needed to figure some things out for herself and not always be told what to do by everyone else."

Caleb sat back in the saddle, rubbing his tired eyes with the palms of his hands. What Blaine said made sense. Caleb had to get away from his own father. He'd traveled hundreds of miles to do it. Heather had only put a few miles between her and the rest of the MacLarens. Now she was back at Circle M. Caleb didn't believe he'd ever return to Oregon and his family's farm.

None of it mattered. He'd put her behind him. Concentrating on building up the new operation kept him busy and his thoughts off the woman who'd haunted him for far too long.

"Makes no difference to me if she figured things out or not. I don't plan to work with her anytime soon. Besides..." Caleb's voice trailed off as he tried to come up with another excuse.

"Besides, you've the new teacher to think about."

Caleb glared at him. "So we are clear, I have no interest in Miranda Harris. It's all I can do to keep up with the work around here. In case it's escaped you, the budget for this place is non-existent. Unless we make a go of it, the family might be forced to sell it off, the same as they might have to call in the note on the Pearce place."

Blaine's back stiffened, his nostrils flaring enough so Caleb knew he got the message. "It'll not be getting that bad. Ian and Ewan won't do anything to hurt the Pearce family. They might let Boyd Doggett go and send one of us over to foreman the place, cut other expenses, but they won't be calling in the note from Big Jim and Gertie Pearce."

When Emma's parents fell on hard times, almost had their ranch taken away by some questionable bank dealings, the MacLarens had loaned them the money needed to keep the place. Unfortunately, the small operation needed to be folded into the larger MacLaren ranch to become profitable.

Right now, the cattle ranch made enough to feed the Pearces, pay Doggett and his men, and reduce the loan a little each month, but it couldn't be considered profitable. It wasn't the same as Circle M or the cattle ranch they and August had purchased from Juan Estrada. Even though they were his close friends, Big Jim might never recover if he had to sign his ranch over to the MacLarens to pay off the debt he owed them.

"I wouldn't count on that, Blaine. The family has expanded rapidly, maybe too rapidly. They'll do what's needed to keep Circle M together, even if it means some tough decisions involving friends."

"How would you be knowing such things?"

Caleb scrubbed a hand down his face. "You and I sat with your uncles, plus Colin, Brodie, and Quinn, when they made the decision about buying the Evanston place. The numbers on the old Estrada ranch and the Pearce ranch were right in front of us. The Pearce place is bleeding money, Blaine." He let out a breath. "It sounds cruel, and I'm not saying I like it, but it would be profitable right away if we incorporate the land into Circle M, use the men we already have, and let the house, barn, and corrals sit idle."

"I suppose you're thinking it's the same with the Evanston place."

Caleb nodded, watching Blaine's reaction. "I do. The MacLarens made a wise decision years ago to keep all the family close by in their own homes, surrounded by open land where they could run cattle and breed horses. Now they've bought the Estrada and Evanston ranches, along with loaning Big Jim Pearce a substantial sum so he and Gertie wouldn't be forced to leave their ranch. All have separate foremen and other expenses that wouldn't be needed if everything was run from one location."

Blaine looked away, rubbing the back of his neck as he thought over Caleb's words. After a while, he nodded. "Aye. I can see what you're saying makes sense. Have you spoken with anyone about it?"

"Colin and Quinn feel the same. They're waiting for the right time to speak with Ian and Ewan. It's hard with Quinn being Emma's husband. Big Jim and Gertie are like second parents to him. The other problem is keeping all this within the family. If word gets out to the banks..." Caleb's voice trailed off.

"Aye. There'd be speculation on how strong Circle M is."

Caleb looked around, admiring the beauty of the southernmost boundary of the Evanston ranch. Buying it was a good decision. Anyone would be proud to own this prime piece of land. The MacLarens had to be smart about how they operated it.

"I'm seeing no reason not to speak with Ian and Ewan about moving the cattle from here to the Circle M. We've only two men here. They could join the outsiders in the bunkhouse."

Caleb grinned. "Outsiders?"

Blaine grimaced. "Aye. We've six men working for us who aren't family, and most of them worked for Estrada. It was a hard decision to bring them on. The two men here would make eight. My pa never would've been agreeing to allow so many outsiders on the ranch."

Blaine's face clouded. His father, Angus, and Quinn's father, Gillis, had been murdered. Both were good men, set in their ways, and trusted their future to family. With their deaths, Ian and Ewan needed to look beyond the numbers in the MacLaren clan if they were going to expand and flourish.

"The wagon train was a long time ago, but from what I saw, Angus was a good man, Blaine."

"Aye. As was Uncle Gillis." He blew out a breath. "I'm thinking you don't know about the latest deal Ian and Ewan got the family in."

Caleb's eyes widened. "Another investment?"

Blaine nodded. "They agreed to being minor partners in a new hotel and restaurant in Conviction."

Caleb groaned, mumbling a curse. "How'd you hear of this?"

"Colin was here yesterday. You were working with the other men and he couldn't stay, but he told me what he knew. He wasn't happy about it."

"And Quinn?"

Blaine shook his head. "Colin didn't say. I'd be guessing Quinn isn't too pleased, either. And Sean, well...who knows how all this will affect him."

Ian's oldest son, Sean, had a gift with animals. His greatest desire was to attend the Highland Society's Veterinary School in Edinburgh. It would be a tremendous opportunity and a great honor for him. Students at the veterinary school also attended the lectures in human medicine at the University of Edinburgh and the Royal College of Surgeons of Edinburgh. It would require a substantial sum and he'd be gone for several years. At nineteen, he'd hoped the family would be in a position to allow him to apply soon.

"Does Sean know about how thin the money is?" Caleb asked.

"He's a bright lad, but quiet. Sean doesn't talk much about what he's thinking. If he knows, he's said nothing to me."

Caleb looked up at the darkening sky, felt the air thicken as it did before a rain. "We should start back to the house."

Blaine rode beside him, their horses moving at a leisurely pace. "You know, lad, it's been a while since you attended Sunday supper."

Caleb glanced at him and nodded. "I was thinking the same. Maybe we should go."

"Aye. I'm thinking we should."

Conviction

"Please, have a seat, Mr. Delacroix. It's a pleasure to have you back in town." Philip Aunspach, the new manager of the San Francisco Merchant Bank local office, stood as Giles walked into the room. "I apologize for not meeting the stage."

Like the two managers before him, Philip had been handpicked by Delacroix for the job in Conviction. He'd risen through the ranks in the main office in San Francisco, starting as a clerk, becoming a secretary before being promoted to reviewing loan requests. Over time, he'd become an assistant manager. All the while, Giles had followed his progress, spending considerable time with Philip outside of work. During this time, Giles discovered something about the man he could use to turn him from an idealist into someone of true worth.

Holding up a hand, Giles shook his head. "There's no cause for an apology, Philip. It means you must be busy."

"More than I imagined when you gave me this assignment."

Giles threw back his head and laughed. "I know you weren't pleased with the news you'd be moving away from San Francisco. You'd always seen your future in the city, not in some dirt town with few of the amenities you'd grown accustomed to."

Shrugging, Philip relaxed in his chair. "It's an opportunity I was happy to accept, Mr. Delacroix."

"Yes, I know. Few men at the bank are offered the chance to grow their experience outside of the confines of those walls. You, though, are special."

Philip's brows furrowed as he tilted his head. "No more special than any of the others."

"I guess we'll see about that, won't we?" Giles' mouth twisted into a knowing grin. "In any case, I'm here to discuss how we grow the bank's business."

Sitting forward, Philip rested his arms on the desk. "It's doubtful that will be a problem, sir. The town is growing rapidly, faster than I anticipated. We're opening accounts at an incredible rate." He opened a ledger to a certain page before sliding it across the desk to Giles. "These are the new accounts in the last month."

Taking the book, Giles studied the information. Flipping the pages, he looked at the accounts before

Philip arrived, comparing the data. Closing the ledger, he pushed it back across the desk.

"Excellent work."

Philip didn't disguise his pleasure at the compliment. "Thank you, sir."

"I would like to point out something, though."

The smile on Philip's face fell away. "What would that be?"

"The number of new accounts is good. Quantity is always good. The amounts, however, need to be higher. The bank wants to attract people with more income and more need for our services. Those are the accounts that make us money."

Philip opened the ledger, studying the columns, understanding what Giles was telling him. "What do you suggest?"

"We need to go after businesses, land owners, and ranchers. Those are the people who are behind the growth."

Rubbing his brow, Philip's forehead creased. "The Bank of Conviction has control of those customers. I've visited some of them. They're friends of the men on the bank's board, do business with them, depend on the association. I'm not sure how successful we'll be at getting them to change."

Crossing his arms, Giles smirked. "We will have to come up with a plan. And I have a few ideas."

"We need to be turning the herd north, Heather. Move them up through the valley." Quinn reined his horse to his left, heading off a few head that refused to stay in the group, then turned back to his sister. "Be more aggressive when they move away, lass, or this will take all day." He kicked his horse into a gallop, riding forward.

Heather pulled the bandana over her face, doing her best to breathe, while mentally cursing her cousin. Colin had told her to ride drag, pushing the herd from the back. It meant eating dust all day—swallowing it, breathing it, and feeling it filter through her clothes. Even a bath couldn't wash it all away. The grit would last for days.

Her younger brother, Bram, and cousin, Fletcher, took the left and right flank positions, closer to the back of the herd. Cousins Camden and Sean rode left and right swing near the front. Colin and Quinn took point, guiding the herd. They didn't need a trail boss for the short trip of moving a few hundred head less than five miles.

Heather knew they'd change positions on the next drive. She also knew they weren't treating her unfairly, and that mattered to her. None of the men made exceptions for her.

"You all right, lass?"

She glanced to her side, peering over the top of the bandana. "Aye, Bram."

"Take my spot on left flank. I'll ride back here."

Heather shook her head. "Nae. I'll not be taking your place. Your turn riding drag will come soon enough." She heard Bram's muffled laugh through his bandana.

"Did Colin let you know you'll be with Fletcher and me, sleeping with the herd tonight?"

His voice was muffled, but not enough for her to mistake his words.

"And why would we be sleeping with the herd?"

"A few head are missing and we've not been able to find them. Colin wants to make certain we've no rustlers picking off the herd."

Heather nodded, feeling a trickle of excitement. No matter how much she'd begged or pleaded, her father had never let her stay with the herd all night. He'd never allowed her on a drive, either. After his death, Quinn and her cousins continued her father's wishes. It appeared things were beginning to change.

She knew Bram couldn't see it, but a smile crossed her face. "Then I'm hoping someone brought enough hardtack and jerky for supper."

Bram laughed. "You may have to wrestle us for it, lass." Waving, he rode off, leaving her to enjoy the way her life seemed to be changing—mostly for the better.

Chapter Six

A Cabin Miles North of Conviction

"Don't misunderstand, boss. I can get the men you want. There are more than you'd think, ready to do whatever is needed for cash. But I need to know what you want them to do."

Giles sat inside the cabin, cradling a surprisingly good cup of coffee, studying the man sitting across from him.

Black Jolly, a man who lived in the shadows, doing whatever he had to for the right amount of coin, was neither black nor jolly. At six-foot-seven, as thin as a willow switch, and with a mustache so full it consumed his upper and lower lips, Black could walk into a room and all conversation stopped. It wasn't his height as much as his eyes. Yellow, like those of a tiger, rimmed in black with a black center. And the ragged scar running from his right temple to the tip of his chin. Even the most hardened man couldn't help but stare.

"For now, all you need to do is hire them. Don't worry about what they'll be doing, Black. Once the men are assembled, I'll have more than enough work to keep their pockets full."

"As well as their stomachs?"

Giles finished his coffee, setting the cup on an old table. "Of course. They'll be supplied with whatever they need. As long as they do what I ask, we'll all be happy with the arrangement. Including you, and I know how difficult you are to please."

Choking out a bitter laugh, he took off his hat and stood, stretching to his full height. "My needs are simple, boss. Pay me what we agreed on. You do that and we'll be fine."

"Have you ever known me not to?"

Jolly stared down at him, his face twisting into a snarl. "No. You wouldn't be here if you'd ever tried to cheat me."

Giles stood, never taking his gaze off him. He couldn't afford to show any weakness in front of a man like Jolly. "I'm a businessman, Black, the same as you. It's real simple. You do the work, you get paid." Reaching down, he grabbed his empty cup, moving past Jolly to set it on a shelf by the stove. "Tell me more about the men you want to hire."

"That's information you don't need. They'll take orders from me."

"How do I know they can be trusted?"

Jolly's yellow eyes narrowed on Giles, darkening in warning. "You doubting me, boss? It ain't going to end well if you don't trust me."

Holding up both hands, palms out, Giles shook his head. "You're right. I don't need to know anything about the men and they don't need to know anything about me. I see no problem, as long as we're clear on that."

Jolly's features didn't change as he walked to the door, bent low, and stepped outside. Settling the hat on his head, he leaned against a post, pulling a cheroot from his pocket. Lighting it, he blew out a stream of smoke as he glanced about the secluded site. A dilapidated barn stood twenty yards away, a well near the side of the cabin, which was in better condition than Jolly expected.

"You own this place?"

Giles nodded as he stepped beside him. "One of my companies. It's not in my name. I don't want anyone to know I own land around Conviction. Will it be satisfactory?"

"It's as good a place as any for me and the men to hide while we're here."

Looking up at the darkening sky, Giles walked down the steps. "I need to head back to town." Grabbing the reins, he mounted his horse, then looked back at Jolly. "You know, you never did tell me if Black is your real name."

Jolly blew out another stream of smoke, shaking his head. "It's not."

Giles leaned toward him. "How'd you get it?"

Finishing the cheroot, he dropped it onto the wooden planks, crushing it out with the heel of his boot. His lips twisted into a feral grin.

"Ma said she'd never known anyone with such a black heart." Without another word, Jolly went back inside, shutting the door behind him.

Conviction

"Will you need anything more from me tonight, Mr. Donahue?"

Bay stopped rubbing his brow with a finger to look up at Jasper Hamm, the young man who assisted August, and now him, in the law practice. Straightening the papers in front of him, he shook his head.

"Nothing more this evening, Jasper. We'll be starting early again tomorrow." Bay glanced back down at the papers.

Jasper continued to stand next to Bay's desk, then cleared his throat.

"Was there something else?"

"Uh...tomorrow is Saturday, sir."

Straightening, Bay nodded. "You're right. It is. Does Mr. Fielder not have you come in on Saturdays?"

"Not usually, sir."

Slapping his hands on the desk, Bay stood, towering over the shorter, slightly built man. "Then I'll make do without you tomorrow."

"If you're certain...I mean, I can come to work if you need me."

"I'm certain. If I find your services are needed, I'll send word."

"Well, then, goodnight, sir."

"Goodnight, Jasper."

Bay watched him close the door, cringing as an image from his childhood popped into his mind. He'd opened his father's study a crack, enough to peer inside without being detected. His father sat at a huge desk, his work stacked in front of him, his glasses low on his nose. At eight years old, and unlike his older brothers, he'd never been allowed in the private room off the entry to his family's opulent home.

Bay had drawn in a breath, building up his courage before pushing the door open to walk inside. He tiptoed all the way to the edge of the desk, setting a hand on it, waiting for his father to notice him.

As the minutes passed without being acknowledged, Bay wondered if he'd made a mistake entering his father's sanctuary without invitation. Without warning, the elder Donahue whipped off his glasses, features twisting, his gaze lifting to collide with Bay's.

"Get out. Now."

Bay's breath caught, his heart racing as he backed up, never taking his eyes off his father. Blinking back the tears at the terse dismissal, he squared his shoulders, lifting his chin.

"Well, then, goodnight, sir." Stepping into the entry, he closed the door with a gentle click.

He'd used the same words then as Jasper had tonight. The circumstances were much different and he knew Jasper would return.

Bay had never again attempted to enter his father's study. He'd refused to step inside when the invitation came at age twelve, six years before he left his family for the last time.

Black sheep was a term he knew well, had grown to embrace after hearing it innumerable times growing up. His older brothers were the golden sons. Bay was the result of a drunken night his father spent with their nanny, who'd disappeared the day after giving birth.

A messed up start to a messed up life, Bay thought as he shook off the memory, lowering himself back into his chair.

"Ah, you're still here."

Bay looked up to see August, his father's old friend, standing in the doorway. The two men couldn't be more different.

Standing, Bay motioned to a chair in front of his desk. "I thought you'd left for your supper meeting."

August sat down, crossing one leg over the other. "Giles won't be meeting me at the Gold Dust for another hour." He rubbed his chin, letting out a breath. "There's something about the man..." His voice trailed off as he gazed toward the window.

Bay walked around the desk, taking the chair next to him. "What are your concerns?"

"I'm not certain. I sent a telegram to the president of the San Francisco Merchant Bank, asking general questions about Giles. The response was what you'd expect."

Bay nodded. "He's a valued colleague of the board, an upstanding member of society, and a generous patron. His wife's father was a founder of the bank and one of the wealthiest men in San Francisco. Oh, and Giles is a close friend of the bank president." Seeing August's eyes widen, he grinned. "I did some checking on the man myself. Since you're the principal share of the Bank of Conviction, I thought it wise to learn as much as possible about the man."

Lifting a brow, August leaned forward. "What else have you learned?"

Standing, Bay walked to a cabinet, pulled out a file, and handed it to August. "He grew up poor—in extreme poverty. His mother raised him. From what the investigator learned, his father was one of the first to come west at the discovery of gold. He left Giles and his mother in a tent city outside Sacramento. The man never sent any money and didn't return."

Reading the pages, August looked up. "There's a gap between his teens and when he married."

Bay leaned his hip against the desk, crossing his arms. "My man is working on it. It's as if Giles disappeared, then reemerged when he met a wealthy young widow who became his wife."

"The report shows he's dedicated to her."

"And his mother moved in with them a few years ago," Bay added.

"So he's devoted to the two women. Fine qualities." August rubbed his brow, pursing his lips.

"Men do exist who love their wife and mother, but engage in questionable activities."

Handing back the file, August stood. "Join us for supper. I'd like you to get a better feel for the man, give me your opinion."

Bay had hoped to go to Buckie's Castle, have a couple whiskeys, before returning to his room in August's house. "Of course. Let me finish a letter and I'll meet you at the Gold Dust."

Walking to the door, August turned back. "I'll be glad when the Feather River Hotel opens."

Bay nodded his agreement. "Have you hired someone to manage the restaurant?"

"I have. I'll say no more now, but believe you'll be quite surprised by my selection."

Bay cocked a brow. "You stole one of the cooks from the White House?"

August chuckled. "Not quite, but I believe you'll find my choice quite unconventional."

Bay went along with the game his boss started. "When are you expecting this mystery man?"

"Not long now. With luck, the hotel and restaurant will be finished in late November. The cook will have time to hire staff, prepare menus, and order supplies in time for the Christmas season."

"He'll have his work cut out for him."

An odd expression crossed August's face before his features stilled. "Certainly. Well, I'll see you at supper."

Bay sat down, amused at the enjoyment his boss took in the secrecy of his new hire. When the man arrived, he was sure it would be one of the top chefs from New York, or perhaps someone August had brought over from France. Fielder only worked with the best, which reminded Bay of how he still needed to prove himself to the man who'd taken a huge chance on bringing him to Conviction. Bay would do everything in his power to make certain August didn't regret it.

Circle M

"You sure you want the first watch, lass?" Fletcher sat next to Heather, both finishing the last of their hardtack, jerky, and coffee.

83

She nodded. "I'll not be sleeping anyway. Might as well be first."

Standing, Fletcher stretched his arms over his head. "I'll leave you to it." Grabbing his bedroll, he spread it out on the other side of the fire, where Bram already snored. "I swear the lad can sleep through anything." Fletcher winked at her. "Wake him first for the second watch."

Heather chuckled to herself. Fletcher and Bram had always been close, though it would be hard for an outsider to know with all their teasing of each other.

Tossing more wood on the fire, she pulled her jacket tight as a shiver ran through her. Within minutes, Fletcher was out, the soft sound of his snoring matching Bram's.

She could see the cattle clearly from where they camped. It was a small herd, easy to guard, for which she was thankful.

Leaning her head back, Heather looked up at the stars, recognizing a few. She wished she'd paid more attention to Caleb when he'd tried to teach her the constellations. He'd insisted knowing them would prove valuable. She'd given him a sharp reply, turning her back to him. Caleb hadn't offered again.

The memory made her think of other times when Caleb had approached her, offering help or advice. Most times, it was when they were with her brothers and cousins, somewhere out on the ranch where anyone could hear their conversation. She never wanted any of them to know how much she liked him. Instead of accepting his help, she allowed her defenses and infamous temper to take control, saying and doing things she now regretted.

Perhaps if she'd talked to her mother or confided in her female cousins, she might have been able to work through what troubled her. It had taken going to another ranch, forming friendships with Mildred Evanston and Levi Abrams, to see herself as others did. She remembered the last words Levi spoke to her before he left.

"Don't dwell on the past. You've got a lifetime to look forward to. Take what you've learned and make the most of it."

How she wished he hadn't left.

Heather hadn't realized she'd almost dozed off until the sound of breaking branches to her left had her eyes popping open. Sitting still, she listened, hearing the noise again. Jumping up, she grabbed her rifle, aiming in the direction of the sound.

"You'd best raise your hands and come out or I'll be shooting." Her loud voice woke Bram and Fletcher, who rose quickly, grabbing their guns.

"What is it, lass?" Bram asked. He instinctively looked at the herd, relaxing when he saw they hadn't been disturbed.

"I heard something out that way." She indicated the direction with the barrel of her rifle.

Fletcher walked around the fire to stand beside her. "Did you see anything?"

"Nae, I—" The sound of footsteps stopped her. She started to move forward, halting when Fletcher grabbed her shoulder. By then, Bram had already taken off in the direction of the noise.

"Stay here and guard the horses. It could be someone trying to draw us away from camp." Fletcher didn't wait for her response, running after Bram.

Seconds later, she heard her cousins yelling, the sound of horses, then nothing. Her body tensed. She didn't want to wait, wondering if Bram or Fletcher had been hit. Thankfully, she didn't have to wait long.

"What happened?" She lowered her rifle, dashing up to them.

Bram glared over his shoulder in the direction they'd come. "Two men. They got to their horses and took off before we could reach them."

Heather glanced over each of them, seeing no sign of injury, then toward the herd. The animals hadn't moved. "Did you recognize them?"

Fletcher shook his head. "Nae. One was tall and skinny."

Bram looked at Fletcher and nodded. "Aye. Taller than any man I can remember seeing. The other was shorter, maybe Fletch's height."

He winced when his cousin slugged his shoulder. At six-foot-five, Fletcher was the tallest of the MacLarens.

Bram rubbed his arm, then ran a hand through his hair. "I'm guessing they were after the horses."

Fletcher nodded. "Aye. If they'd wanted the cattle, they'd have been coming from the other direction."

Resting the butt of her rifle on the ground, Heather looked around as her heart rate began to slow. "Only two?"

Bram nodded. "Aye. There could be more."

Fletcher scrubbed a hand down his face. "We should all be staying awake tonight."

Bram nodded. "I'll not be getting back to sleep. Heather, why don't you try to rest? Fletch and I will keep watch."

She shook her head. "Nae. I'll not able to sleep after this." Walking to the fire, she threw on more wood, then grabbed the empty coffee pot. "I'll make some fresh. It's going to be a long night."

Chapter Seven

"Don't be forgetting to get the new tools from the blacksmith." Blaine stepped away from where he'd finished hitching the horse to the wagon for Caleb's trip to town. "We'll need to be taking some of the tools to Colin tomorrow."

Climbing onto the seat, Caleb picked up the lines, glancing at the early morning sun. "I won't. Maloney's, Ferguson's, and the blacksmith. Do I need to get anything at the feed lot?"

"Nae. You could always grab a bottle of whiskey at Buckie's. Put it on the MacLaren account." Blaine lifted his brows, grinning.

"The bottle in the house is still almost full."

Blaine chuckled. "You've not checked it in a few days, lad. I've had a wee bit since we shared the bottle earlier in the week."

Caleb shook his head. "Must not have been too little, but I'll get a bottle. Anything else?"

"Nae. I'll be seeing you this afternoon."

"Sooner, if the supplies and tools are ready."

Slapping the lines, Caleb took the trail to town, glad for some time to himself. He needed more space than the MacLarens, who seemed to draw energy from the constant banter and bickering within the family.

Caleb thought of the conversation he and Blaine planned to have with Ewan and Ian after supper tomorrow. He didn't think they'd get much resistance to closing the Evanston house and merging the cattle with the existing MacLaren herd. The same with the old Estrada place. He already knew they wouldn't touch the Pearce ranch, not as long as Big Jim and Gertie wanted to stay. Their foreman, Boyd Doggett, did a good job, but his skills were wasted on such a small ranch.

He knew Brodie had been struggling with the decision to continue as sheriff or return to the ranch, where the family needed him. Perhaps Boyd could take on some of the work, giving Brodie more time to make a decision. Caleb resolved to stop at the jail to speak with his friend.

The outskirts of Conviction came into view. Within minutes, he'd joined the other wagons and horses on the main street. Saturday mornings were busy, especially when one of the steamers came up the Feather River from Sacramento. The ships often docked on Fridays or Saturdays, carrying supplies the ranchers needed. Most importantly, they brought passengers who either planned to start a new life in Conviction or visit, spending their money in the hotel, restaurant, and other businesses before moving on. Judging by the number of people on the boardwalk, Caleb figured the River Belle or another steamship had arrived.

Pulling the wagon to a stop, he jumped down. Bounding up the steps, he opened the door of the general store.

Clarence Maloney nodded at him from behind the counter as he helped a woman with her purchases. "Good morning, Caleb. You're in town early."

"Morning." As Caleb reached the counter, the woman turned.

"Hello, Mr. Stewart."

Removing his hat, Caleb smiled. "Miss Harris. It's a pleasure to see you again."

"As it is to see you. Have you come to town for supplies?"

"Yes, and some other errands." He looked down at the counter, seeing soap, some fabric, and other items. "Appears you're doing the same."

"Saturdays are the only time I have to do my shopping."

Clarence cleared his throat, getting their attention. "Do you have a list for me, Caleb?"

Fumbling to get the list out of his pocket, he handed it to Clarence. "I'll also need some potatoes."

Reading, he glanced at Caleb. "This won't take long." He looked at Miranda. "I'll see you next Saturday, Miss Harris."

"Thank you, Mr. Maloney." Miranda sucked in a breath, looking up at Caleb. "Well, I suppose I should leave you to your business."

Caleb's mouth opened before he'd thought things through. "If you have no plans, perhaps you'd consider joining me for dinner at the Gold Dust." If her face hadn't lit up at the invitation, he might have regretted his rash action.

"I'd love to."

He nodded, still not certain why he'd made the offer. "Would noon suit you?"

"It would. Should I meet you there?"

"If you don't mind."

"Not at all. I look forward to it, Mr. Stewart. Goodbye...for now."

Caleb massaged the back of his neck, watching her leave. He had no business asking her to dinner, but the way his invitation pleased her made him glad he'd spoken up. She seemed like a nice lady and he knew, from speaking with August, she hadn't had an opportunity to make friends. Maybe she'd realize that was all he offered and not expect anything more. He winced. Somehow, he doubted it.

"Tell me about the work you do at the ranch, Mr. Stewart." Miranda sipped her tea, sparing little attention to the boiled ham and vegetables on her plate.

Caleb finished chewing the bite of roast beef, swallowing it down with coffee. "Not much to tell. I'm working at the old Evanston ranch with Blaine MacLaren and a couple ranch hands. Most every day is the same. We take care of the cattle, make repairs. Not very exciting."

A smile curved up the corners of her mouth. "Well, to someone who grew up in the city, it sounds quite exciting. Is it dangerous?"

"Only if you don't know what you're doing."

"And you do?" Miranda asked.

He nodded, picking up his coffee cup and taking a sip. "I've learned from the best." He speared another piece of roast, putting it into his mouth.

"The MacLarens?"

Chewing, he thought about living at Circle M and all they'd taught him. He'd been fortunate to have them take him in as part of their family. Setting down his fork, he pushed his plate away.

"They've been very generous to me. I owe them a great deal."

Miranda took another bite of her boiled ham. Looking up, she cocked her head. "Do they pay you for your work?"

Caleb's eyes widened for an instant before he lifted a brow, his features showing a hint of amusement. "I'm not considered a slave, if that's what you're implying."

Dropping her fork, Miranda's face reddened. "Of course not. I didn't mean anything of the sort. I'm so sorry if my question offended you." Picking up the napkin, she dabbed at the corners of her mouth.

"What *did* you mean?"

She shrugged, placing her napkin back on her lap. "I don't know about ranching, but I've seen places where people work for food and shelter. There's no way for them to get ahead when they're stuck in places like that." Letting out a breath, she leaned toward him. "Tell me how it works on a ranch."

Leaning back in his chair, Caleb crossed his arms. "It's not much different from any other job. They provide a place to stay, food, and a wage that compares with other places I'd work as a ranch hand. The difference is the MacLarens treat me like family. If I'm sick, they pay Doc Vickery. My horse goes lame, they give me another one, the same as they'd do for Blaine or any of the others."

Her brows furrowed. "What about the other men who aren't family?"

He shook his head. "There aren't many. From what I've seen, they're more than fair with everyone who works for them."

"Would either of you like some pie?"

Neither had noticed the waiter walk up.

Miranda smiled, shaking her head. "Not for me, thank you."

"I think we're finished. I'll take the bill, if you have it." Caleb reached into his pocket, pulling out some bills. He held them up for Miranda to see, a wry grin on his face.

Biting her lip, she shook her head. "I shouldn't have said anything."

Caleb handed the money to the waiter. "You're always welcome to ask questions, Miss Harris. Don't be surprised if the answer isn't what you're expecting." Standing, he pulled out her chair, escorting her outside. "It's been a pleasure."

"Thank you for dinner, Mr. Stewart. It was wonderful to see you again." Stepping away, she hesitated a moment before turning in the direction of the boardinghouse.

Caleb watched until she opened the door and stepped inside. He felt dueling pangs of relief and regret as she moved out of his sight. He'd enjoyed their meal, even if her continuous questions caught him off guard. They were honest, not meant to ridicule or judge him. He also knew how hard it was to make friends in a new town. During the week, her days were filled with teaching. He wondered what she did to keep herself busy at night and on weekends.

Living at Circle M meant he had little time to be alone. There were days all he wanted to do was saddle Jupiter and ride for miles. A few times, he and Heather had worked together herding small numbers of cattle. Those had been the best days. Unlike most, he'd never let her surly attitude or brisk manner get to him. He'd seen through her bravado, knowing her need to prove herself to her family.

And she hated doing it in front of him.

"Caleb!"

Turning, he saw Brodie across the street, waving at him. Dashing between wagons and horses, Caleb made his way to him.

Brodie clasped him on the back. "What brings you to town?"

Caleb pointed down the street to the wagon. "Maloney's, Ferguson's, the blacksmith."

Brodie cocked a brow. "And Miss Harris?"

Glancing behind him at the boardinghouse, he shook his head. "It's not what you think."

"I'm not thinking anything, other than she's a comely lass. And she's single."

Caleb sent him a warning look. "I saw her at the general store and asked if she wanted to share a meal. There's nothing more to it."

Brodie grinned. "All right, lad. I'll be taking your word for it. Do you have time to come inside for a bit?"

"I do. In fact, there's something I want to talk with you about."

Brodie rubbed his chin, considering Caleb's suggestions about the ranch. "I've no problem supporting your ideas for the Evanston and Estrada lands. There's no sense keeping the houses and barns in repair, and I think the uncles will agree. You're right believing the Pearce ranch shouldn't be touched while Big Jim and Gertie still live there."

"Have you heard how Big Jim is doing?"

"He isn't doing well. Gertie's been trying to convince him to move to town to be closer to the doctor."

Caleb's face sobered. "The last I spoke with Quinn, he thought Big Jim was improving."

"I'm thinking they don't want Emma and Quinn to know how bad he's getting. She's the only child they have left, and they still feel the need to protect her."

Caleb leaned back in the chair. "I don't think he ever recovered from being shot."

"Or their son's death. I know Quinn still misses Jimmy."

Nodding, Caleb let out a breath. "Colin said they were best friends."

"Aye, since right after we arrived. Now, enough of this talk."

"I agree," Caleb said. "How are you doing with your search for new deputies?"

"Good news. I've hired two."

"That's great news, Brodie."

"Aye." Pulling out a drawer, he grabbed a piece of paper, handing it to Caleb.

"You expect me to read these scratch marks," he snickered, trying to make out Brodie's writing.

"So now you'll be mocking me?"

"Do *you* even know what this says?"

Brodie grinned. "Aye. It's the names and backgrounds of the new deputies."

"Seth Mon...Mont..."

Brodie stood, walking around the desk to pull the paper from Caleb's fingers. "Seth Montero. He used to work for Juan Estrada."

"Does he have experience as a lawman?"

"Nae, but neither did I when the town council hired me."

Caleb rubbed his forehead. "True. I don't recall him in the group of men who stayed on after Estrada sold the ranch."

"Seth found work on a ranch near Sacramento. A deputy he knew mentioned we were looking. The lad took a chance and rode in yesterday." Brodie glanced back down at the paper. "The other lad is Alex Campbell. Fought for the North, then rode west. He saw a note posted at the general store in Crocker, Nevada, and rode over."

"Didn't we ride through there on our way back from Oregon?"

"Aye. It's a nest for outlaws. I'm surprised the old man who owns the general store even posted it. They don't like lawmen in Crocker." Brodie walked to the window, looking out. "They started work this morning."

"You still looking for more?" Caleb asked.

"One, maybe two if I get approval from August. Do you know of someone?"

"Wish I did." Standing, Caleb walked to the door. "Will you be at supper tomorrow?"

Brodie's brows lifted. "Aye. Will you be there? I know the family's been missing you."

Smirking, he shook his head. "Most of the family."

Brodie moved around the desk, stopping next to Caleb. "Colin's been telling me Heather's changed since coming back."

"Why would you think I care?"

"You've not said anything, but we all know you care for the lass."

Caleb shook his head. "Not as I once did. There's no future pretending anything can come from believing otherwise." He looked away, sucking in a breath. "I'd better get back before Blaine comes looking for me."

"I'll be seeing you tomorrow, though?"

Nodding, Caleb opened the door. "You will."

Checking the contents of the wagon, Caleb climbed onto the seat, picking up the lines. Steering the wagon down the street, he turned north, riding along the river on his way to see the progress restoring the stores in Chinatown burned down by the mob. The amount of improvement surprised him. People still worked, replacing burned wood with new, installing new windows, painting, and hanging signs. A couple businesses looked ready to reopen.

Having seen what he wanted, Caleb turned the wagon toward home. Relaxing, he thought of his meal with Miranda. She'd made no attempt to hide her interest in him, which made him cautious about developing a friendship. If he didn't still have feelings for Heather, no matter how futile he knew they were, he might be attracted to the pretty schoolteacher.

He wouldn't ignore her, but had no intention of leading her on. Maybe he'd change his mind in the future. For now, he'd concentrate on work, time alone, and a chance to voice his feelings about the ranch to Ewan and Ian.

Blaine and Brodie supported his ideas. He believed Colin, Quinn, and the rest of the family would, too. If they did, it would mean he and Blaine would return to the main ranch—Blaine to live in his mother's house, and Caleb to live...well, he wasn't sure where. While Heather was gone, he'd stayed in her mother's home. They had more than enough room for him to move back in. With Heather there, though, he had no desire to be under the same roof.

The MacLarens had never built a large bunkhouse, only a cabin suitable for four men. All beds were taken. He knew Colin would invite him to stay with them. It was the largest of the homes, with the most bedrooms, and had been the place all the MacLarens lived until the other houses were built. At least four bedrooms were vacant, which made it the best choice. He loved Kyla like a mother, and he knew she treated him as another son. He just wished it were farther away from where Heather lived.

Whatever decision was made about the Evanston and Estrada properties, he'd figure a way to make it work for him. And he'd begin planning his own future. The day would come when he'd have to make a choice—continue living at Circle M with no prospect of ever owning a piece of land, or venture out, create a life of his own away from the family he'd come to regard as his own.

For now, he'd accept his good fortune. He'd work hard, learn all he could, and save as much of his wage as possible. When the day finally came to make the difficult decision, he'd be ready. At least that was what he'd keep telling himself.

Chapter Eight

Circle M

Colin, Bram, Fletcher, Camden, and several others stood on the lowest rung of the fence, watching Quinn readying to mount the horse for the third time. Laughing among themselves, they placed bets on how long he'd stay on this time.

"Any of you lads who bet against me will be regretting it," Quinn yelled after he quickly checked the cinch, then slid his left boot into the stirrup and mounted. He'd barely made it up when the horse started bucking. His right hand gripped the reins, concentration focused on the animal. Unlike the previous two rides, Quinn stayed centered in the saddle this time, his weight low.

Sean joined the others at the fence, leaning over the top. "Finish it up, lad!"

Colin clasped him on the back, not taking his gaze off Quinn. "How's the mare?"

Sean gave him a weary grin. "She'll be foaling tonight, I'm certain of it."

Colin chuckled. "That's what you've been saying since yesterday."

"Aye." He looked at the others along the fence, all cheering and whooping their support for Quinn. His face sobered when he looked at Colin. "She's a small mare with what I'm thinking is a big foal. We're going to be needing all the help we can get." Sean looked up at the sky, as if offering a silent prayer. He shook his head. "I've not done this before. I'm afraid we'll lose the mare and the foal."

The hoots and yells from the others drew their attention long enough to see Quinn still atop the now exhausted horse. A few more feeble attempts at bucking and the animal stopped, snorting, pawing at the ground, but under Quinn's control.

"The lad has a magic touch when it comes to gentling horses."

"Aye, Sean, he does." Colin waved at Quinn, then turned back to his cousin. "We all know you'll do all you can for the mare and foal. No one will be blaming you if you can't save them."

Sean shook his head. "I'll not be losing them." He started to turn away when Colin grabbed his arm.

"I'll be staying with you in the barn for as long as it takes."

"Nae, Colin. Fletch and Bram will be helping me. The lads and I will be taking turns in the barn."

"Make certain each of you comes in to eat. If you don't, my ma and yours will come looking for you."

A movement behind Sean caught Colin's attention. "It's about time you lads showed up."

The rest of those around the corral turned to see Blaine and Caleb rein their horses to a stop, then slide to the ground. Camden dashed ahead of the others, studied Blaine's face, then turned to Colin.

"Aye. It is our brother. I almost didn't recognize him." Slapping him on the back, Camden turned to Caleb. "Ma will be pleased you came today. She and the lasses have outdone themselves."

Caleb grinned. "It could be beans and it would be better than what we've been cooking for ourselves." He looked beyond them to the corral, seeing Quinn leading a horse toward the fence. "What have you boys been up to?"

"Quinn's been showing us his skills at busting a horse. I think the lad has already convinced Ewan and Pa we don't need to a hire a specialist." Sean looked at Colin. "I'll be getting back to the barn."

Caleb watched Sean leave, cocking a brow at Colin. "A specialist?"

"Aye. A horse buster who rides from ranch to ranch breaking horses. Ewan believes it would be better to pay five dollars per head than to risk one of the lads getting hurt. Quinn isn't keen on bringing in someone from outside to tame our horses. I'm guessing we'll be discussing it at supper tonight."

"What do you think?" Caleb asked, watching Quinn groom the horse he'd broken.

Placing his hands on his hips, Colin shook his head. "Quinn, Fletch, and Bram are the three who bust them now, and each time I pray they don't get hurt. Maybe a specialist would be best, especially with the number of mustangs and wild horses we've added to the herd. We've enough for the contracts with Lime Point Military Reservation and Fort Anderson, plus a large remuda for ourselves. The lads don't have time for their regular chores and busting all the horses."

Caleb glanced at Quinn. "How long did it take him to break that one?"

Colin looked up at the sun, gauging the time. "Maybe half an hour. A specialist gentles six to ten horses a day. I've no doubt any of those lads could keep the same pace. It's their safety I'm worried about. We can't afford for any of them to be laid up."

The sounds of approaching riders had them turning to the trail from town, Colin taking several steps toward them. "It's Brodie and Maggie." He squinted into the distance. "August and Bay Donahue are with them, along with the bonny Miss Harris."

Caleb pursed his lips, settling his hands on his hips. He tried to ignore the churning in his gut as the wagon with Miranda approached. She was pretty, as Colin said, and smart.

"Ah, the lasses have seen them." Colin nodded over his shoulder to where several of the MacLaren women stood on the front porch, waving at the wagon and riders.

Caleb's gaze landed on Heather. The first thing he noticed was the dress, a sight he'd almost never seen. Then he noticed her hair, the way she'd clipped it at the back with long tendrils falling over her shoulders. Last, he realized her attention wasn't on the wagon or riders. All her attention was focused on him, an almost wistful expression on her face. He wanted to go to her, ask what she was thinking. Before he could move, Colin's hand clamped down on his shoulder.

"You've a decision to make, lad."

Drawing in a breath, Caleb shook his head. "You're wrong. Heather made her choice and it wasn't me."

Cocking his head, Colin looked at him. "From what I've seen, the lass has made no choice. There've been no lads asking to court her."

Glaring at him, Caleb turned back toward the wagon. "You misunderstand. In her own way, she made a choice. No matter what her future held, it wouldn't include me. I've accepted it. Now it's time for me to think of a future beyond your prickly cousin."

"Does it include Miss Harris?"

Shaking his head, Caleb shot him a grim smile. "There's no room for a woman in my future. At least not right now. We've lots of work to do on the ranch, and that's where all my energy will go."

He said no more before walking up to where August, sitting between Maggie and Miranda, stopped the wagon. "Mr. Fielder, it's good to see you again." Touching the brim of his hat, he nodded at Miranda and Maggie. "Ladies. May I help you down?"

"I'll help Maggie, Caleb." Brodie walked to the other side of the wagon.

"Miss Harris?"

She moved to the edge of the seat, resting her arms on his shoulders. "Thank you, Mr. Stewart."

Setting her down, he didn't allow his hands to linger on her waist before stepping back. "How was the trip out?"

"Wonderful. It's a beautiful drive from town to Circle M. I'm surprised to see you here today. Heather said you don't come back often."

Caleb's gaze narrowed. "Heather?"

"Well...yes. I came to Sunday supper one other time and sat next to her. She's such a lovely woman, although I don't understand her desire to work alongside the men."

"It's what she loves." He took her elbow, guiding her toward the house. Looking up, he noticed Heather, talking to Kyla, glancing at him and Miranda. He didn't know what he expected. A flash of jealousy perhaps, but her features remained unchanged. "Do you know the women?" he asked as they approached the steps.

"Oh, yes." She smiled up at the ladies who stood on the porch.

"Then I'll leave you here." Caleb dropped his hold on her elbow, tipped his hat, then glanced once again at Heather before heading back to the corral.

"Caleb!"

Turning around, he smiled at Opal and Pearl, two of the three orphaned sisters the MacLarens adopted. Opening his arms, he laughed as they ran up to him.

"You've been gone so long. We thought you might not be coming back." At fourteen, Pearl was the youngest, thin as a reed, and preferred wearing pants to a dress, much the same as Heather.

"Aunt Kyla said he'd be back, Pearl." Opal had been much like her younger sister until she turned sixteen. She now tended to wear a dress and preferred helping Colin and Sarah with their son, Grant, rather than working around the ranch. Slipping her arm through his, she looked up at him. "When are you coming back, Caleb? We all miss you."

"I miss everyone, too. There's a lot of work to do and I go where I'm sent. Right now, that's the old Evanston place. Where's Coral?" Caleb asked. Usually the oldest wasn't too far away from her sisters.

Opal placed a hand over her mouth, giggling. "She's watching for Deke."

Caleb's brow lifted, his attention on Opal. "Deke Arrington who works at the saddlery?"

"Uh-huh. She's sweet on him." Giggling again, she pointed to the house where Quinn and Emma lived with his mother and siblings. "See. There she is."

Looking over his shoulder, he spotted Coral sitting on the porch railing, staring at the trail from town. Rubbing the back of his neck, he smiled.

"Is Deke invited for supper?"

Opal nodded, sliding her arm from Caleb's. "Aunt Audrey invited him. I think he's sweet on Coral, too."

Caleb shook his head. "Well, I'll be." He had a hard time thinking of Coral as twenty. She was no longer a girl, capable of deciding who she cared about.

Looking back at Kyla's house, his gaze halted on Miranda and Heather standing next to each other, talking as if they'd been friends for years. Crossing his arms, he reconsidered his decision. Maybe coming for supper wasn't such a good idea.

The sound of a bell and Kyla's shouts about supper being ready stopped him from doing what he wanted—grabbing Jupiter and riding back to the Evanston ranch.

Opal and Pearl each took one of his hands, tugging him toward the house. "Come on, Caleb. You can sit with us."

"I'd like that." He hoped that would be true. Knowing the aunts, they'd already have seats figured out for everyone, and with the way his luck was running, he'd be right between Miranda and Heather.

Caleb shouldn't have even thought it. On one side sat Heather, doing her best to ignore him, which wasn't hard since Bay sat next to her. On the other side was Miranda, doing all she could to get and keep his attention.

He'd learned she'd grown up an only child in a house with rigid rules and high expectations. Miranda had been courted by one young man who didn't impress her in the slightest. Coming west had been her way of getting out from under her parents' suffocating home and away from the inappropriate suitor. After that, Caleb's attention had begun to wane, his ears picking up bits and pieces of conversations between the men around the table.

"I think the lad has a good idea," he heard Brodie say. "Why spend money and time repairing houses and barns we don't need?"

"And what do you think, Colin?" Ewan asked.

"The idea has merit. We merge the herds and bring everyone here."

"It would mean enlarging the bunkhouse." Ewan looked down the table at his brother, Ian, who'd been listening.

Blaine nodded. "Aye, but it's an easy job."

"And you, Quinn. What do you think?"

"The same as the others, Uncle Ewan. Caleb's idea is sound."

Ewan looked around the table, knowing several of those who'd want a say couldn't hear the conversation. Seeing his wife, Lorna, and Ian's wife, Gail, emerge from the kitchen, each carrying pies, he grinned. "Then I'll be bringing it up over whiskeys...after we've finished dessert."

A poke in his side had Caleb looking over at Heather, quirking a brow. "Did you want something?"

"Don't be daft, Caleb. Of course I do or I wouldn't be jabbing you."

Sitting back in his chair, he crossed his arms. "Well, you have my attention."

"What idea is Uncle Ewan talking about?"

He explained his idea, seeing her nod. Picking up his cup, he took a sip of coffee, waiting for her thoughts.

"Aye, it is a good idea." Lifting her chin, Heather locked her eyes on his. "Except the part about you returning. It's too bad you couldn't stay at the Evanston ranch."

Choking on the last swallow, he set the cup down. "Yes, it is. If it helps, I promise to stay as far away from you as possible."

Her eyes sparked for an instant before she nodded. "See that you do, lad. I'll not be wasting my time working around you."

If the front door hadn't burst open, he would've told her he had no desire to work around her, either.

One of the newer ranch hands yanked his hat off his head, walking to the table. He looked at Ewan.

"Sorry to interrupt your meal, sir, but we've got a problem."

They'd all been surprised when the ranch hand explained about the fire at the original Estrada hacienda, the missing cattle, and the wrangler who hadn't been seen since breakfast.

Ewan didn't hesitate to give the order for everyone to saddle their horses and be ready to ride in ten minutes. He sent the ranch hand back instead of waiting for the rest of them.

Heather immediately stood, her chair falling over in her haste.

"Where do you think you're going?" Caleb crossed his arms over his chest, glaring at her. "You aren't riding with us, Heather."

"Of course I'll be coming with you." Heather picked up her skirt, racing to the front door. "I'll change and meet you in the barn."

"Nae, lass, you won't." Ewan grabbed her arm. "You'll be staying here with the women and children."

"But—"

"I'll have no sass from you on this. We've no time to wait." He looked at his wife. "Lorna, will you and the others be all right while we're gone?"

She shot him a stern glare. "Of course. Would you be thinking we're weak females, unable to manage with you lads away?"

Dropping his hold on Heather's arm, he held up his hands. "Nae, love." Walking to her, he placed a kiss on her cheek. "Keep everyone here. Thane will be watching the barns while we're gone."

At fourteen, Quinn's younger brother had expected to ride along. It wouldn't be long before he'd be old enough, putting himself in danger the same as his older brothers and cousins.

Lorna nodded. "Thane's a good lad. He'd warn of anything suspicious." She followed him outside, stopping next to the others who were staying behind.

Mounting his horse, Ewan motioned to the other men. "Let's go."

Caleb reined Jupiter in a circle, coming to a stop in front of the porch, his hard gaze on Heather. "Do not follow us." When she didn't respond, he leaned toward her, his voice low and firm. "Do you hear me?"

Swallowing the bile in her throat, she nodded, her body shaking in anger. Caleb had no right telling her what to do. And to reprimand her in front of her family made her blood boil.

Resting fisted hands on her hips, she stared back. "I'll be doing what Uncle Ewan asked," she ground out, feeling her face heat.

He stared at her a moment longer, nodded once, then reined around, hurrying to catch up with the others.

"It's wonderful that Caleb is so protective of you. It must be like having another brother." Miranda smiled sweetly, yet the tone of her voice told Heather her thoughts might be moving in another direction.

"I've enough older cousins and brothers. I don't need Caleb Stewart trying to be another."

Clasping her hands in front of her, Miranda watched the men disappear down the trail. "Well then, perhaps he's interested in something more."

Heather snorted, crossing her arms over her chest. "Believe me, the lad isn't looking for anything more from me. He doesn't like me, and I'm not feeling friendly toward him." She shook her head, her lips forming a thin line.

"Well, if you're certain..." Miranda's voice trailed off, but not before Heather heard the interest in her tone.

She thought about saying something more, maybe a type of warning, when her mother walked up.

"The lads will be fine, Heather. Now, I'll be needing your help in the kitchen." Audrey nodded toward the door, then left, expecting them to follow her back into the house.

"Don't be feeling you have to help us." Heather took a few steps toward the front door, stopping at Miranda's voice.

"I can't leave until Mr. Fielder gets back, so I might as well help you inside. Besides, it will give me time to learn more about your fascinating family."

Heather bit her tongue, forcing herself to calm down and not respond. She reminded herself she wasn't angry at Miranda or any of her family. It would do no good to take her frustration out on them. Instead, she'd save her rage and irritation for another time when it could be directed at the right person.

Right now, that person was nowhere around. He rode north with her family, risking his life to help whatever threatened the Circle M. The thought cooled her annoyance...somewhat.

When he returned, she'd set him right. Heather wasn't some simpering female, like Miranda Harris. And she was no longer the young woman who faced everyone as if they were her enemy. She'd changed, and the time had come for Caleb Stewart to understand it.

Chapter Nine

Caleb's eyes widened as the group reached the top of a hill overlooking the Estrada hacienda. In the late afternoon light, all he could see was smoldering embers surrounding charred adobe walls. The two story home had been destroyed, along with the barn and most of the bunkhouse.

Ewan nudged his horse in front of the others, his jaw working as he surveyed the damage. "There's nothing we can do, lads. The house and barn are gone. It's time to find our cattle."

"I'd suggest we divide into groups, Uncle Ewan."

"Good idea, Colin." He glanced over his shoulder. "Split into two groups. Colin, Bram, Brodie, Sean, and Bay will ride north. Quinn, Caleb, Blaine, Fletcher, Camden, and Deke will ride west. Ian, August, and I will be continuing to the hacienda to see if there's anything we can salvage and talk with the ranch hands. Maybe one of them saw someone." He glanced up at the sky, gauging the time. "Meet back at the hacienda two hours after sunset."

"And if we find the cattle, Da?" Brodie asked.

"Send a rider to the hacienda."

Quinn motioned to those in his group. "Let's go."

Caleb rode between Blaine and Quinn for a couple miles, his mind switching between thoughts of who had set the fire and wondering if the same people rustled the cattle. Remembering something Fletcher had mentioned, he leaned toward Quinn.

"Fletch said a couple men snuck into their camp a few nights ago."

Quinn nodded. "Aye. Heather was on watch when she heard someone."

Caleb's brows creased. "Heather?"

"Aye. The lass was guarding the herd with Fletch and Bram when she heard noises. The lads followed two men to their horses, but couldn't stop them." Quinn reined his horse slightly south, then continued west.

Following his lead, Caleb caught up to him. "Fletch said he didn't think they were after the herd."

"Nae. The three sat up the rest of the night, but no one approached the cattle. They don't know what the men wanted. It couldn't have been good or they'd have approached the camp, not run off."

"Do you think what happened today is connected?"

Quinn nodded. "Aye, Caleb. I do."

"A hundred head is a lot for two men," Caleb said as they approached a stream, Quinn reining to a stop.

"I'm thinking they were scouts for a larger group of rustlers. Probably followed them the next morning when they merged the cattle into the larger herd." Quinn shoved his hat back, looking at the others. "Fan out, lads, but keep in sight of each other.

Nobody go off alone. Fire once in the air if you've found them, twice if there's trouble. I'll be at the farthest point north, and Fletcher will be the farthest rider south. The rest of you lads spread out between us."

Caleb followed Quinn, stopping fifty yards away to begin the search. Reining Jupiter left, then right, he listened and watched for any signs the herd had been driven in this direction. The more ground he covered, the less he believed they'd moved the herd west. It wouldn't be easy to hide a hundred head, and harder to cover the trail of that many cattle.

As darkness spread, his mind shifted to thoughts of Heather. Caleb hadn't meant to come down so hard on her about going with them, and he hadn't planned to give her a warning in front of the other women. But he hadn't anticipated his protective reaction at her insistence on going with the men, or the way his gut twisted at the thought of her in danger.

Walking Jupiter over a narrow creek, and as much as he wanted to deny it, Caleb accepted his feelings for Heather hadn't changed. As infuriating as he found her, she was the only woman who stirred his blood, captured his interest and held it. The grim reality was he'd never get over her by staying at Circle M.

Given the comments at supper, and with the Estrada ranch burned to the ground, he had little doubt they'd make the decision to close the Evanston house, merging the cattle with the rest of the herd. His plan had been accepted, yet it had also sealed his fate. He and Blaine would be moving back to the main ranch. With both Brodie and Jinny living with their spouses in town, Ewan's house would have plenty of space for him. No matter. It still wouldn't be far enough away from Heather.

He'd wait until the decision had been made on the Evanston property, then speak with Ewan and Ian. With a recommendation from them, he'd be able to find work at almost any ranch within a thousand miles.

Instead of a sense of foreboding at the direction of his thoughts, he felt a sense of peace. Maybe this was the way it had always been meant to play out. Once he'd arrived at Circle M, Caleb thought his journey had ended. Now he realized it had only begun.

Circle M

Heather, Emma, Sarah, and her sister, Geneen, hurried outside at the sound of an approaching rider. A minute later, Maggie, a few months pregnant with her and Brodie's first child, joined them. The women had put the younger children to bed long ago, then began their vigil, sending up prayers for the safety of all the men.

Fires weren't uncommon. Losing a hundred head and discovering a ranch hand had gone missing were unusual and cause for concern.

Heather couldn't help herself from thinking of the men who'd stalked their camp a few nights ago, wondering if they had anything to do with what had transpired today. She'd said nothing to the other women. No sense causing them more worry.

"It's Mr. Donahue." Heather hurried down the steps. "Do you have news?"

Stopping his horse, he slid to the ground, tossing the reins over a nearby rail. By now, all the women had assembled outside, waiting as he took Heather's elbow and guided her back up the steps.

"I'm afraid it's not good. The hacienda, barn, and bunkhouse are gone, and we haven't been able to find the missing cattle."

"And the ranch hand?" Kyla held out a glass filled with whiskey.

"Thank you, ma'am." Accepting it, he shook his head. "He hasn't returned." Tossing the alcohol back, he handed the empty glass to Kyla. "August is a little ways behind me. The other men are staying. They want to start early to look for the missing man and renew the search for the cattle. I'll be rejoining them, but I wanted to give you the news."

"I'll be going with you."

Audrey stepped beside her. "Nae, Heather, you won't."

"But, Ma, they'll need every available rider."

Audrey shook her head. "What they need is for us to prepare food for Mr. Donahue to take back with him and to know we'll be taking care of everyone while they're gone."

Placing her fisted hands on her hips, Heather glared at her mother. "You've plenty of help here, Ma. I can be of more help out there with them, searching for the cattle."

After a few moments of uneasy silence, Bay cleared his throat, looking at Heather. "Miss MacLaren, your Uncle Ewan was quite specific that you not go against his orders. I believe he suspected how you'd react and wanted to make sure you didn't ride back with me."

Throwing her hands up, Heather stomped into the house, letting the door slam behind her.

Shaking her head, Audrey offered Bay a weak smile. "She's a passionate lass."

He nodded. "It's understandable. Her family's in danger and she wants to help. From what I've heard, it seems she is quite capable in many ways."

"Aye, Mr. Donahue, she is. As are most of the women. If I'd be judging their expressions correctly, I'd say Emma, Geneen, and Coral would join Heather if they saw an opportunity. They're all excellent riders and quite proficient with guns.

"Well, let's get you some food to take back. The men will be having a long night and a longer day tomorrow."

"Heather, you must settle down. Ewan has his reasons for wanting us here."

"Aye, Geneen. He sees us as weak females." Heather pounded a fist into her lap, looking at the group of women sitting with her in the living room. "It isn't right, Emma. You ride and shoot as good as Quinn."

Emma straightened the folds of her dress, trying to control her own agitation at the situation. Before marrying Quinn, she'd worked from sunup to sundown on her parents' ranch, riding with the men, doing the same work. She now worked with Fletcher and Bram in their horse breeding part of the ranch, having little to do with the cattle or threats to the family.

Reaching over, Emma touched Heather's arm. "As much as I'd like to be alongside him, I believe Quinn and the others are doing what they think best. Remember, there's over a thousand head at the Evanston place, and my parents have several hundred head at their ranch. With most of the men at the Estrada place, we're all that's left if the rustlers move this way before the family returns."

Heather's eyes flashed. "There are only two men left at the widow's place."

"And only Boyd Doggett and a few ranch hands at my parents'." Emma bit her lower lip, then stood, pacing to the window. "I wonder if we should send word to them about what happened."

"You'll be doing no such thing." Kyla walked into the room, crossing her arms. "When Mr. Donahue left, he promised to send word of what the lads found."

"But we don't know when, Aunt Kyla." Heather stood, her shoulders slumping as she joined Emma by the window. "Someone should warn them about what happened."

Kyla walked toward them, glancing at the other women who watched her. "If we've no word by noon tomorrow, we'll send word to the men at the old Evanston place and to Emma's parents." She gave Heather a hard stare. "It'll be Audrey, Lorna, Gail, and me deciding who goes. So don't be pestering us about it." None of them would go up against the four elder MacLaren women. Once their minds were made up, they could be even more resolute than Ewan and Ian.

Audrey stepped beside Kyla, nodding her agreement. "We've already discussed tonight. I'd suggest those of you on watch get your guns and find your positions. After four hours, wake your replacement. The rest of us will get what sleep we can."

Heather trudged to a back bedroom where several of the women would be sleeping. She'd requested the second shift, although she might as well have taken both. There'd be no sleeping tonight. Not bothering to slip out of her dress, she lay down, placing an arm over her eyes. Without conscious effort, an image of Caleb appeared. This wasn't the intense man who'd glared at her just before leaving to join the other men. Tonight, she pictured him around a campfire, a cup of coffee in one hand, laughing at the banter of the other lads. No one could question how handsome he looked with his broad smile and deep laugh. In her mind, she saw him stand, tossing out the rest of the coffee, then made his way across camp to his bedroll.

She'd never allowed herself to fantasize any further. Tonight, though, she pictured him taking off his boots, sliding out of his trousers, and opening his shirt. His tapered waist and muscled thighs had her balling her fists at her sides. Heather had seen him working without a shirt many times. The vision seemed almost too real, enough to send heat coursing through her limbs. She imagined running her hands over his shoulders and chest, feeling the taut muscles.

Closing her eyes, Heather pictured his lips, wondering what it would feel like to have them brush against hers. An odd tightening of her chest caused

Heather to suck in a deep breath, shoving the thought aside.

"What would he think if he knew I'd never been kissed?" she whispered to herself.

"Did you say something, Heather?"

She shot up, her eyes adjusting to the darkness to see Emma across the room. So caught up in her fantasy, she'd forgotten Emma would be sharing the room with her.

Clearing her throat, Heather shook her head. "Nae. Just thinking of the men."

Staring out the window, Emma's determined gaze fixed on the full moon. "I have to believe Quinn and the others will be all right. They'll find the missing man and the cattle, then be safely back here tomorrow evening." Turning her head, she looked at Heather. "You should think about telling Caleb how you feel."

Heather's jaw dropped. "Caleb?"

Taking off her shoes, Emma ignored the feigned surprise. "Caleb...the man you've been in love with since he came to the ranch. Don't you think it's time you put him out of his misery?"

Heather clutched her stomach, her throat thickening at what Emma's words implied. Did everyone know how much she cared about him, how much she missed being around him?

"I've no idea what you mean."

Emma lay back on the bed, making no attempt to stifle a huge yawn. "You can deny it all you want, as I tried to do with Quinn. In the end, you'll wish you'd talked to Caleb."

Before Heather could reply, she heard the soft, steady sounds of Emma breathing. She'd already fallen asleep.

Lying back down, Heather's body hummed with nervous tension as she thought of what Emma said. She thought of Caleb's anger at the thought of her riding with them to the Estrada hacienda. His stern reaction made her think he believed it his job to protect her.

It had taken time, but she now realized the full degree of her feelings for Caleb. At one time, she knew he felt the same. She no longer felt such confidence. Confessing her love could be the start of a real future for them. It could also lead to humiliation.

Blood began to pound in her temples as fear and indecision wrapped around her. She wished Levi had stayed so she could express her confusion to him. He'd always given her good advice, known what she needed to hear.

Uncertainty whirled around inside her head. Maybe sleep would help ease the chaos of her thoughts. Closing her eyes, Heather willed herself to sleep.

Four hours later, she still stared at the ceiling...no closer to a resolution.

Caleb sat by the fire, cradling a cup of coffee in his hands while the others finished saddling their horses. He'd been ready to ride since well before sunup, thoughts of their missing ranch hand, the stolen cattle, and Heather warring for space in his brain. The last kept him awake into the early morning, until he'd succeeded at shoving her image from his mind.

Quinn walked up, setting a hand on Caleb's shoulder. "The lads will be going out in the same groups, looking for both the cattle and the ranch hand. Any suggestions on where to start?"

What they'd seen last night left no doubt the cattle had been taken. That many head didn't go missing without help from two-legged predators. And unless their ranch hand had gone in with the rustlers, no one believed they'd find him alive.

Standing, Caleb tossed out the last of his coffee. "If it were me, I'd go where we'd least expect it."

"East..." Quinn let the word trail off, knowing the implications.

Shrugging, Caleb looked at the Boundary Mountain range that split California from Nevada. "So far, there's been little snow. If they can drive the herd over the grade to Crocker, they'll be out of danger. They'll sell the cattle, divide the profits, and nobody will ever know."

Quinn nodded. Caleb, Brodie, and Quinn had been through there with Sarah and the three orphans on their journey back to Circle M from Oregon. Control of Crocker rested in the hands of outlaws—individuals and gangs who didn't care for strangers and shunned normal values. They operated by shooting, then asking questions.

"It could take them two weeks to make the trek."

Caleb tightened his gunbelt around his hips. "Then we'd best get going."

Quinn walked over to where Colin stood with Ewan, Ian, and Brodie. The discussion didn't last long before he returned to Caleb.

"Our group will go east toward Crocker. Ian will be coming with us and Ewan with Colin's group. They'll be returning here tonight, unless they find the cattle. Then they'll drive them to the main herd."

"And us?" Caleb asked.

"If needed, we go as far as the edge of Crocker. We're not to go into the town. If we don't find the cattle by then, we head back to Circle M."

"It could be several days," Caleb reminded him.

Quinn nodded. "They've given us three days to return, then they'll be looking for us."

Caleb's jaw hardened. He hated to lose a single head. To have a hundred taken ate at him. "Then we find those miscreants fast and get the herd back on our land."

A faint smile tilted up the corners of Quinn's mouth. "Aye, lad. That's what we do."

Chapter Ten

"They're going to Crocker?" Heather's hand flew to her mouth. "That's outlaw country."

"Yes, ma'am." The ranch hand who'd notified them of the fire nodded, nervous fingers twisting the brim of his hat as he looked around the circle of women. "One group is heading east and the other's riding north. The ones headed to Crocker have three days, then they're to return to Circle M—with or without the herd."

Looking around at the other women, Heather decided there was no point in hiding her concern. "And Caleb Stewart...which group is he with?"

The ranch hand didn't quite meet her gaze. "Why, he'd be with Quinn's group, ma'am, going over the mountains." He rattled off the names of the men in each group. "I'm to stay here and help out."

Kyla stepped forward. "I'm sorry, but I don't recall your name."

"Victor Rhimes, ma'am. But everyone calls me Vic."

"Aye, Vic it is. If you'll wait a minute, I believe we have a job for you."

"Yes, ma'am."

She motioned for Audrey, Lorna, and Gail to join her across the room. "I'd be thinking Vic is the right person to ride to the ranches and to town to let Sam and the deputies know what's happening."

Lorna nodded. "I'm surprised Sam hasn't sent anyone out to check on Brodie and Maggie."

"Aye, but with Brodie here, he's a busy man. So, we're agreed?" Kyla asked, seeing the other three nod their approval before returning to speak with Vic.

"We'd like you to ride to the old Evanston ranch, Vic, then to the Pearce place, and finally to town to see Sam Covington. They need to know what happened. Let them know we're doing fine here and not to worry about us."

"Yes, ma'am. I'll get going right away." Nodding at the women, he hurried outside, mounted, and took off to the Evanston property.

Heather paced a few feet away, then turned to face the others. "I'm not liking this. No one knows how many men took the cattle. We've seven men going east and six north. It's not sounding like good odds."

Audrey walked to her, placing a hand on her daughter's shoulder. "Give the men some credit, lass. They've been taking care of the ranch, and us, a long time. We must trust them."

"Aunt Audrey. There's a rider coming." Coral headed out the front door, stopping at the edge of the porch as a heavyset man with a red beard, dressed all in black, reined his horse to a stop. Looking behind her, she saw most everyone had joined her outside.

Taking off his hat, he looked around, not bothering to dismount. "Ladies, I'm Giles Delacroix. I've heard you've had some problems out at the Estrada property and thought I'd see if it's been straightened out."

Kyla studied the man, unease rolling through her. Taking a few steps down the porch, she looked at him. "I'm Kyla MacLaren, Mr. Delacroix. I believe we met months ago at the community dance."

"I well remember, Mrs. MacLaren. As I recall, your sons, Colin, Blaine, and Camden, were also at the dance, as were many of the women I see this morning."

She glanced over her shoulder at her family, then back at Giles. "You've a good memory, Mr. Delacroix. I do believe all the women were there."

"And the men...have they returned?"

Kyla felt another prickle of unease flash through her. She wondered how he'd heard of their misfortune so quickly. "They're rounding up the strays now. We expect them to return soon."

"Is that so?" He looked around again, not hiding his skepticism. "I heard a man might have been killed."

Crossing her arms, Kyla cocked her head to the side. "Aye, there's a man missing. I'm thinking he's looking for the cattle, the same as the others. We've no reason to believe he's dead, Mr. Delacroix. Unless, of course, you have reason to think he is."

"Why no, Mrs. MacLaren. Just recounting what I heard in town."

Heather stepped forward, settling her hands on her hips. "Where'd you hear the news, Mr. Delacroix?"

"From August Fielder early this morning. He said he'd brought Miss Harris back late last night after seeing the remains of the Estrada hacienda." He shook his head. "Such a shame to lose such a wonderful old home."

Heather glanced at Emma and Geneen, who stood on either side of her. They all knew the decision to abandon the hacienda would've been made last night, even if the fire hadn't started.

Emma stepped forward. "As you can see, Mr. Delacroix, we're all doing fine here. I'll let Ewan and Ian know you came by to check on us."

"As I recall, you're Quinn's wife. Your parents are Big Jim and Gertie Pearce, correct? So good to see you again."

Something in his manner caused a shiver to run through her. "Yes, they're my parents. You do seem to have an extraordinary memory for only meeting us once."

His chuckle seemed forced. "It's a flaw, I'm afraid, Mrs. MacLaren. Well, as you said, everyone seems well. If there's anything I can do, please don't hesitate to ask for my help. I'm staying at the Gold Dust." Settling his hat on his head, he smiled.

"Ladies. Please have Ewan and Ian contact me when they return."

"We'll do that, Mr. Delacroix." Emma waited until he'd ridden far enough away not to hear. She turned to the others. "I don't like that man."

For the first time in two days, several of them laughed.

"I'm believing we're in agreement with you, lass," Audrey said. Turning to Kyla, her face grew serious. "Something's not right. I can feel it." She touched her chest, the same as she'd done the day her husband, Gillis, and Kyla's husband, Angus, had been murdered. Since that day, Kyla had learned to take Audrey's premonitions seriously.

Straightening, Kyla spun around, her gaze locking on Heather. "I want you, Emma, Geneen, and Coral to change into your work clothes. Get your rifles, then saddle your horses."

"What is it, Aunt Kyla?" Heather asked, her heart pounding.

"Audrey has a feeling..."

The four young women glanced at Audrey, then nodded. Two seconds later, they burst into action, doing as Kyla asked.

"What is it, Jupiter?" Caleb worked to control his horse, an animal who spooked at nothing. An instant later, Quinn's horse danced around, snorting as it tried to turn away.

Getting Jupiter under control, Caleb's gaze searched the area, his eyes locking on a spot several yards away. "There...up ahead."

Quinn looked where he indicated, muttering a curse.

"Holy..." Fletcher reined hard when his horse tried to bolt. "Easy, lad." Leaning down, he stroked the gelding's neck. "Easy."

As Deke, Blaine, Camden, and Ian arrived, they worked to control their own horses, the animals' sense of smell alerting them to danger. They looked in the direction where Caleb and Quinn stared. Not twenty yards away, a body hung from a rope.

"Our ranch hand." Ian dismounted, handing his reins to Deke. "Stay here, lad. We need to get him down."

Deke and Fletcher took care of the horses while the other men took cautious steps around the trees and low bushes, stopping a few feet away from the body.

"Do you recognize him, Quinn?" Ian asked.

"Aye. He's one of ours."

Ian nodded, then looked at Blaine and Caleb. "Cut him down, lads. Camden?"

"Aye, Uncle Ian."

"Get one of the horses. We'll be taking him back with us."

"What about the cattle?" Fletcher rode alongside Ian as they took the trail back to the Circle M. They'd tied the body onto Camden's horse, the least likely of the animals to spook. He'd doubled up with Blaine for the ride back.

"I'm hoping Brodie's group finds them. If not, we let them go."

"Caleb might still be right about them going over the mountains."

"Aye, Fletch, he might be. We've not enough men to take the body back and still continue the search. We've done what we can for now."

Caleb and Quinn rode at the back of the group, talking in low voices as they made their way back to the ranch. Neither wanted to give up searching for the cattle, but Ian's decision had been made, and they'd abide by it.

"I'm thinking of leaving Circle M, Quinn." Caleb didn't know why he let the thought spill out of his lips, except maybe to get a reaction.

Quinn chuckled, shaking his head. "Aye, lad. And I'm thinking of running for governor."

"And a fine governor you'd be."

Glancing over at Caleb, he saw the somber expression on his friend's face, then frowned. "You're serious."

Sucking in a breath, Caleb let it out in a slow rush of air. "I am."

Scratching the back of his neck, Quinn hesitated a moment, his face blank. "You can't just leave, lad. You're family."

Reining Jupiter to a stop, Caleb rolled his head from side to side, trying to ease the tense muscles in his shoulders. Quinn watched him, waiting.

"I feel the same about all of you. The problem is I'm not family. If I want a future, a place of my own, I can't stay."

Quinn's nostrils flared, his jaw tightening as he studied Caleb. They'd become close over their time together. He trusted him as much as any of his family. There was no way he'd let Caleb walk away without an argument. "This is about Heather, isn't it?"

Caleb let out a weary sigh. "I've been considering this for a while. It's not about anyone but me, Quinn."

"You might be telling yourself that, but I don't believe it."

He'd known this would be hard. Caleb thought telling Quinn, the MacLaren he felt closest to, would be the best way to deliver the news. Now, he wasn't so certain.

Scrubbing a hand down his face, Quinn shook his head. "You've a place here, lad. The family needs you...now more than ever." Looking back toward the trail, he saw the others had stopped, Ian regarding them with a frown. "I'm asking you to think on this some more. We've enough land to carve out places for everyone, and that includes you."

Caleb snorted. "I'm not looking for charity."

Quinn's face reddened. "Charity!" he barked out. "You work as hard as the rest of us, harder most days. Ewan, Ian, and everyone else knows it. They see you as a part of the family, not someone in need." He blew out a frustrated breath. "You've become a brother, lad. We'll not be letting you leave without serious conflict."

Caleb's jaw slackened. "You'd fight me over this?"

"Aye. If pounding sense into you is the only way to change your mind, I'll be the first in line."

Throwing back his head, Caleb laughed. "I'm not fighting you or anyone else."

Quinn smiled. "It's a good decision you've made."

Caleb's brows furrowed in confusion. "What decision are you referring to?"

"To stay, lad. If you won't be fighting us, it means you'll not be leaving."

"Quinn, I don't think—" Caleb shut his mouth when Ian rode up.

"Are you lads coming?"

Quinn shot a quick look at Caleb, then nodded at Ian. "Aye. We just had a few things to straighten out."

Ian cocked his head. "You've finished then?"

"Aye."

"No."

Quinn and Caleb answered at the same time, causing one of Ian's brows to lift.

"Well then, I'll leave it to you lads to finish this later." Reining his horse around, he rode away, knowing they'd follow.

"This isn't over, Quinn."

"Aye, Caleb, it is."

"I'm still not certain what Aunt Kyla expects of us." Geneen rode next to Heather, her mind still reeling from the sight of the destroyed Estrada hacienda a couple hours before. They'd been keeping a steady pace since leaving the house, determined to locate the group led by Colin.

Heather did her best to shove aside the anger she felt at whoever set the fire. She wanted to find them and make them pay. Glancing at Geneen, she cleared her throat. "Aunt Kyla and Ma want us to follow the lads who've ridden north in search of the cattle."

"I still don't understand why when Uncle Ewan ordered us to stay away."

"Ma has a bad feeling about what's going on with the cattle. When she's got a feeling, we listen."

Geneen stared at her, shaking her head as Emma and Coral came up beside them.

"I know it sounds strange, Geneen, but whenever Audrey would get agitated about something, Gillis would listen." Emma looked at Heather, who nodded for her to continue. "He said her instincts were better than anyone he'd ever known. She had a very bad feeling for several days before he and Angus rode off together. Audrey warned them, begged Gillis not to go. It was the one time he didn't listen. They were murdered the same day. We always pay attention when she says something doesn't feel right."

Geneen bit her lip, doing her best to understand. She'd ridden to Circle M with the group from Oregon, been there the day Colin and Quinn learned their fathers had been killed while they were searching for Sarah. Still, she'd never quite understood Audrey's premonitions.

"How does she know it has to do with our men? What if it's about those we left at the ranch?" Geneen asked.

"God help whoever tries," Coral smirked.

"Aye, Coral." Heather looked at Geneen. "Have you ever seen them when they're angry?" She kicked her horse, picking up the pace.

"Once," Geneen answered, urging her horse on to match the others.

"What about angry *with* guns in their hands?" Heather asked.

Shaking her head, she laughed. "I know I wouldn't want to be their target."

"Trust me," Emma said. "Those four women can handle a rifle as well as any of the men. They'll keep everyone safe. I'm certain of it."

Coral opened her mouth to say something when Heather reined her horse to a stop, holding up her hand.

"Listen." Heather leaned in the direction she'd heard the sounds. "It's cattle." She smiled at the others. "The lads must be up ahead." Starting forward, she reined up at Emma's warning.

"Wait. Look over there." Emma pointed toward a hill a good distance away. "What do you see?"

Narrowing her gaze, Heather leaned forward. "Looks like a group of men. Five, maybe six. It's hard to tell."

"I count six. Do you recognize any of them?" Coral asked.

Heather shook her head. "We're much too far away. But if they found the cattle, those lads aren't ours. They'd be with the herd."

"My guess is they're the rustlers. We need to get closer." Emma leaned forward, whispering to her horse, who started forward. "We should keep close to the trees so they don't see us."

Heather agreed, reining her horse behind Emma. "And until we know who they are, be ready to shoot."

Chapter Eleven

"We've all the missing cattle." Colin shifted in his saddle, looking for signs of the men who'd taken the herd. "It makes no sense there'd be no one guarding them." He and Brodie rode point, Bram and Ewan at the flank positions, and Sean and Bay riding drag. The rains several days before, as well as the fact they traveled over land covered with low-growing grass, kept the dust to a minimum.

Brodie rested his hand on the handle of his six-shooter, feeling a sense of unease. "Aye. This doesn't seem right. I'm going to let the lads know to be extra careful. I've a feeling this isn't going to be as easy as it appears."

Continuing toward Circle M's main herd, Colin kept his gaze moving over the rolling hills and boulder formations, watching for any sign of trouble. Unlike the day before, they had no trouble finding the herd that morning. There were no guards posted, no men watching for the MacLarens. Every instinct he had pointed to a trap. But where?

What he couldn't figure out was why someone went to the trouble of moving the herd at all. If they wanted to go after the men, there were easier ways to do it than burning down the hacienda and driving a hundred head of cattle several miles north. None of it made sense.

"The lads are ready. They know to be on watch."

Colin nodded. "And what of Ewan?"

Brodie glanced behind him at his father. "Da is going to take Bay's place on drag."

Colin shook his head. "Bay doesn't have the experience to ride flank. If Ewan wants to change, have him come up here and take my spot."

"According to Da, he's ridden flank on other drives before. Another bit of information about the gunfighter we didn't know."

Colin chuckled. "And how did Ewan find this out?"

"It wasn't anything Bay offered. August told him. Seems the lad worked on a ranch on his journey from back east to Conviction. That's why he was eager to ride along when he heard about the fire."

"A gunfighter, ranch hand, and lawyer. He's an interesting lad."

Brodie nodded. "That he is. I'm thinking we should take him to Buckie's Castle"

"Aye, I'm thinking the same."

Even his concern about who took the cattle didn't stop Brodie's mouth from tilting into a smile. "Soon."

"I see three of the rustlers. Where'd the others go?" Emma slowed as they got to the edge of the stand of trees, then slid to the ground. Holding the reins, she looked at the others, who'd also dismounted, grouping themselves together.

Heather stared at the last spot she'd seen the group of six men. Three were still on the opposite hillside, kneeling, staring in the same direction. She followed their gaze.

"There." Heather pointed toward a large grouping of rocks down the hill. "They're hiding among the boulders."

Emma's brows narrowed. "But why?" Then she gasped, seeing the herd moving directly toward the rustlers. "They're setting a trap."

Geneen stepped up beside her. "We have to stop them."

Heather looked over at her. "We'll never hit them from here. We have to get closer."

"On foot." Emma led her mare back into the trees, then pulled her rifle from its scabbard. The others did the same. "We stay low, come up behind the three men still on the hill. When we shoot them, the other three will hear the shots."

"And race back up the hill?" Coral asked Emma.

"With luck. But the shots will also alert our men."

Heather nodded. "Emma's right. If we can get those on the hill, our lads will know there's a trap.

We'll never get to the ones hiding in the boulders without being seen."

"Then we need to get moving before our men get any closer." Geneen checked her rifle, grabbing more shells and stuffing them into the pocket of her jacket. "We're coming up behind them. If we hurry, they won't suspect anything until it's too late."

The four looked at each other, their determined expressions hiding the fear racing through them. Without a word, they moved, making a wide arc and staying as low to the ground as possible. The late morning sun beat down on them, offsetting the chill from the early November breeze, and causing another problem.

Emma stopped, crouching down, looking behind her. "Keep your rifles out of the sun. We don't want them seeing a reflection."

"Aye. Now go," Heather urged, watching the herd come closer to the men hidden in the boulders.

Within minutes, Emma stopped again, dropping onto her stomach. "We can get them from here."

Heather flanked her on one side while Geneen and Coral settled into position on the other.

"I'll take the one on the far right," Heather said.

Emma nodded. "The one next to him is mine."

Geneen sucked in a breath, letting it out in a slow whoosh. "Coral and I will aim for the third man."

Emma glanced at all three. "Just be sure to stay down. They won't see us in the grass—at least not soon enough to get off good shots before we do."

"All right then, lasses." Heather held up her gun, aiming at her target.

Emma did the same, forcing herself to relax. "Everyone ready?" The instant they answered, she counted. "One, two, three."

The sound of four rifles discharging at one time ripped through the quiet countryside. Two men dropped, the third staggered, then fell when a second shot caught him in the chest.

"Holy..." Geneen sputtered, looking at the herd. "The cattle..."

Heather, Emma, and Coral whipped their heads in the direction of the cattle, hearing the sounds of scared animals.

Emma jumped up, her heart pounding. "They're stampeding."

Heather stood, grabbing Emma's arm to keep her from rushing forward. "The lads will be fine. Look." She pointed toward the men. "They're letting the herd go and taking cover. We must continue down the slope and try to get closer to the other men."

Not long ago, Emma had been badly injured in a stampede. Quinn had been with her. The memory still haunted her, causing nightmares and nights where she couldn't sleep at all.

Geneen screeched as a bullet hit the ground in front of her. "Get down! They've seen us."

Heather dropped, yanking Emma down beside her. Aiming her rifle at the cluster of boulders, Heather fired. The others did the same, unloading their weapons until they were out of bullets, then reloading.

The remaining rustlers fired wildly up the hill, then turned to fire at the men on the other side.

"Why don't they surrender?" Geneen reached into her pocket, reloading her rifle once more.

As soon as the question left her lips, the area quieted. The women didn't speak, listening and watching for any movement around the boulders.

"I think I see Colin and Brodie." Coral supported herself on her elbows, watching as the group of MacLaren men made their way toward the rocks. "There's Uncle Ewan."

"I see Bram and Sean. And Mr. Donahue is alongside them." Geneen got to her knees, keeping her rifle trained on the last place she'd seen the rustlers.

When the area remained quiet, Heather stood, followed by Emma and Coral. All raised their rifles to their shoulders.

"Let's move closer." Emma started edging forward, one slow step after another, her gaze searching for any signs of life among the rocks.

"Look, Colin is motioning to us." Coral took several steps forward. "He's waving his arms. I think he wants us to get down."

Not five seconds later, gunfire landed within feet of the women, causing them to drop. Another barrage of shooting lasted less than a minute before all went still.

Heather raised her head, searching for her brother, Bram, but she was too low to get a good look. Waiting a few more minutes, she slowly rose to her feet, once again aiming at the rocks. Seeing Brodie climb to the top of one of the rocks and wave at her, she lowered her gun, looking at the others.

"The lads have them."

"Thank God," Emma breathed out. Pushing up, she stood next to Heather, rifle lax at her side.

For a minute, the four women simply stood next to each other, taking in the full scope of what had happened.

"We did it." Coral looked at Heather, placing a hand on her stomach, feeling a wave of nausea as she thought of what they'd done.

"Aye, lass. We did." Heather placed a hand on Coral's arm. "Are you all right?"

Nodding, she drew in a slow breath. "I just never, um...never..."

"Neither have the rest of us, lass. I'm hoping we'll never have to do it again." Heather squeezed Coral's arm lightly, then let go.

"I suppose we should see if any of the rustlers are still alive." Emma's voice sounded resigned, knowing it was their duty to check for survivors.

"Coral, do you want to stay here?" Heather asked.

"No. I'm a part of this and I'll see it through."

The four started down the hill toward the first three men they'd shot. They reached the spot the same time as Colin, Brodie, and Ewan.

"You did this, lasses?" Ewan asked, kneeling by one of the men to check for any signs of life.

Coral forced herself to look at the bodies, her stomach roiling. An instant later, she turned away, racing several steps from the others to wretch into the scrub. Within seconds, Geneen and Heather joined her. Emma seemed the only one who could look at the bodies without the sight sickening her.

Emma's face hardened. "Yes, Uncle Ewan. We did. We knew no other way to warn you of what we found." She glanced at Heather, Coral, and Geneen, glad to see them walking back toward the group.

"Well, lasses, you shot real well. Those lads are already growing cold." Ewan stood, looking at the four young women. "I left instructions for none of you to leave the ranch. Now you'll be telling me why you went against my orders."

Emma let out a breath, licking her lips. "It was Audrey." She thought of Quinn's mother, her mother-in-law, Emma's respect for the woman's premonitions growing.

Ewan's brow's furrowed. "What about her?"

"Mr. Delacroix heard of what happened and came to the ranch. Something about his visit bothered her. When she spoke with Kyla, they decided we should ride out and warn you."

Colin stepped next to Geneen, placing a comforting hand on his sister-in-law's shoulder. "Aye." He nodded as understanding dawned. "One of Aunt Audrey's hunches."

Heather glanced at the bodies, then back at the men. "She was quite agitated, wanting us to leave right away. She seemed to be feeling sick at what she felt."

"But she couldn't explain the danger. Only that we needed to warn you." Geneen placed a hand on her stomach, looking at Colin. "I'm glad they ordered us to come."

Brodie listened to the conversation as he searched each body for clues as to their identity. Standing, he shook his head. "They've nothing on them to say who they are. Did you see horses?"

Emma nodded. "Yes. They must've run off. What of the other men?"

"They'll not be causing us any more problems, lass." Ewan took off his hat, swiping an arm across his brow.

Brodie walked several paces up the hill, scanning the area for any sign of the horses. "We need to find their horses. Maybe there is something in the saddlebags to indicate who they are."

"Or who put them up to this," Colin hissed out.

"Let's get the bodies taken care of, then look for the horses." Ewan looked at Heather. "Where are yours?"

"A couple hundred yards back. At least that's where we left them."

"Get them and ride back to join us." Ewan let his gaze study the three bodies before turning away. "There's a lot to be done before we round the cattle back up and start for home."

"A couple more miles and we'll be home. I'm anxious to see Emma." Quinn took a sideways look at the man who rode next to him.

Deke Arrington had come to town to join his uncle in the saddlery business. At first, everyone thought he had an interest in Jinny. Quinn now believed the man had his sights set on another MacLaren woman.

"Pearl says you've been spending some time with Coral."

Deke's face shifted toward Quinn, his expression going still. "A little."

"And what does *a little* mean, lad?"

Returning his attention to the trail, Deke didn't answer right away. After a moment, he shot a quick look at Quinn. "I like her. Right now, that's all there is to it."

"It's the same as you said about Jinny."

"Jinny's heart was never available, Quinn. She and Sam belong together."

Quinn couldn't dispute it. From the first time Sam met Jinny, he made no secret of his interest. Being that Brodie was his boss, and Jinny's brother, it took him a little while to make his intentions known. Then fate had jumped in, forcing the couple to part while Sam took care of some unresolved issues from his past.

"Aye, they do. Are you thinking you and Coral belong together?"

Deke's jaw tightened. "As I said, I like her. For now, that's all I'm willing to say."

"Then I'm expecting you to be careful with her. I'll not be having her hurt by your attentions if you've no plans to carry them through. I'm hoping you understand me, Deke."

Looking over, Deke saw the hard lines on Quinn's face, the warning look in his eyes.

"I understand you, Quinn. It's not my intention to hurt her."

"Intentions mean nothing when we're talking about lasses. Actions and what you say are what they rely on. You'd best be careful with both."

Caleb rode a few feet behind them, hearing the conversation, knowing Quinn's warning was all too real. He thought of what Pearl and Opal had said about Coral, how she was sweet on Deke. It appeared he felt the same about her, but like many men, he wanted to take his time, make certain his feelings were more than a passing fascination.

Caleb had gone through the same with Heather. Unlike Coral, who he suspected did have feelings for Deke, Heather made her dislike of Caleb clear. Accepting it had been hard, but necessary. Even if he had decided to leave the ranch, it didn't lessen his need to protect her, keep her as far away from danger as possible.

He breathed a sigh of relief, knowing Heather was safe at the ranch. The same sense of longing Quinn expressed to see Emma washed over Caleb. The difference was Quinn would spend the night with his woman, while Caleb would be alone.

"Not long now, lads," Ian called from the front. "Fletch and Cam, when we get there, take the ranch hand's body around back of the barn."

"Do you plan to bury him in the ranch plot, Uncle Ian?" Fletcher asked. They had a family plot with two headstones. One for Angus and the other for Gillis. A small distance away, they had a ranch plot for those who died on the ranch but had no family to claim them.

"I'll be asking the other men if he has family. If not, then aye, we'll have a service for him here." Ian's nostrils flared at what the rustlers had done to their man. "Then we'll find who did this and make sure they pay."

Camden nodded. "Aye. They'll be paying all right. I'm wondering if the other group found the cattle."

"If so, it won't be long before we know. It's doubtful they'll stay out more than a couple nights before coming back." Ian looked over his shoulder at Quinn. "Brodie will need to see the body. Maybe he'll have some ideas about who did this."

Quinn's expression didn't change. "Maybe. Although I'm doubtful anyone knows why, except the men who killed him." Looking ahead, he saw the last bend in the trail, the ranch house and barn coming into view. "A few more minutes."

As they rode into view, the men saw the women rush outside, then down the steps, waving. The smiles on their faces froze when they spotted the body draped over Camden's horse.

"Who is it, Ian?" Gail walked up to her husband, hugging him when he slid to the ground.

"The missing ranch hand."

"Shot?"

"Nae, Gail. Not shot. We'll be discussing it later."

Quinn dismounted, tossing the reins over the rail before dashing up the steps. A few minutes later, he came back outside, looking at his mother, Audrey.

"Where's Emma?"

"And Heather," Caleb asked, looking around.

The women cast quick glances at each other, although no one spoke up.

"Ma, where's Emma?"

Audrey took the steps up to the porch, looking at her son. "I'm sure she and the others are fine."

Quinn's lips thinned, his eyes flashing. "Where is my wife, Ma?"

"Well now, we had a visitor while you were gone." Kyla joined them. "Mr. Delacroix came to check on us. Something about his visit bothered your ma. We had to make a decision."

Caleb hurried up the steps, facing Kyla, knowing in his gut this had something to do with Heather. "What decision?"

"You know how serious we take Audrey's instincts."

Both men remained silent, although judging by their expressions, they were doing their best to rein in their anger.

"She sensed danger, although she didn't know what. Right, Audrey?"

Swallowing, she nodded. "Aye. The same as I felt the day Angus and Gillis were killed. I couldn't ignore it."

"And neither could we." Gail stepped next to them.

Kyla nodded. "Bay told us your group was headed east, up the mountains. We weren't going to send the lasses there."

"Which lasses and where did you send them?" Caleb's voice was strained, his fists clenched.

"Geneen, Heather, Emma, and Coral, of course. The lasses who can ride and shoot the best."

At the mention of Coral, Deke pounded up the steps.

"Where'd you send them, Mrs. MacLaren?" Deke asked, his shaky voice betraying his feelings.

Kyla lifted her chin. "To where Bay told us the second group was going to look for the herd. North, beyond the Estrada hacienda."

Quinn tore his hat off, tossing it onto a chair. "So you just let the lasses ride into danger, not knowing what they'd be facing? Ma, what were you thinking?"

Audrey took a slight step forward, glaring at her son. "Don't you be taking a tone with me, Quinn MacLaren. I was thinking of protecting our men, and the best chance of that was to send the lasses to warn them. Those four ride and shoot as well as any of you, and better than some. If there was a warning to be delivered, they were our only hope of doing it."

"When?" Caleb asked.

Kyla looked up at him. "This morning."

Turning away, Quinn mumbled a curse as he ran a hand through his hair. Taking deep breaths, he looked back at Caleb and Deke. "We'll grab food, then be going after them."

"But, Quinn—"

"Nae, Ma. I'll not wait to see if they ride back. We'll be going now, and don't try to stop us."

Chapter Twelve

"I'm ready, Quinn." Caleb finished filling his saddlebags with the food the women had prepared, swallowing the piece of bread Kyla handed him. They'd done nothing else except fill their canteens and double check the cinches of their saddles.

"So am I." Deke walked up to them, holding the reins of his horse.

Swinging up into the saddle, Quinn gave a brief nod to his mother, who stood on the porch with her hands clasped in front of her. "Let's go."

The three rode north, touching the spurs lightly to the sides of their horses, moving into a gallop. Ian and the others in their group, except for Brodie, volunteered to ride along. He needed to get back to town and his wife, Maggie.

Quinn refused their help. They were needed at the ranch. Even though he knew the women would object, whoever killed their man was still out there. He had no intention of leaving the women alone to face them.

They continued for no more than thirty minutes when riders approached from the north.

Caleb reined up Jupiter. "It's Colin and the lads. And the women are with them."

"Aye, they are." They didn't miss the relief in Quinn's voice. He saw Emma lift her arm, then drop it to her side. Quinn moved forward, his gaze locked on her.

Within minutes, they'd met the group, Quinn dropping to the ground and running to Emma. Lifting his arms, she put her hands on his shoulders, letting him pull her out of the saddle. Wrapping his arms around her, he tugged her to him.

"Ah, lass. You scared me." He whispered the words against her ear. Placing a hand under her chin, he lifted her face. "I thought..." Words failed as he looked into her eyes.

"I'm fine, Quinn." Getting on tiptoes, she leaned up, kissing him. "We're all fine."

Caleb watched, then moved his gaze to Heather. She stared at him, causing his heart to beat almost painfully in his chest. Nudging Jupiter forward, he rode up next to her.

"Are you all right?" He studied her, seeing no wounds or other injuries. What he wanted to do was run his hands over her, discover for himself that she was fine.

"Aye, Caleb. I'm fine."

"I know you're wondering what happened, and we'll be explaining it all." Ian motioned everyone to circle around him. "For now, all I'll be saying is we found the cattle and merged them with the rest of the herd. The ranch hands at the Estrada place are watching them." He glanced at each of the women. "And we might not be here now if the lasses hadn't come to our rescue. Now, I'm tired and ready for food. I'll save the rest for later." Turning his horse around, he headed toward the ranch, the others following.

Quinn didn't let more than two feet separate him from Emma on the ride back.

Although they didn't touch or say more than the few words, the same held true for Caleb and Heather.

Deke rode behind Coral, never dropping his gaze from her back.

By the time they reached the ranch, they were all exhausted. Blaine, Fletcher, Camden, and several of the younger MacLarens took care of the horses as the riders made their way into the house.

After accepting greetings, they sat around the table, the men digging into the food while the women stared at their plates.

Audrey placed a hand on Heather's shoulder. "You're not hungry, lass?"

Shaking her head, Heather leaned back in her chair. "Nae, Ma. I'm tired, but don't think I'll be sleeping much." She looked at Caleb, who sat next to her, offering nothing except a grim expression. "I'm thinking I'll walk outside for a while." Pushing back her chair, she ignored the curious expressions.

Caleb didn't move, not knowing if he should follow or allow her time alone. The sound of Quinn clearing his throat had him shaking his head before glancing at his friend.

"You should go out with her, Caleb. From what Colin said, it's been a hard day for all the lasses." Quinn placed a hand over Emma's, leaning over to kiss her cheek. Like Heather, she hadn't taken a single bite of her food.

"Maybe I will." Caleb stood. Grabbing his hat from a hook by the door, he walked outside in time to see Heather disappear into the barn. He struggled with what to do. Quinn said it best—the women had been through a lot, seen too much, and would carry the memory with them forever.

When they arrived at the ranch, Colin had taken Quinn, Caleb, and Deke aside, explaining what happened. As irritated as they were about the women being sent out to warn the men, they couldn't be more proud of them.

Maybe that was what he should tell Heather before mentioning his decision to leave. He knew it wouldn't matter to her, but telling her before anyone, except Quinn, seemed right. Then he could leave with a clear conscience.

Blowing out a shaky breath, he placed his hat on his head, walking to the barn. Inside, he saw what he expected. Heather stood at Shamrock's stall, talking to her mare as she'd speak to anyone.

"I thought I'd find you here."

Startled, she turned around, resting her back against the stall. "What are you doing out here?"

Walking up to her, he leaned against the stall, keeping a couple feet between them. "Same as you. Getting some fresh air."

She didn't respond, choosing to turn around and watch Shamrock.

"Are you all right?"

She choked out a strained laugh, shaking her head. "Nae."

"Killing a man isn't easy, no matter how good the reason."

Giving him a slight nod, she let out a breath. "Nae, it isn't."

They stood in silence for several minutes, watching Shamrock move about the stall. Caleb knew Heather would let her mare out into the back pasture before returning to the house, and he was determined to wait her out.

He had some things to say before he left.

"How is Miss Harris?"

Caleb turned toward her, surprised by the question. "I've no idea, other than seeing her when she came for Sunday supper."

Glancing at him, she shook her head. "You know what I'm asking."

Frowning, he shook his head. "No, I don't. I've spoken to her a few times, nothing more. You seem to know more about her than me."

Worrying her lower lip, she lowered her head. "August said he thinks you might be courting her."

Choking out a laugh, Caleb shoved his hat back from his forehead. "I assure you, I'm not courting Miss Harris." He watched as she continued to stare at her boots. "Would it bother you if I did court her?"

Her head whipped up. "Aye...I mean, nae..."

Chuckling, he touched her cheek. "Which is it, Heather?"

Eyes wide, her lips parted. "Nae," she breathed out.

"Are you sure?" He felt her shudder as his thumb caressed her lower lip.

"I, um..." Her voice caught as he continued to smooth his thumb across her lip, sending chills through her body. No man had ever touched her like this. She'd never been kissed, and other than hugs from family and friends, no man had ever held her. Caleb's light touch made her feel things she'd never felt before.

Inching closer, he lowered his head a little, forcing her to look into his eyes.

"You know what I think?"

Her head moved back and forth slowly, her eyes still fixed on his.

"I think you don't want me to court Miss Harris, do you?" When she didn't respond, he leaned to within an inch of her face. "Heather?"

He stood so close, he felt her shudder, sensed the heat radiating between them. Lowering his head, he brushed his lips across hers, surprised when she didn't push him away. Instead, her breathing became erratic, her eyelids lowering, encouraging him to continue.

"Heather..." he whispered against her lips as his mouth settled over hers.

As soon as Caleb stepped into the barn, she'd fought her body's response to him. His presence made her feel excited, anxious, scared, and so many other things she couldn't define. They hadn't been alone together for so long, she'd forgotten his effect on her. It had always been this way and was the main reason she'd spurned his interest. She had no idea what he expected or how to react. Pushing him away, acting as if she hated him, had been her only defense.

Focusing on Shamrock, she'd done her best to ignore him. She'd answered his questions, hoping he'd give up and leave. Instead, he seemed to settle in, determined to wait her out.

Heather's mistake had been bringing up Miranda. The question had popped out of her mouth before she could stop it, and she hated to admit the importance of his answer. Acute relief overwhelmed her when he claimed to have no interest in the other woman. Then Caleb had moved forward.

When his finger moved down her cheek, her body vibrated. An overwhelming need to lean into him swamped her, stealing her ability to think and talk. She had no experience with men, nothing to guide her when he brushed his lips against hers. The feeling had been exquisite.

When he'd claimed her mouth, Heather's first thought had been to push him away, slap his face in indignation. She couldn't summon the anger.

Instead, she felt her hands creep up his arms to his shoulders, gripping them when he wrapped his arms around her. She'd never felt anything so wonderful or excruciatingly tender. His lips were soft, yet firm and controlling. He knew what he was doing, while all she could do was hang on and hope he didn't recognize her total lack of experience.

All her life she'd competed with the MacLaren men, fought hard to secure a place as a competent and respected ranch hand. She'd thought it was all she ever wanted...or needed.

As Caleb's mouth continued to work its magic, her body heating to an almost unbearable degree, she accepted there was much more she needed to learn.

Feeling his hands move to the small of her back, she arched into him, tightening her hold around his neck when his lips moved along her jaw, down her neck, to the tender hollow of her throat. Squirming, trying to get closer, a moan escaped as he brought his mouth back to hers.

Intense pleasure claimed her when his tongue lightly grazed the crease of her lips, causing her to open. Moaning against his mouth, hungry for something, although she didn't know what it was, she writhed against him. His hands settled on her hips, holding her in place as he continued his tender assault.

She didn't know how long they'd stood there before he raised his mouth from hers, gazing into her eyes. His warm breath caressed her as he placed a gentle kiss on her forehead. Releasing his hold, he stepped away, leaving her with an unfamiliar sense of loss.

Breathing heavily, he reached out, stroking her cheek. A bemused smiled tipped up the corners of his mouth when he saw the confusion in her eyes.

"We have to stop, sweetheart, before we do something we might regret."

"Regret?" The word whispered from her lips.

Stepping closer, he cupped her face with both his hands, kissing her once more. "Go too far."

Her brows furrowed before his meaning became clear and her eyes widened. "Oh..."

His gaze heated seeing her flushed face, hearing her labored breathing. "Someday, though, we will make love, Heather." Reaching out, he slipped a strand of lose hair behind her ear. "You can absolutely count on that."

To Heather's disappointment, Caleb had already left when she returned to the house. It didn't surprise her he'd decided to stay in one of the empty bedrooms in Ewan's house. With both Brodie and Jinny married, each living in town with their spouses, they had plenty of space.

"Are you all right, lass?" Audrey looked up from where she worked on the hem of a dress.

"Aye, Ma. I'm fine."

"You're looking a little flushed. You're not ill, are you?"

Heather touched her face, feeling a slight warmth, although being ill had nothing to do with it. "Nae, I'm not ill."

Setting down the dress, Audrey stood, walking up to her. "I'm sorry for what you had to do today."

"It had to be done, Ma. If we hadn't been there, the lads might've been shot, maybe killed."

"Aye. Instead, you four lasses had to kill others to protect them. It shouldn't have been necessary."

"But it was, Ma." Quinn walked into the living room from the kitchen with Emma, his arm around her waist. "And you can't be blaming yourself for sending them out. You made the right decision."

Blowing out a breath, Audrey nodded. "Aye, but it wasn't an easy thing to ask of them."

Quinn dropped his arm from around his wife's waist, moving up to hug his mother. "Not much is easy. We are all doing the best we can, making hard decisions. The one you made today saved our lives." Turning, he looked at Emma and Heather. "The lasses did well today. And, as much as it pains me to say, shot as well as any of the MacLaren men."

Heather's face lit up, as did Emma's. A compliment such as this didn't come often.

"Now, lasses. Don't be getting big-headed over this."

"Us?" Heather smiled. "We've known our skills are as good as yours for a long time, Quinn. It was the lads we had to convince."

His face turned serious. "And don't be bragging about this. Killing a man is never something to brag on."

Heather's face sobered. "Aye, it isn't."

Emma looked at Quinn. "Do you think we'll find out who hired them?"

"I don't know, lass. Only three of the horses were found, and there was nothing to identify the men. It may be they're nothing more than what it seems."

"Rustlers," Emma whispered.

"And killers," Heather added.

"Aye. They may have seen us coming, abandoned the herd to set a trap. They would've known we'd drive the herd south, so they found a good position and waited."

Audrey shook her head. "But why kill the ranch hand and set fire to the hacienda, Quinn? Those make no sense."

Quinn nodded. "Aye, they don't. Sometimes there's no explaining how people like that think."

"Evil never makes sense." Emma stepped up to him. "We need to figure out who those men were and if someone hired them."

Heather nodded. "Aye. There may be more than the six we saw."

Bram walked in from outside, stopping when he saw the dire expressions. "Is there something wrong?"

Quinn shook his head. "We've been talking about those who died and if there might be more who weren't a part of the trap."

Bram took off his hat, setting it on a hook. "I've been wondering the same. We leave early tomorrow morning with the wagon to fetch the bodies. We'll take them to the undertaker's, then fetch Brodie. Maybe someone in town will recognize them."

Heather glanced at Bram before looking at Quinn. "Will we be going with you?"

"Nae, lass. You've done your part. Only Colin, Bram, and Fletch are going. The rest of us are needed here. You, Emma, Coral, and Geneen will be helping with the herd."

"Really?" Emma asked, her voice laced with excitement.

Quinn smiled. "Aye, lass. We've been thinking it's time we used your skills more than we've been doing...at least until more men are hired."

Emma looked at Heather. "We should go tell Coral and Geneen." They started for the door before Quinn called them back.

"Colin already told them. Seems they're as excited as you."

"Of course they are, Quinn. Except for Heather, the rest of us have only been going out maybe one day a week. We can do so much more." Emma stood on tiptoes, placing a kiss on his cheek.

Bram shook his head. "I don't know why you lasses are so excited. It's hard work out there."

Emma glared at her brother-in-law. "And you think what we do around here isn't hard?"

Holding up both hands, Bram took a step away. "I know you work with Fletch and me with the horses, and Heather's been out with the cattle. It's just...I don't know...dangerous to be out there every day." His gaze met Emma's. "You know how dangerous."

Emma nodded, the memory of the stampede that almost killed her still fresh in her mind.

Heather stepped next to her younger brother, placing a hand on his arm. "Emma and I are ready, and I know Coral and Geneen are, too. Don't be worrying about us, Bram." The words made her think of Caleb and what he'd say when he heard the women would be out with the cattle. "Does Caleb know?"

Quinn shot a knowing look at her. "Aye, lass. He isn't thrilled, but agreed it was for the best. He and Blaine will be moving the Evanston herd back here tomorrow. I suggested you go with them. That will give them five riders, including the two ranch hands still there."

Her chest constricted, thinking of working alongside Caleb. Heather felt herself shiver, remembering the two of them in the barn less than an hour ago. Her lips still tingled from his touch.

"Did you hear me, lass?" Quinn asked, a slow grin spreading across his face.

"Aye. I'll be ready in the morning." Swiping hair off her face, she moved to the stairs. "I should be getting to bed then."

Quinn nodded, the smile still on his face. "Aye. I'm certain Caleb will be wanting an early start tomorrow. Sleep well."

Chapter Thirteen

Caleb stared at the ceiling, his arms tucked behind his head. After the last couple days, he'd thought falling asleep would be easy. He hadn't expected the way his body still hummed from being with Heather. Holding her had been far better than any of the many fantasies he'd created.

He hadn't expected her to react to him the way she did, or the blistering passion. Given her quick temper and independent ways, Caleb thought she'd push him away, not pull him closer. He'd wanted to continue, let her know the depth of his feelings.

It had taken all his willpower to break the kiss and step away. He'd known the instant he touched her lips she'd never been kissed before, not that he expected anything different. She'd spent her life competing with men, doing her best to prove herself to her father, Gillis. After his death, Heather had pushed harder, doing all she could to draw attention to her work. It had alienated her family. No one wanted to work with her, except Caleb.

He'd volunteered to ride with her when others hesitated, made sure she wasn't out on the range alone. She tended to go off by herself—Heather's way of proving to the others she didn't need them to do her job. Her decisions were often foolish, putting her, and others, in danger. When Mildred Evanston offered her a job, it had been a relief to everyone, except Caleb.

According to Quinn, Colin, and others, the time there had mellowed Heather. Other than their brief time in the barn, Caleb had yet to see it. He'd planned to leave as soon as the MacLarens decided to close the Evanston ranch and move the cattle. The events of the last few days made his choice more difficult.

In the morning, he, Blaine, and Heather would join the men still there, round up the cattle, and move them into the main herd. By tomorrow night, he'd be free to leave.

He found himself facing a dilemma. After kissing Heather, he no longer knew if that was what he wanted. Caleb also wasn't sure he should stay.

The Heather he knew could change moods on a whim. He'd seen it, experienced it, and refused to rely too much on a few kisses, no matter how passionate.

They'd be together tomorrow, the next day, and the following. He had plenty of time to decide if Heather could still be a part of his life.

Closing his eyes, Caleb felt himself drift off with the vague image of a future he couldn't quite perceive.

"Blaine, Heather...are you ready?" Caleb sat atop Jupiter, waiting outside the barn as the other two finished saddling their horses. He'd gotten three hours of sleep before a slice of early morning sun peered through the curtains. Slipping into his pants and shirt, he'd downed a cup of coffee before preparing to ride. It would be a long day. One he wanted to get behind him.

"Aye." Blaine reined up next to him.

Heather rode out of the barn a few seconds later, holding the reins in one hand while pushing her hat down with the other.

They'd yet to acknowledge each other. Caleb had Jupiter saddled by the time she collected Shamrock from the pasture. She'd made no effort to look at him, keeping her face turned away. After Blaine joined them, any opportunity they had to talk about the night before vanished.

Caleb looked at each of them. "It's going to be a long day. Ewan and Ian want us to move the cattle over to the main herd, then return with a wagon for the tack and tools."

Ready to move out, he rolled the heels of his boots into Jupiter's sides. Caleb rode in front, Blaine and Heather behind him. He could hear them talking, even if he couldn't make out the conversation. Every once in a while, Heather's laughter echoed down the deserted trail. Not a giggle like some women, but a rich, throaty sound that reverberated through him.

He fought the urge to look behind him, join in the fun, but thoughts of last night stopped him. She'd ignored him all morning. Then again, he'd done the same.

If he pursued something with Heather and it didn't work out, he'd be the one leaving with his pride and heart exposed. If he left now, it would be a clean break without anyone getting hurt.

Things were getting complicated, and he didn't like complicated.

Caleb shifted in the saddle, looking over his shoulder. "The ranch is up ahead."

"Oh, my God!" Heather's words flew past him, Shamrock galloping toward the Evanston house.

Brows furrowing, Caleb shot a look at Blaine, who shrugged. "I've no idea what's gotten into the lass."

"I guess we'll find out." Caleb continued to the house, seeing Shamrock near the barn, a horse he didn't recognize a few feet away, and the two ranch hands in a nearby corral. Heather was nowhere in sight.

Then he heard it—male and female laughter from inside the barn. The calm façade dissolved as jealousy gripped him. Nostrils flaring, he dismounted, charging forward, stopping when Blaine grabbed his arm.

"Lad, you need to calm yourself. If I can see you're looking for blood, so can whoever is inside."

Blaine tightened his grip when Caleb tried to pull away. Both were evenly matched in size and weight. In a fight, either one could come out the victor. Fortunately, it didn't get that far.

Caleb sucked in a deep breath. "You go inside and see who she's talking to. I'll go speak with the men, let them know to saddle up." Nodding toward the corral, he strode off, his boots pounding into the dirt.

A few feet from the gate, he stopped, placing his hands on his hips. After a moment, he scrubbed a hand down his face, wondering what had just happened to him. He never lost his temper without cause. Glancing back at the barn, he shook his head at his antics, mumbling a thanks to Blaine, who stopped him from making an utter fool of himself.

Lifting a hand at the men who'd stopped their work to watch him, he turned back toward the barn. As he got closer, he heard Blaine's uninhibited laugh, then Heather's. Stepping into the dark interior, he allowed his eyes to adjust.

Between Heather and Blaine stood an older man, tall and wiry, his thick black hair tinged with silver. The deep lines on his rugged face indicated years in the sun. Caleb guessed his age could be anywhere between forty and sixty.

"Caleb." Blaine motioned him over.

Stepping toward them, he stopped a couple feet from the stranger, holding out his hand. "Caleb Stewart."

The man grasped his hand in a strong grip, pumping it once. "Levi Abrams. I used to be the foreman here."

Caleb's eyes widened. "I've heard of you, Mr. Abrams."

"Call me Levi."

Nodding, Caleb glanced at Heather, then back at Levi. "I heard you quit."

"I did." He leaned against a stall, pulled a pipe from one pocket and a pouch of tobacco from another. "It didn't take me long to realize I had nowhere to go." Stuffing the pipe, he tamped it down with a light touch, then held it at his side.

Heather slipped an arm through Levi's, a broad smile flashing across her face. "So he came back."

Caleb's lips twitched when he looked at her. "I can see he did." Transferring his attention back to Levi, his face sobered. "Are you looking for work?"

He nodded. "A man has to eat."

Heather's face lit up. "I'm certain we've work for you at Circle M. Don't you think so, Blaine?"

Her cousin nodded. "We can always use another good lad." Blaine glanced at Caleb.

"They're right, Levi. There's more work than men to handle it. But some things have happened that might change your mind."

Levi's gaze narrowed on Caleb. "I've got plenty of time. Let's go outside and you can explain it all to me."

176

Levi walked to his saddlebags, opening one to pull out a large box. Opening it, he pulled out a stick with a red tip, then brought his pipe up to his mouth. Striking the match against his belt buckle, he lit the pipe, puffing a few times before blowing out the smoke.

"Got these in San Francisco a couple weeks ago. Other than Annabelle, they may be the best purchase I ever made." Levi chuckled, slipping the box back into the saddlebag.

Lifting a brow, Caleb looked at Heather.

She smiled. "His Springfield 1861 rifle. Calls it Annabelle." Shrugging, Heather looked back at Levi.

Taking another puff from his pipe, Levi looked at Caleb. "Now, tell me all about the changes and how I can help."

They congregated on the porch, Levi with his pipe, Heather sitting next to him, Blaine and Caleb leaning against the railing. After listening to them describe the changes, Levi nodded, blowing out another wave of smoke.

"Yep. Lots of changes. Sorry to hear about the Estrada hacienda. Juan invited Mildred, her husband, and I over for supper one time. It was quite a place." Levi settled back in the chair. "Always thought it was a good decision for you MacLarens to buy the place. Some of the finest grazing land north of Sacramento. Those springs and streams up north flow down into the dryer pastures, creating ponds. All that water is controlled by the people who own the land. Real smart move to buy it from Juan."

"We didn't buy it all, Levi."

He nodded. "I remember that. Estrada still holds enough to live on and run a few cattle."

Blaine shifted his feet, crossing his arms. "Aye. It was a fair deal. We own it with August Fielder."

"I seem to recall that."

Heather turned sideways in her chair. "As you can tell, we've big plans and can use your help, Levi."

"The lass is right." Blaine straightened, looking out at the two men fixing part of the corral. "You might as well come along today so we can make it official with Ewan and Ian."

Letting the tobacco burn out, Levi stood, stepping to the edge of the porch to tap his pipe against the railing. "So, you boys tired of gabbing or are you ready to get that herd and take them north?"

"Just waiting on you, old timer," Caleb joked, eliciting a gasp from Heather and a laugh from Blaine.

"Old timer, is it?" Levi smiled. "We'll see if you still can say that at the end of the day."

"Six men, Black. How the hell did you lose all six of them?" Giles kicked an already broken chair across the room, cursing as he paced back and forth. "The job was to take the cattle, move them off MacLaren land, change the brand, and sell them."

Black leaned against the doorframe, undaunted by Giles' display of anger. "That's the instructions I gave them. Seems the men changed the rules on their own."

Cursing again, he lowered himself onto a chair. "I heard about it this morning when the bodies were brought to town. I happened to be across the street when the wagon pulled up to the undertaker's. Half the town walked over to look inside. Those men were riddled with bullets."

Shrugging, Black nodded. "I was supposed to meet them last night. When they didn't show, I went looking for them. Found their bodies, no horses, and the herd was gone."

"I'm trying to drive them out of business, not create a bloodbath." Giles shivered, remembering the first dead body he'd ever seen. He'd pushed his best friend into fighting an older boy who'd been bullying everyone. The friend didn't want to fight, but Giles talked him into it. The bully had landed a devastating blow to his friend's jaw, snapping his head and breaking his neck. They were only ten. From then on, Giles did whatever he could to avoid killing to get what he wanted. Sometimes, though, accidents happened.

"The MacLarens have stretched themselves too thin. Purchasing the Estrada and Evanston places, loaning money to the Pearce family, and investing in the new hotel have created a large amount of debt. The slightest push could achieve my goal."

"Of buying their land." There was no inflection in Black's voice. He didn't care a whit about their debt, the property, or who died. All Black cared about was getting paid and riding out before the law caught wind of him.

"Correct. Not getting into gunfights with their men." Raking a hand through his hair, Giles leaned back.

"By the looks of the bodies, it seemed there were two groups who discovered our men. One group came down from the hills, the other from the opposite direction. I'm thinking those were the ones with the herd." Pulling a cheroot from his pocket, he lit it, inhaling deeply. Blowing the smoke out, he looked at Giles. "Cattle ain't going to work a second time. They've got too many men watching."

"I suppose you have other suggestions. After all, if this doesn't work, you don't get paid."

Black's features hardened enough for Giles to know the man didn't like being threatened. "The job will get done and you'll have your land."

"Fine. Tell me how that happens."

"They've got several ponds in the northern part of the property. It's where they keep the main herd and where the cattle drink." Black lifted a brow and waited.

After a few quiet moments, Giles' eyes widened. "You want to poison the water?"

Black nodded.

Standing, Giles rubbed the spot between his eyes, trying to relieve the throbbing ache he had since seeing the bodies.

Black walked over to the stove, grabbed a cup, and filled it with coffee. Turning back to Giles, he took a sip. "It's easy enough to do."

"You've done this before?"

"I've done a lot. That's why you hired me." He stepped toward Giles. "You don't want to hear the details, then leave."

Shaking his head, Giles crossed his arms. "Go on."

"You don't plan to run cattle on the land, right?"

Giles nodded.

"Then we poison one of the smaller ponds. It'll take longer, but you'll get your land without killing any men."

Shaking his head, Giles turned away. "Too much time. There must be another way."

Black finished the coffee, then smirked. "There is, but I don't think you have the stomach for it."

Waving a hand, Giles' face grew serious. "As long as you don't intentionally murder, I don't care. Poison the pond and do whatever else you have to." He walked to the door, pulling it open. "Just don't let anything fall back on us."

Stepping outside, Giles closed the door behind him. Mounting his horse, he turned toward town, his mind moving from one problem to another. He'd gotten a telegram the day before about his ailing mother. She'd taken a turn for the worse.

Several years before, when she'd been robust and healthy, he'd moved his mother into his wife's house. Not long afterward, she'd taken ill. Hiring the best doctors and a full-time nurse had done little to identify the illness or relieve her constant pain. He hated watching her deteriorate, knowing he could do nothing.

His dear wife had been a godsend in more ways than one. He'd picked her carefully, culling through the rich San Francisco widows until he found one who suited his purposes. Rich, no children, no other relatives, and a pristine social standing. Courting and marrying her had taken little time. Giles planned to use her money and connections to increase his own wealth and social stature. Manipulating her had been far too easy. What he hadn't expected was to fall in love with her.

When his mother moved in, his wife took to her as if she were her own. Watching them together softened his heart, though not enough to change the dreams he'd sought for so long. Giles wanted his own wealth, not just what he'd married into. He'd grown tired of the snide remarks and innuendos about how he achieved his money. So he'd done his research.

Conviction's location on the Feather River, the rich soil and expansive pastures made it one of the best places west of Denver to raise cattle. Driving them to market was easy with the rapid expansion of San Francisco and Sacramento. And the people just kept coming. He saw no end to the opportunities. But you had to own the land.

Giles had waited, watched as the MacLarens sunk more and more money into the ranch, creating debt they could handle, assuming everything fell in their favor. The weather, the market, water—all the pieces had to fit. It would take just one major problem to topple their plan and make them vulnerable.

He'd seen it happen many times. Banks were wonderful when you were doing well. When you weren't, their friendship and money dried up. It was time the MacLarens experienced the harsher side of staying prosperous, and he was the perfect man to provide the lesson.

Black watched from the window, then glanced over his shoulder. "It's safe for you to come out now."

The woman pushed open the door, emerging from a small storage space at the rear of the cabin. "What an insufferable man. I don't know why you put up with him."

Chuckling, he walked up to her, stroking a hand over her hair. "Money. The man pays well, and that's all I care about."

The woman nodded, placing a hand on his arm. He looked down at it and frowned, but didn't make a move to shove it away. She was the only person who could make him smile, who he allowed to touch him. No one else dared. She'd never seen him as the dangerous predator he'd become. For that, he was grateful.

"So now you'll be poisoning the cattle?" She shook her head.

"Again, for the money."

"I know how much you've made, Black. You could put all this behind you and live comfortably the rest of your life." She sat down in an old, splintered chair, her dress catching on one of the rough edges. "You could start over."

"I suppose you'd follow."

"Only if you'd want me to." She tilted her head and smiled.

He walked to her, tugging on a strand of hair. "We'll talk after I'm finished with Delacroix."

Crossing her arms, her bottom lip jutted out. "That's what you said the last time."

Dropping her hair, he folded his arms across his chest, staring down at her. "You help me finish this job with Delacroix, and I'll make you a promise." She looked up at him, her round eyes wide with hope. "We'll get out of this hovel and start fresh."

Chapter Fourteen

Bay pinched the bridge of his nose, reading the telegram in front of him. He'd been catching up on paperwork since six that morning. The pile on his desk might have lessened if his assistant, Jasper, hadn't kept adding to the stack.

Accepting the position to partner with August in his law firm had been too good to ignore. Closing the door on his past, focusing on the reason he'd attended law school, had been an easy decision to make.

Instead of the matching revolvers he preferred when working for ranchers, he now strapped a single Colt around his waist. The two rifles usually secured in his saddle scabbards were replaced with one, and his shotgun leaned against the wall in his office. He had no desire to return to a life of protecting the range, no matter the money offered.

The telegram in front of him was a temptation, nothing more. At least once a week, he received an offer such as the one on his desk. An outlandish sum had been offered by a cattleman in Texas if Bay would rid him of the rustlers and land grabbers who dogged him. Bay didn't hesitate to wad the telegram into a ball and toss it into the trash.

"I see you're right back at it." August walked into Bay's office, taking a seat. "I heard about the ranch hand."

"They found him hanging from a tree miles from the Estrada hacienda and the stolen herd."

"Were you part of the group who shot those six men?" August's tone held no recrimination. His years as a lawyer had schooled him to get all the facts before judging.

"I assume you saw the bodies."

"Hard to miss, laid out in front of the undertaker's. I'm glad Brodie was there to answer questions or the townsfolk might have jumped to conclusions. Dare I ask how many you killed?" August steepled his fingers under his chin, his gaze narrowing on Bay.

"Two, and I was glad to do it. They hid in the rocks with a direct aim at us. If it hadn't been for the MacLaren women, we might be the ones being prepared for burial." Standing, Bay walked to the window, glancing at the new hotel down the street. "A burned structure, one dead ranch hand, stolen cattle, and six dead rustlers. I've been trying to make sense of it all and have come up with nothing. If the ranch hand had been found at the Estrada place or with the cattle, it would make more sense. Instead, he was miles away. And why did the rustlers leave the cattle unattended? We rode over a hill and there was the herd, no one guarding them. Why try to kill us, and why abandon the herd?"

Leaning forward, August rested his arms on the desk. "You're the one with range war experience. I'd think you'd have some ideas."

Rocking on his heels, Bay massaged the back of his neck, then turned from the window. "Could be unrelated. Maybe the ranch hand came upon some men who killed him for the fun of it. The fire could've been a distraction while the rustlers took the cattle."

"Two separate events?" August asked.

"It's possible." Bay sat back down, staring at a spot on the wall behind August. "Taking the cattle north makes sense. They could split the herd up, rebrand, and move them to a buyer. They were almost off MacLaren land when they chose to abandon them and wait for us." His gaze traveled to August. "They knew we'd be coming."

"Any rancher would go after his missing cattle."

"Of course. But the rustlers wouldn't leave them unguarded." Bay rubbed his chin. "I think they used the cattle as bait to draw us in. I don't believe they had any intention of moving them off MacLaren land."

August's brows furrowed. "To what end?"

Bay opened a drawer, pulling out a piece of paper and sliding it across the desk. "Look at this and tell me what you see."

Pulling spectacles from his pocket, August picked up the paper, leaning back in his chair. After a few moments, his brows lifted. "Where did you get this information?"

Bay hesitated, weighing how best to describe how he'd come into possession of the data. "I got an offer. It included what you're looking at."

"Explain." August laid the document on Bay's desk.

"I wish I had an explanation for you, sir. The document was shoved under my office door while I was out with the MacLarens. Nothing else, just what you see. Jasper has no idea how someone got inside our offices, but it happened."

"I gather you think this has something to do with what is happening at Circle M."

Bay nodded. "If the numbers on the MacLarens are accurate, it wouldn't take much to push them into a position of it being difficult to pay their debt. Destroying property, taking their cattle, killing off family members all work toward putting them in a tough position to fulfill their obligations."

August picked up the paper again, scanning the numbers, his jaw tightening. Shaking his head, he tossed the papter back onto the desk. "Who do you think gave you this data?"

"I've no idea."

"Why would they do it?"

"I have three theories. One, whoever left this knows you're a partner with the MacLarens and sought to cause doubts about my decision to work with you. Two, it could be meant as a warning to the MacLarens that they're vulnerable. Although I believe they're astute enough to know the financial risk they've taken."

"And your third theory?"

"Whoever left this knows who is behind the activities at Circle M and wants us to start looking for answers. In truth, I believe it's a combination of the last two."

August nodded. "I agree. It's a warning and an appeal to do what we can to find the person behind all of this. Where do we start?"

"There are only a few people who have access to this information." Bay pointed to the paper.

"Those who are employed at my bank." August didn't hide the disgust in his voice.

"Or someone who got it illegally."

August watched Bay's expression. Over the years, he'd become adept at discerning people's thoughts by small changes—lifting of a brow, downturn of lips, tightness around the eyes. Bay showed none of these. Instead, August saw a man in intense thought, considering what to do next.

"There's one person I've met since arriving in Conviction who might provide us with some insight."

"Who?"

"With all due respect, sir, I'd prefer to talk to the person first."

"Understood, but I expect to speak with you again on this within the next couple days. If someone is trying to drive the MacLarens off their land, I want to figure out who and stop them."

Pulling a pocket watch from his pocket, August stood. "If you have time, I'd like you to accompany me to the docks. A steamer is coming in and there's someone on it I'd like you to meet."

Bay waved his hand over the mountain of paper on his desk. "I'd like to, sir, but I've got so much to attend to today."

August chuckled. "I know what you have on your desk. It's the work I had Jasper pass along to you."

Bay offered a sheepish grin, shaking his head. "Still..."

"This won't take long. Trust me. It will be worth your while. Just let me grab my hat and I'll meet you out front in a few minutes."

His mouth twisting into a wry grin, Bay watched August leave. Lifting his coat off the rack, he slipped it on, checking the gun strapped around his waist, a habit he had yet to break. Picking up his hat, Bay stopped by the window to look out at the almost completed Feather River Hotel down the street. It reminded him of the last entry on the list of accounts for the MacLarens—their percentage ownership in the new venture.

They were a good, hardworking family. People he'd come to like and respect. Anger rushed through him at what was happening to them. Whether random acts or a concerted effort to take their ranch away, Bay vowed to do all he could to discover who was behind the threats and bring them to justice.

Circle M

Blaine reined up alongside Heather as they finished merging their herd into the larger one. "Good work today, lass."

Her gaze kept moving, keeping watch for any stray animals while also looking for Caleb. "Aye. It was a good drive."

"When you're ready, you'll be heading back to the house with the two ranch hands. Caleb, Levi, and I will be riding back to get the tools and tack."

Shaking her head, she leaned toward him. "Nae. I'll be going with you."

"You'll not be going this time. Three is more than enough to do what's needed."

"Then I'll go with Caleb and Levi. You can head back to the house." She started to turn away when Blaine reached out, grabbing Shamrock's reins.

"Lass, it's not your decision to make. Ewan put Caleb in charge of the work today and the lad's made his decision. You'll be meeting the ranch hands up the trail." Blaine let go of the reins, but not before seeing the anger brewing behind her eyes. "Lass, you've got to take orders, the same as the rest of the lads. If you don't, Ewan and Ian will see that you don't ride out with the men for a long time."

Sucking in a breath, she looked around, refusing to meet Blaine's gaze until she had her temper under control. She'd been doing better, not letting pride get in the way of her desire to be out on the range with the rest of the men. Glancing up, she nodded.

"I'll be heading back now then." As she turned toward the house, Blaine called after her.

"Don't be taking this personal, lass."

Pursing her lips, she nodded once, then continued to where the men waited for her at the top of a hill. During the drive, she'd gone over the events of the last few days, spending considerable time reliving her brief time alone with Caleb. He'd made no mention of it happening again, if he liked it or didn't. The fact is, he'd said little to her at all.

He'd positioned himself at point while she rode drag. Blaine had told her it was because Caleb knew she'd push the herd along, saving them time on the drive. When they'd crested the hill, seeing the main herd and MacLaren ranch hands, Heather had focused her attention on keeping the cattle together. She'd lost track of Caleb during the merge and hadn't seen him since. He'd taken off without a single word to her, sending Blaine with the message for her to return home. It hurt more than she'd expected. What bothered her most was knowing the other lads would have no problem accepting his orders, not caring one way or the other if he delivered it in person. Why did it bother her so much?

The annoying voice inside her head clarified what she didn't want to believe—she loved him.

She'd known it for months, choosing to push Caleb away instead of dealing with emotions she didn't know how to control. Last night, she'd finally surrendered, letting him know, in her own way, how she felt. Riding back to the house under the bright glare of today's sun, she realized it may have meant much less to him than it did to her.

Caleb and Levi had ridden ahead to Circle M to hitch a wagon. If they hurried, they could return to the old Evanston place, load the wagon, and be back home by supper. It also gave Caleb a chance to speak with Ewan for a few minutes about Levi. Although the elder MacLaren didn't commit, Caleb felt certain they'd find a place for the man.

"You lads ready to go?" Blaine rode up alongside the wagon as Kyla came down the porch steps.

"I just need to put Jupiter away, then I'll be ready."

"I'll be taking care of your horse, Caleb. You three go ahead now. We'll have supper waiting when you get back." Kyla grabbed Jupiter's reins.

"Thanks, Kyla." Climbing onto the seat, Caleb picked up the lines, looking at Blaine. "Did you talk to Heather?"

"Aye. The lass isn't too happy with you, lad."

Caleb lifted a brow, his face clouding. "And why's that?"

"Heather was thinking she'd be the one riding back with you and Levi to pack the barn. By the time I left, she seemed fine."

"You didn't have her ride back alone, did you?"

Blaine chuckled. "I'm not daft, lad. She's riding back with the two ranch hands. Although, after what happened yesterday, I've no doubt the lass can take care of herself. You might consider setting aside your differences now that you'll be working together more often."

Caleb hid a smile, aware Levi sat atop his horse a few feet away. What happened the night before was between him and Heather. "I'll consider it, Blaine."

"You do that." Touching spurs to his horse, Blaine took the trail south.

"Do you and Heather have some things to work out?" Levi leaned on his saddle horn, his gaze narrowed.

"No more than any two people who work together."

Levi studied him, pushing his hat away from his forehead. "You sure that's all it is? 'Cause that girl means a lot to me. I'd hate to think you might be doing something to hurt her."

Caleb's grip tightened on the wagon lines, his body still. He'd heard a lot about Levi, never meeting the man before today. One thing he did know— Heather had taken to him right off, considered him family. If nothing else, Caleb respected the man for that reason alone.

"I'd never intentionally hurt Heather, Levi. On that, you have my word."

Nodding, Levi straightened. "Your word is good enough for me."

Caleb blew out a relieved breath, his shoulders relaxing when he realized Levi had no intention of questioning him further, at least not now.

"Then we'd better catch up to Blaine before the lad gets lost." Slapping the lines, the wagon moved out.

It wasn't a long trip, but it gave Caleb a chance to think through what Blaine had said about his conversation with Heather. It hadn't occurred to him his decision would upset her, but one never knew with Heather. No matter what Quinn and Colin told him about how she'd changed, Caleb knew she still had a temper, one she released without warning. He'd been the recipient too many times to believe it wasn't still a part of her.

When they met up with Blaine, Caleb intended to ask a few vague questions, enough to learn what Heather had said. Maybe he should've delivered his decision in person, explained his reasons.

He'd purposely avoided her today, keeping as much distance between them as possible. It hadn't been easy, and he now believed it had been a mistake. It was obvious she had little experience, and knowing Heather, she'd be confused by his silence, maybe angry at the way his orders had kept them apart.

"Pull the wagon over here, lad."

Caleb shook his head, surprised they'd already reached their destination. Nodding, he pulled the wagon alongside the barn's entry, tied the lines, then hopped down. As he walked inside, he vowed to take her aside tonight. She deserved better than how he'd treated her today.

Conviction

"Ah, there it is." August looked south, seeing the steamship coming up the Feather River from Sacramento. "Won't be long now."

"You said the restaurant manager would be here soon. Is this the reason you wanted me here? To meet him?"

August glanced at him, then looked away. "I believe you'll agree the person I hired is more than capable of making the restaurant a success."

Bay chuckled. "I've no reason to doubt anyone you hire."

August nodded at him, hoping it proved to be true.

Several minutes later, the steamer docked, deckhands securing the lines, while workers crowded around to unload the cargo. It took another ten minutes before passengers began to disembark.

Bay watched with disinterest. He had a desk piled high with work and a puzzle he had to sort through regarding the MacLarens. Little time existed to stand around waiting for a man he'd only see in passing when he ate at the hotel.

"I believe that's our passenger." August pointed to a group of three people. A man standing to one side of the gangway, an elderly woman waiting for help to reach shore, and a lone woman standing at the ship's rail, a wide-brimmed hat covering her face as she studied the crowd.

"I'll be right back."

Bay watched August hurry to the gangway, crossing over toward the man. Growing bored, he looked away, his gaze focused on the repairs made in Chinatown after the riot. The leaders were serving time in jail near San Francisco, sending a clear message to the townsfolk about gang violence. With two extra deputies, he knew Brodie felt more comfortable dealing with an angry crowd in the future.

"Bay."

He turned at August's voice, then froze, his breath seizing in his chest, throat tightening.

"I'd like you to meet Miss Suzette—"

"Gaznier," Bay breathed out, interrupting August's introduction.

"Why, yes. I understand the two of you have met before."

Bay forced his gaze away from Suzette long enough to nod. "Met. Is that what she told you?"

The smile on August's face stilled, as did the tentative one Suzette had been holding in place by sheer determination. Taking a deep breath, she stepped forward, holding out her hand.

"Hello, Bay. It's been a long time."

Glancing at August, he turned his attention back to the young woman. She was as beautiful as he remembered, and no doubt just as deadly as when he'd fallen in love with her.

Ignoring her hand, Bay shook his head. "Not long enough." Turning on his heel, he strolled away as the pain he thought he'd left behind years before returned, strangling his breath and crushing his heart.

Chapter Fifteen

"We're so glad you could join us for supper, Mr. Abrams." Audrey passed a platter of meat to him.

"If you don't mind, ma'am, I'd prefer you call me Levi."

A smile lit her face. "Then you'll call me Audrey."

"Done." He forked a thick piece of beef, setting it on his plate. "This sure does look good. I haven't had a home-cooked meal since I left for San Francisco."

"Did you see Mrs. Evanston when you were in San Francisco, Levi?" Heather sat on his other side, Caleb next to her. "She promised to write, but I've received nothing."

Swallowing a piece of meat, he nodded. "Mildred stays real busy. I saw her several times. She misses the ranch, but is adjusting to life in the city. Her friends have her wearing fancy dresses and hats."

Heather smiled. "Most women wear bonnets, Levi."

"I'm not talking about those pretty bonnets you ladies wear. She went out and bought herself a hat with feathers and ribbons, and well...I'm not sure what all. Sure didn't look the same all gussied up like a big city lady. But she's happy and that's what matters. You ought to go out and visit her, Heather. I know she misses you."

"Maybe someday, when there isn't so much work at the ranch."

"I suppose you've heard of our troubles, Levi." Ewan sat at the end of the table. He'd already offered him a job, which Levi didn't hesitate to accept.

"Caleb and Blaine told me some of it. Hard to believe they hung a man for doing his job." Levi shook his head. "Rather be shot than end up like that."

"Aye. I'd not want to be going that way." Ewan put another forkful of food into his mouth, chewing slowly.

A loud knock at the front door drew everyone's attention.

Caleb stood first. "I'll get it." Opening the door, he stood aside when the same ranch hand who'd alerted them about the fire stepped up to him.

"I need to speak to Ewan and Ian."

Caleb nodded toward the table. "Ewan's here, but Ian's having supper down at his place." He motioned to the table.

"Sorry to bother you at supper, Mr. MacLaren, but we've got another problem."

"What is it, lad?"

The man glanced around, drawing in a breath. "It's the cattle."

"More are missing?"

"No, sir. They're dead."

Heather stood at the edge of the porch, her hands clenched at her sides, watching as the riders headed north. "We should be with them."

Stepping beside her, Caleb leaned against the rail. "Ewan wanted a small group. No sense taking everyone and leaving the ranch vulnerable."

Bram, Blaine, Fletcher, Camden, and Sean rode out with Ewan and the ranch hand. All he could tell them was at least six animals were dead, all near a pond just north of the burned-out hacienda. It had taken him two hours to ride south and alert the MacLarens.

Caleb let his gaze wander over Heather. Before supper, she'd changed into a yellow cotton dress, her light brown hair in a clasp at the back of her neck, tendrils framing her face.

"I worry about them."

"I'd expect you to. Just remember, they know what they're doing."

She looked at him. "They could've waited until morning."

Caleb chuckled. "You know Ewan well enough to understand he wasn't going to wait. In his place, I wouldn't, either."

"Aye, you're right."

He started to reach out, let his fingers brush across her cheek, then pulled back. There were things he needed to say and he'd never get a better chance. Walking to the swing, he sat down, motioning to the spot next to him. When she hesitated, he held out his hand.

"Sit down, Heather. You've had a long few days."

Making her way to him, she glanced around before sitting down, keeping as much distance between them as possible. She knew Quinn and Emma had already gone to bed, as had her mother. The thought of them being alone again sent shivers through her. She clasped her hands together so Caleb wouldn't see them shaking.

"Are you cold?"

She shook her head.

Stretching out his long legs, he relaxed, resting his arm along the back of the swing. "I should've explained to you why I wanted you at the house after we moved the herd."

Stiffening, she shrugged, not looking at him. "Ewan put you in charge. It was your decision."

"Still, I should've been the one to tell you." Grasping a strand of her hair, he rolled it between his fingers. "I purposely stayed away from you today."

She shifted toward him, her eyes wide. "Why?"

Letting his fingers graze the back of her neck, he felt her shiver. "I didn't want Blaine or Levi suspecting anything."

Her eyes softened, her voice breathless. "And what would they be suspecting, Caleb?"

His mouth tilted up at the corners. "Well, I'm not sure." His fingers on her neck tightened, edging her toward him. "Maybe because I can't stop watching you." Lowering his head, he brushed a kiss across her lips. "Or that I can't keep my hands off you." Feeling no resistance, he inched closer, taking full possession of her mouth.

Moaning into his mouth, Heather rested her hands on his arms, gripping him as if she never wanted him to stop. The warm heat of his mouth triggered a quivering sensation that traveled through her body and down to her toes, settling in her belly.

She moved her hands behind his neck, her fingers playing with the silky strands of his hair as she squirmed to get closer. Both his arms were clamped around her, yet she still didn't feel close enough.

Heather felt his taut muscles shift as he lifted her, settling her on his lap, never breaking their kiss. The action caused her already quivering belly to ignite as waves of heat flashed through her. His hands were everywhere—moving over her back, up her arms, then gripping her hips in a gesture so possessive, she sighed in pure pleasure.

Breaking the kiss, he drew in a shuddering breath. "Ah, Heather...you've got me burning for you," he whispered.

Looking up, she stroked his stubbled face, her eyes glassy. "Show me what to do."

The plea hit him square in the chest. Although he had some experience with the ladies at Buckie's Castle, Heather was innocent, untouched by any man but him. He wanted to treasure her, teach her all he knew, bring her passion to life. The bigger obligation was to take care of her, not let emotions carry them so far they couldn't turn back. He needed time to come to terms with his future, while she needed to be sure her feelings for him were more than passing lust.

Lowering his head, he kissed her once more, hot and passionate with a promise he wasn't sure he'd be able to keep. Drawing away, he loosened his hold, tucking her head under his chin.

"We'll give this time, Heather. Once you're certain I'm the man you want to teach you, I'll show you everything."

Pulling back, she looked up at him, a question burning in her eyes.

"But it won't be tonight. Not until I know you're sure of your feelings."

Confusion flashed across her face before her features stilled. Licking her lips, she placed a kiss on his chin, moving along his strong jaw, then back to settle her mouth over his.

Cupping her face with both hands, he let her explore, his body igniting to a point he felt ready to explode. She was all he'd ever imagined and more. Her passionate response to his touch caused his heart to pound painfully in a chest already tight with need. Lifting his lips from hers, he drew in a ragged breath.

"You're making we want things you're not ready to give."

She shook her head slightly, uncertainty in her eyes. "I don't understand."

Blowing out a breath, he stroked a finger down her cheek. "Then I'll be clear. You make me want to strip off your clothes, lay you down, and not let you up until daybreak. Is that clear enough?"

Her lips parted, eyes widening at his meaning.

The corners of his mouth tilted into a wry grin. "I see it is." Lifting Heather off his lap, he set her on the seat, then stood. Holding out his hand, he helped her up, placing his hands on her shoulders.

"I care a great deal for you, Heather, but I won't be taking advantage."

She'd never felt so nervous or uncomfortable. Even her first cattle drive didn't scare her this much. "You're confusing me, Caleb. Do you want to give this a try or not?"

It was all he'd wanted since he'd first met her. He didn't understand why he hesitated when she finally stood before him, ready to give their relationship a chance.

"If you're agreeable, I'd like to take it a day at a time."

Her gaze shifted away, her expression blank for a long moment before she looked at him again. "A day at a time it is, Caleb Stewart. But I'll be warning you...I'm not a patient woman."

His head fell back as he let out a loud rumble of laughter, his entire body shaking. "Ah, darlin', I never thought of you as having patience."

Punching him lightly in the arm, her lips twitched before she joined him in laughter. "I'll not have you thinking me a shrew," she said, although a smile brightened her face.

Wrapping an arm around her waist, he hauled her to him for one more heated kiss before stepping away. "I've never thought you a shrew, darlin'. Petulant, opinionated, cantankerous..." This time, he moved fast enough to avoid the punch, laughing as he bounded down the steps. "I'll see you in the morning, sweetheart," he called over his shoulder, chuckling again when he spotted her at the edge of the porch, hands on hips, a peevish expression on her face.

Hearing the front door close, he found himself wondering if a life with her would always be filled with surprises, arguments, and laughter. If so, he figured it could be a pretty good life after all.

"Poisoned..." The word rolled from Colin's lips, his mouth twisting in anger.

Sean nodded. "Aye. If I'm right, the pond was tainted with arsenic."

"How many head?" Quinn asked, taking a seat in the living room of Ewan's house. They'd all congregated there early the following morning.

"Twelve. Five heifers, all close to calving. The rest were steers." Sean cradled the cup of coffee in his hands. "I could be wrong about the arsenic. I've been reading about it, though, and it's the one thing making sense."

Sean read everything he could about cattle and horses. Illnesses, breeding, and general care—every topic fascinated him.

He looked at Ian. "If it's all right with you, Da, I'll be riding into town this morning. I want to send a telegram to a doctor in San Francisco who works with cattle."

Everyone knew Sean had formed a friendship with the doctor, a man who'd visited August Fielder a couple years ago. Even though it was a new field in America, he'd encouraged Sean's curiosity about becoming a veterinarian. The doctor was the one who suggested he apply for admission to Highland Society's Veterinary School in Edinburgh.

Ian nodded. "Aye. It's a good idea, Sean. You should be speaking with Doc Vickery or Doc Tilden, also. They may have some answers."

"What you're saying is someone poisoned our cattle." Caleb sat forward, resting his empty cup on the table, his gaze on Sean.

"Aye. It could be intentional. It could also be natural poisoning."

"What do you think, lad?" Ian asked.

"I'm thinking the men who took the cattle, hung our ranch hand, and burned the hacienda also poisoned our water."

Ewan nodded his agreement. "Bram, Blaine, Fletcher, and Camden stayed with our other men. They'll be moving the herd a little south, posting more guards around the watering holes." He looked at his brother. "We'll be needing more lads, Ian. At least until we find who's responsible."

Quinn stood, glancing around the room. "I'll ride out with Levi."

"I'll be going with you." Colin walked over to him.

"Nae, Colin. You'll be riding into town with Sean. Put the word out we're looking for more men, and let Brodie know about the poisoning."

Caleb placed his hands on the table in front of him, pushing to his feet. "I'll ride out with Quinn and Levi."

"What of us?" Heather sat at the dining room table with Emma, Geneen, and Coral, as well as Sarah and the older MacLaren women.

"You'll be staying here, lass." Ian looked at Quinn. "Send word if you need more help, and the lasses will ride out."

Quinn nodded. "Aye, Uncle Ian." His gaze moved to his wife. He didn't miss the disgruntled expression on Emma's face.

Ian ignored the women's dissatisfied looks. "Colin, you'll need to be hiring at least six lads. Bring them back with you today."

"If I can find them."

"Do what you must. Even if they've no experience, they can stand guard."

Colin nodded, rubbing his jaw as he glanced at Sarah. He knew the events of the last few days worried his wife. "Aye, Uncle Ian."

"What of my parents, Uncle Ian? They should be warned." Emma sent an anxious glance at Quinn.

Ian leaned toward Ewan, speaking in hushed tones before looking at Emma. "You and Heather ride over this morning. Ask Boyd Doggett if he has any lads he can spare," he said, mentioning the Pearce foreman.

Emma nodded, letting out a relieved breath, as Ian continued.

"Geneen and Coral, you lasses and the rest of us will be keeping watch here." Standing, Ian picked up his hat and headed toward the front door before turning back. "We'll be finding the lads responsible for this." Slamming his hat on his head, Ian walked outside, Ewan close behind him.

As the others filed out to prepare for the day, Caleb lagged behind, waiting to speak with Heather.

Getting her attention, he nodded toward the study a few feet away. When she followed, he closed the door behind them, fingering the brim of his hat.

She looked at him, seeing lines of worry around his eyes. "What is it?"

Caleb's lips pursed. "I want you to be careful riding with Emma to the Pearces'. If you're approached by anyone you don't recognize, get out of there."

Merriment danced in her eyes. "Are you worrying about me now?"

He took a step toward her. "I've always worried about you, Heather. Whatever is going on is serious."

The amusement left her face, a tinge of red coloring her cheeks. "Aye, it is, but I'm not an eejit. I know to be careful."

"I'm not saying this because I think you're stupid, Heather. Quite the opposite. I understand how much killing those men bothered you." He looked away, sucking in an unsteady breath before pinning her with a hard stare. "I'm hoping you'll never have to do it again." His features softened. "I'm also hoping to sit next to you at supper tonight."

Swallowing her initial frustration, Heather wrapped her arms around her waist. "You'll not be back here tonight. You'll be guarding the herd, the same as the other lads."

A grim smile spread across his face. "True, but you understand my meaning." Reaching out, he placed a hand behind her neck, pulling her forward. Lowering his head, he kissed her. "Promise me you'll be careful," he whispered before kissing her again, drawing it out this time.

Moaning against his mouth, he felt her nod. "Aye, I'll be careful."

Resting his forehead against hers, he let out a relieved breath.

"I'm expecting you to be careful as well, Caleb."

Lifting his head, his gaze met hers. "So you *do* care about me."

Pushing away, she laughed. "Perhaps a wee bit."

He tilted his head to the side. "Only a wee bit?"

"Well..."

They jumped apart at the sound of the door opening, Audrey poking her head into the study. "Ah, there you are, lass." Her knowing smile landed on Caleb. "Emma's waiting for you. Should I be telling her you'll be a while longer?"

Caleb brushed a hand across his mouth, hiding his smile.

Heather clasped her hands in front of her as she shook her head. "Nae, Ma. Tell her I'll be coming right away."

"Be safe today...both of you."

Watching the door close, they looked at each other and laughed.

She put a hand to her mouth to stifle the sound. "I'm thinking she knows."

Leaning down, Caleb couldn't pass up one more kiss before settling his hat on his head. "I'm thinking you're right."

Chapter Sixteen

Heather and Emma glanced over their shoulders, waving to the men before the trail turned toward the Pearce ranch. They hadn't ridden more than a mile when Emma reined her horse closer to Heather.

"It is true?"

Heather's brows furrowed. "Is what true?"

"You and Caleb, of course."

Heather's mouth opened, then closed, her mind flashing back to last night and this morning in the study. "I'm not sure what you're saying."

"You don't have to tell me, but Quinn went downstairs last night and heard noises on the porch. When he looked out the window, he saw you and Caleb on the swing, and well...Quinn said, well...you probably don't want to know exactly what he said."

Heather closed her eyes, biting her lower lip, then looked over at Emma. "Was the lad's face all red, his eyes shooting fire?"

Emma laughed, nodding. "I've never heard him say some of the words that came out of his mouth last night. Of course, when he calmed down, he couldn't apologize enough."

Sucking in a breath, Heather thought of Caleb and Quinn riding together toward the herd. Her stomach churned, thinking of what Quinn might do.

"Did he tell you what he saw?"

Emma's sympathetic expression was all the answer Heather needed. "Truly, he didn't tell me much. Just that you were in Caleb's lap and...well, you know...kissing and such."

Reining up, Heather turned Shamrock around, her stomach churning. "I'd better be going back. I need to explain before Quinn kills him."

Emma stopped next to her, shaking her head. "Quinn won't kill him. He and I had a long talk before he finally got back into bed." Her lips twisted in a grimace. "Although when he woke up this morning, it was the first thing he mentioned, so maybe he'll just rough him up a bit. He loves Caleb like a brother. Besides, everyone knows he's been sweet on you for a long time. Deep down, I'm pretty certain Quinn is happy for you."

Placing a hand on her stomach, Heather bent over the saddle, sucking in air.

"Are you going to be sick? If so, you'd best get down." Emma slid off her horse, walking around to try and take Shamrock's reins from Heather's hand.

Tightening her grasp, Heather shook her head. "Nae, I'll be fine."

"Are you sure you don't want to get down, walk around a bit?"

"Nae, Emma." She cast a worried glance along the trail. "Are you certain we shouldn't be riding back?"

Shaking her head, Emma sighed. "Quinn is not going to kill Caleb, but I'm certain they'll talk. They're grown men. What could possibly happen?"

"What the..." Caleb sat up, rubbing his jaw and shaking his head to clear the spots before his eyes. "What'd you do that for?"

Quinn stood over him, fisted hands on his hips. "You and Heather," he sputtered.

Looking up at him, Caleb cocked his head to one side, still massaging his jaw. "What about me and Heather?"

"I saw you last night, on the swing. The lass is my sister...*my sister*!"

Jumping to his feet, Caleb took a tentative step toward him, mindful of the distance between them. "I know who she is, Quinn."

"You'll not be taking advantage of her."

Caleb touched his lip, then looked at the blood on his finger. "I know that, too."

"And you'll not be hurting her."

"I've no intention of hurting her. What you saw is as far as I intend for it to go." *Until I've made up my mind about the future.*

Scrubbing a hand down his face, Quinn pointed a finger at him. "Does the lass know you're talking of leaving?"

The air left Caleb's lungs. "I haven't told her."

Quinn had been silent during the ride north. After the two of them had split with the others, riding to one end of the herd, Quinn stopped, slid to the ground, and before Caleb knew what was coming, hauled him off Jupiter, landing a fierce blow to his jaw. Staggering backward, Caleb landed on his butt, blood trickling from a cut on his lip, his face throbbing. He still felt dazed, but at least he knew the cause of Quinn's anger.

"Then you've decided to stay." It wasn't a question, but a demand.

Stretching his jaw, Caleb studied his friend, judging how much of the anger remained. He didn't blame him for his concern. Quinn and Heather were close, protective, and unforgiving to those who threatened the other. They also valued honesty.

"I don't know."

Mumbling a curse, Quinn turned away, pacing several feet before whirling back to face Caleb. "You've got to tell her what you've been thinking."

"Not yet." He bent to pick up his hat, which had flown off his head with the first punch.

"What do you mean *not yet*?"

Slapping the hat against his thigh, he jammed it on his head, his own temper beginning to take hold. "Just what I said. I'll tell her, but now isn't the time."

Quinn's voice hardened. "It's as good a time as any. The lass won't take it well if you keep secrets from her."

"You're right." Grabbing Jupiter's reins, he swung into the saddle. "She's unpredictable on her best days. I'll tell her when I'm ready."

Staring at the ground, Quinn shook his head. "You're an eejit, Caleb."

A bleak smile crossed his face as he waited for Quinn to mount up. "I've been told that."

Quinn spun his horse around, concern etched on the corners of his mouth and eyes. "You hurt her and I'll have no choice but to kill you."

The threat, delivered with deadly resolve, had Caleb flinching. "And I'd let you."

He saw Quinn's eyes widen before he turned Jupiter toward the herd and rode off.

It had taken some persuasion before Emma could talk Heather into continuing to her family's ranch. When she'd offered to ride on alone, allowing Heather to follow the men, she'd declined.

"It was a few kisses, certainly not what you and Quinn did."

Emma groaned at the reminder. "Maybe not, but Quinn won't see it that way. He'll assume the worst.

It's the way older brothers are with sisters. Jimmy was the same."

An eerie silence followed at the reminder of Emma's dead brother and Quinn's best friend.

"He was a good lad. Quinn took his death very hard."

Nodding, Emma kept her eyes focused on the trail. She missed her brother as much as Quinn did. Their mutual love of Jimmy was one of the bonds holding them together.

The pounding of horse's hooves coming toward them caused them to stop, both reaching for the rifles in their scabbards. Settling them on their laps, the women waited, seeing a man they didn't recognize ride up and stop several yards away. Before he had a chance to speak, they'd lifted their rifles, aiming them toward the man.

"Don't be coming any closer." Heather glanced at Emma, seeing the worry on her face. Both knew the trail they rode went straight to the Pearce ranch with one narrow fork going to town. Only the Pearce family and other locals knew of the rough trail. The man could only be coming from Emma's parents' place.

He reined his horse back a few feet, then held up his hands.

"Where are you coming from?" Emma asked, her arms quivering under the weight of the rifle.

The man scanned the trail behind them, glad to see they were alone.

Lowering his hands, the man rested one on his thigh, not far from the gun strapped around his waist. "The Pearce place. I had some business with Big Jim and his foreman."

"What kind of business?"

His gaze shifted between the two before landing on Emma. A feral smile spread across his face. "Well, now, I don't think that's any of your business."

Heather's aim moved to the man's chest. "We'll be deciding that for ourselves." She saw the hand on his thigh twitch. "Don't you be moving any closer to your gun."

Raising his hand, he clasped the saddle horn.

"At least he's not a complete eejit," Heather whispered to Emma. "What was your business with Big Jim and Boyd?"

"Talking land and cattle, nothing more, li'l lady. Big Jim has land and I have money to invest. A business proposition."

Heather cringed at the look on his face. He'd said nothing to warn them off, yet she couldn't help feeling the threat he presented.

"My guess is they sent you on your way." Emma lowered the rifle enough to give her arms a rest.

"You must know them."

Emma wanted nothing more than to wipe the smirk off his face. "Everyone in these parts knows Big

Jim and Gertie. And everyone also knows they have no desire to move off the ranch."

He nodded, leaning forward. "That's what they told me. Seems I'll be taking my money somewhere else."

Emma shook her head. "Not on this trail. You'd do well to turn around. Just before the Pearce ranch, there's a narrow trail going southwest. It'll take you to town."

Scorn twisted his lips. "I heard this was the way to the Circle M."

"You heard wrong." Emma moved her rifle, indicating he should move along. "We'll be coming behind you, so don't think about turning back this way."

"You ladies aren't being too hospitable now, are you? I heard people were real friendly in these parts."

"You must have heard wrong." Shamrock began to dance around, making it hard for Heather to hold her aim. When the man shifted in the saddle, she shot a worried look at Emma, seeing her raise the rifle back up.

Emma directed her aim at his heart. "It's time you headed off."

For a long moment, the man didn't move, his eyes narrowing to slits. An instant later, the hard lines on his face softened before he threw back his head and laughed.

"You ladies aren't much for bargaining, so I guess I'll head back. Southwest at the fork?"

"Aye, that's what she said." Heather let out a relieved sigh when he picked up the reins, turning his horse around. Just as he was about to ride off, she called out to him. "What's your name?"

He shifted in the saddle, jaw tight, his features hard as granite, lips curling into a sneer. In Heather's mind, the look represented pure evil.

"Black."

"That's all he said?" Emma sat next to her father, Heather on her side, and the foreman, Boyd Doggett, across from them.

Big Jim Pearce nodded. "Told me and Boyd he came into some money and was looking for land. I told him my price. He countered with an amount so low I almost threw him out right then. I wasn't interested in haggling any further with someone out to steal my land." He glanced at Heather. "Although I might consider letting the MacLarens steal it someday." The big man winked at her, earning himself a smile. Everyone knew their ranch would pass to Emma. As Quinn's wife, the ranch would essentially be operated by the MacLaren family.

"Now, Big Jim, you stop teasing poor Heather." His wife, Gertie, walked in from the kitchen, placing glasses of lemonade in front of each of them, looking at her husband. "Are you certain it was the same man who came by here?"

Downing the lemonade in a few big gulps, Big Jim nodded. "Called himself Black. Don't think there are two men like him in this area."

"Have you ever seen him before?"

"No, Emma, and neither has Boyd."

Emma's gaze shot to the foreman, a man she'd grown to respect. "What did you think of him?"

Shrugging, Boyd leaned forward, resting his arms on the table. "Tallest man I've seen in a long time. Imposing. Wears his gun low, which had me on edge."

Heather's eyes widened. "Do you think he's a gunfighter?"

"Could be. More like a gun for hire. I'm thinking that's where he came up with all this money he's itching to spend." Unlike Big Jim, Boyd took slow sips of his lemonade, his eyes narrowed, as if in concentration. "I was ready for him to leave before he got off his horse."

Gertie snorted. "Takes you a long time to warm up to anyone, Boyd."

"True enough, but this one's trouble. Did you say he took off toward town?" Boyd looked at Emma, taking another swallow of lemonade.

"He took off at a gallop and got so far ahead, we didn't see him make the turn. All I know is he didn't come back our way."

Big Jim leaned back in his chair. "Black isn't the reason you rode all the way out here. What's going on?"

Heather rolled the glass between the palms of her hands. "We've lost more cattle."

Big Jim lifted a brow. "More rustlers?"

"Poison." Heather's response got everyone's attention. "At least Sean thinks it is. We lost twelve head, five were heifers almost ready to drop."

"Damn..." Boyd muttered, rubbing a hand along his chin.

"The uncles asked us to come warn you and see if you might have any men to spare until Colin hires more lads to help us."

"They asking in town, Heather?" Boyd asked.

"Aye. He and Sean rode to town this morning. Colin will be looking for at least six."

Big Jim looked at Boyd. "What do you think?"

Boyd thought a minute, his jaw working as he considered how they'd be able to help. "I'll ride over. You can spare me for a couple days. That will give Colin a chance to hire some more men."

Nodding, Big Jim laid his hands on the table and pushed up. "You can ride back with Emma and Heather, assuming they plan to return to Circle M today."

"We do, Papa."

Boyd stood, heading toward the door. "Then I'll grab the gear I'll need and saddle my horse. I'll also let the men know what's going on. Give me thirty minutes."

"You get yourself ready, Boyd. I'll talk to the men. I'd feel better knowing you'll get back to Circle M well before dark." Big Jim grabbed his cane, following Boyd outside.

When the door closed, Emma looked at her mother. "How's Papa doing?"

Fiddling with the edge of the tablecloth, Gertie shook her head. "Not good. He seems to get weaker every day."

"Maybe we shouldn't be taking Boyd with us." Heather gathered the empty glasses, placing them on a tray. "We can make do without him."

"No. Your family needs help. If I know my husband, he wants Boyd to go. If he could, Big Jim would go himself."

"Has he seen a doctor lately?"

"Doc Vickery or Doc Tilden rides out about every two weeks to check on him, although I hate to trouble them. If only he'd agree to ride in with me." Sighing, Gertie stared out the window. "He's putting up a strong front today, but as soon as you leave, he'll lay down and not get up for hours, maybe not until tomorrow morning. He sleeps downstairs most nights because he can't climb the stairs. His appetite is gone, so he keeps losing weight." Closing her eyes, she tried to will her tears away, but they wouldn't obey. Breathing out a shaky sigh, she swiped the moisture from her cheek. Even in the worst of times, Gertie always held herself together, refusing to be anything but strong.

Emma's heart broke, knowing what it cost her mother to show weakness in front of her and Heather. Reaching out, she placed her hand over her mother's. "You can't lose hope, Mama. What if we took him to San Francisco, had another doctor look at him?"

"I've tried. He simply refuses to go. Says when it's his time, he'll accept whatever God decides, and for me to accept it, too. Sometimes I just don't understand the man."

"Ach." Heather waved a hand in the air. "All lads are too stubborn. I'm thinking their pride and stubbornness will be the end of most of them."

Emma put a hand in front of her mouth to hide a grin. "You're not thinking of one man in particular, are you?"

Biting her lip, Heather stood, picking up the tray, ignoring the question.

"I'm ready to go when you two are." They hadn't even heard Boyd come through the door.

"We're ready." Standing, Emma walked around the table, giving her mother a hug. "I'll come visit again as soon as I can. Maybe between the two of us, we can talk Papa into making the trip to San Francisco."

Gertie dropped her arms from around her daughter, taking a step back. "Come visit, but we won't waste our time trying to convince him to go. The doctors here are real good and he trusts them."

"If that's what you want, Mama."

Walking to them, Heather hugged Gertie. "We'd best be leaving. I know the lads will appreciate Boyd's help."

Following them out, Gertie watched while Emma said goodbye to her father, then waved as the three rode away.

Taking slow, measured steps up to the porch, letting the cane provide support, Big Jim stood next to Gertie. Putting an arm around her, he pulled her close.

"Our girl's all grown up."

"That she is, Gertie. And I couldn't be more proud of her."

Leaning up, she kissed his cheek. "I'd best get inside and finish fixing dinner. The men will be hungry soon."

Closing the door behind her, Gertie thought of her husband's failing health and all the trouble at the Circle M. A flash of fear speared through her, causing her to stop.

In her heart, she knew it wouldn't be long before she lost Big Jim. It hadn't occurred to her she might lose her daughter, too. With all the trouble, including the shooting Emma played a part in, her mouth suddenly went dry. She'd already lost her son. Certainly, she couldn't lose all her family.

The thought haunted her through the rest of the day and into the early evening. At bedtime, she knelt, clasped her hands together, and prayed harder than she'd done in a long while.

Chapter Seventeen

Conviction

Bay studied the document once more, rubbing his brows as he concentrated on the numbers. Whoever gave this to him had gone to a lot of trouble and had access to more than would be available in one place. He'd first thought it came from one source. Now he wasn't so certain. The bigger puzzle was the information had been given to him.

Pushing away from his desk, Bay shrugged into his coat, folded the paper, and slid it into a pocket. Checking the time on the tall grandfather clock, he winced. It was too late to find who he sought at their office. He'd have to wait until tomorrow.

August and Jasper left earlier, leaving him to lock the office, which suited him fine. He preferred working in the quiet evenings when the others had gone home. Tonight, though, he felt agitation coil within him. Cattle were dying, people were being threatened, and he didn't have the answers he sought.

His stomach growled, reminding him he hadn't eaten for hours. Instead of riding back to August's, hoping the cook would prepare him something, he reined his horse past the almost finished Feather

River Hotel. Dimly lit lanterns were still ablaze inside, casting light on a lone figure huddled over a table. A figure he knew all too well.

He'd avoided Suzette since she'd arrived, refusing to discuss their past with August while doing his best to forget she'd traveled across the country to work at the new restaurant. Somehow, August discovered they had a past and hired her, thinking Bay would be pleased with the decision. Given the way they parted, he doubted Suzette would've been the one to tell him.

Unlike him, he felt certain she knew who awaited her in Conviction. He had no idea why she wanted to be near him and, after all this time, didn't care. Bay wanted nothing more than to avoid crossing her path.

Stopping in front of the Gold Dust, he slid to the ground, tossing the reins over the rail. As he stepped onto the boardwalk, he had a clear view of those inside the restaurant, a tiny smile forming when he saw the man he sought. Maybe tonight would turn out fine.

"Do you mind if I join you?" Bay stood next to the table in the dining room, his hand resting on the back of a chair.

Setting down his cup of coffee, Philip Aunspach stood, his hand stretched toward the chair. "Please do. It would be a pleasure to have company. Most nights I eat alone at the boardinghouse or here."

"Neither are bad choices."

"But the restaurant in the new hotel will be better." Philip sat back down, draping the napkin across his lap.

"Why are you so certain?" Bay asked, then wished he hadn't. The answer seemed clear in Philip's eyes.

"Have you met the woman who'll be managing it?" He didn't wait for Bay to answer. "If her beauty is any indication of her culinary skills, I believe we're looking at a future of fine dining."

"As good as you found in San Francisco?" Bay asked.

Philip nodded. "Possibly. I'll give you my opinion once it opens."

"You've met her then?"

"I stopped by this morning to introduce myself. She's, well..."

"Distant?"

Philip snapped his fingers. "Yes. Professional, courteous, but distant. Sounds as if you've had the pleasure of meeting her."

Bay had no intention of opening up about his past with Suzette. "Briefly. August and I met her when the steamer docked."

The server appeared, preventing Philip from responding. "What may I get you?"

"Coffee and the same as what Mr. Aunspach is having."

Making a quick note on a piece of paper, the young man nodded. "Yes, sir."

231

Bay waited until he hurried off, relaxing back in the seat. "I've been meaning to talk to you, find out how you're doing at the bank."

"Checking on your competition?"

Chuckling, Bay shook his head. "It's my boss who owns a good portion of the Bank of Conviction, not me."

"True, but I'm certain you've already made a commitment to his bank." Philip shrugged. "I'd do the same in your position."

"Ah, now, that's where you're wrong. I've an account there, of course, but the remainder of my funds are still in another bank back east. I believe it's always good to weigh your options, especially in a new town. Don't you agree, Philip?"

His face sobered. "Why, yes. I've come to believe that more and more since arriving in Conviction. The longer I'm here, the more fascinating the inner workings of a small town become."

Both men paused as the server appeared with Bay's meal and coffee.

"Here you are, sir. Let me know if I can get you anything else."

Nodding at him, Bay inhaled the rich aroma of stew. "Their selection is small, but the food is usually good." Taking a bite, he chewed slowly, then swallowed. "Refresh my memory. How long have you been with San Francisco Merchant Bank?"

"Three years, all of it in San Francisco. I never intended to leave, but the opportunity here came up, and...well..." He shrugged, letting the thought trail off.

Scooping up some potatoes, Bay nodded. "And you've been in Conviction a few months?"

"That's right. Mr. Delacroix has been extremely supportive since my first day with the bank. He made certain the other executives knew who I was and understood my capabilities. And even though there were several gentlemen who'd been with the bank longer, he's also the one who convinced the board I was the right choice to take over as manager in Conviction."

"Interesting. And now Delacroix is here. Isn't it unusual for a board member to travel out to a remote location such as Conviction?"

Something in Bay's tone had Philip on edge. Forcing himself to relax, his gaze darted around the restaurant, as if he had to be careful about what he said.

"Perhaps. The man has strong connections in San Francisco." Philip paused a moment before saying more. "In truth, his wife is the one with the money and social influence. I believe her uncle is a major shareholder and is also on the board."

"I'm certain you're quite loyal to Delacroix."

"As much as you are to August Fielder."

Picking up his coffee, Bay cradled the cup, considering Philip's comment. "I've known him a long time. He's a good man. I've found no reason not to be loyal." He watched as Philip's throat worked, his jaw tensing. Pinning him with a hard glare, Bay cocked his head to one side. "I'm sure you can say the same of your boss."

Unable to meet Bay's pointed stare, Philip looked down at his plate. Setting down his fork, he lifted his head. "Delacroix is a complicated man. Let's say I'm still learning about him."

"Fair enough." Taking a few more bites, Bay pushed his plate away. "I'm certain you've heard about the troubles at the Circle M."

Picking up his coffee cup, Philip shrugged. "The same as everyone in town, I heard about the shooting of six men."

"Rustlers," Bay corrected.

"Yes, rustlers. If rumor is to be believed, the MacLaren women played a part in the men's deaths."

Bay nodded, thinking of that day and how close the men had come to being ambushed. "The rumor is correct. If they hadn't arrived and spotted the rustlers, several of us might not have made it out alive."

Philip's brow lifted. "You were there?"

"I was. And I'm in the women's debt."

"I heard the men attempted to steal close to a hundred head."

"You heard right. Did you also know several of the MacLaren cattle were poisoned?"

Philip sat back, his spine stiffening. "When did that happen?"

"Yesterday. They were all drinking from the same pond. Colin and Sean MacLaren rode into town this morning to speak with Brodie."

"I don't know much about ranching, but it's my understanding poisoning can be from what they eat, the water source..." His voice trailed off at the sight of Giles walking into the restaurant.

Noting the strained expression on Philip's face, Bay glanced behind him. Seeing Giles, he looked back at Philip, lowering his voice. "Sean believes it was intentional. Perhaps arsenic."

"Arsenic?"

Bay nodded. "They're hiring more men."

"I thought I might find you here, Philip." Giles looked between the two, his gaze settling on Bay. "Good evening, Mr. Donahue. I didn't know the two of you were acquainted."

"Mr. Donahue has been asking questions about our bank," Philip interjected before Bay could respond. "Seems he has some additional funds to bring out from back east."

Pulling out a chair, Giles sat down, not waiting for an invitation to join them. "We're always interested in new customers, Mr. Donahue. Perhaps I can help. I'd be happy to meet with you...tomorrow perhaps?"

A wry grin formed on Bay's face. "I'm afraid my schedule is quite full tomorrow, Mr. Delacroix."

"Then another time."

"It's not necessary." Bay glanced at Philip, then back at Giles. "I'm certain Mr. Aunspach will be able to answer all my questions." Bay nodded at Philip, seeing his lips draw into a thin line.

Giles looked between the two, then smiled. "Quite right. Perhaps we can talk another time."

"Perhaps." Bay stood, pulling out some money and placing it on the table. "Gentlemen, it was good to see both of you. Enjoy the rest of your evening."

Stepping into the cool night air, Bay felt a small measure of success at what he'd learned. He'd always been a good judge of men. Studying Philip, his posture, the tone of his voice, the way he acted when Giles joined them, Bay knew his initial instincts were correct. All he had to do was apply the right combination of incentives and pressure to get the young bank manager to talk.

"It was so nice of you to invite me for supper tonight, Maggie."

She smiled at Miranda, waving a dismissive hand. "I'm sure eating alone at the boardinghouse every night must get tiring. And it's nice to have company. Brodie works long hours."

"Will he be joining us tonight?" Miranda continued to slice the roast beef, laying it on a serving platter.

"He will."

The words were out a few seconds before the door opened and Brodie walked inside.

"Miss Harris. What a nice surprise." He removed his hat, setting it on a table near the door before walking over to Maggie and kissing her cheek. "You'll be staying for supper?"

"Yes. If it's no bother." She set the knife aside, picking up the platter to place it on the table.

"Nae. It's good to have you here. Maggie's cooking is better than what you'd be finding at the boardinghouse."

"I'm certain it is."

"I'll be washing up, Maggie."

She glanced over her shoulder. "Don't take too long. Supper's almost ready." She lifted a bowl of potatoes, handing them to Miranda. At almost five months pregnant, Maggie found herself slowing down a little. Naps had become a welcome part of each day.

"When is the baby due?" Miranda set the bowl next to the platter.

"Doc Tilden says not for four more months."

"And it couldn't come soon enough," Brodie said, walking back into the kitchen. "She sleeps half the day and still has little energy at night."

Maggie gently shoved him, feigning irritation. "I'll have you know I slept no more than an hour today." Walking to the table, she placed the vegetables down. She waited as Brodie pulled out Miranda's chair, then hers before sitting down himself.

"I heard your house will be ready in another week." Maggie passed the meat to Miranda.

"Yes. I can't wait to move in." Sliding meat onto her plate, she handed it to Brodie. "The boardinghouse is nice, but it will be wonderful to be in my own home."

Maggie looked at Brodie. "Colin and Sean came by this morning looking for you."

He nodded, the relaxed mood slipping from his face. "Aye. They came to the jail with some more news."

The fork stilled partway to Maggie's mouth. "What happened?"

"They found a dozen dead cattle near one of the ponds. Five were heifers ready to calve."

Brows furrowing, she set the fork down. "Shot?"

"Sean believes they were poisoned."

"Who would..." Her sentence trailed off as Maggie thought about the shootings, fire, and rustling. "It can't be the same men. They were all killed."

"Aye, but there could be more. We don't know who's behind it, but I will find out."

"What are you going to do?" Miranda asked.

"First, we have to know for certain the cattle were intentionally poisoned. The lads stopped at the jail again before riding back to the ranch. Sean spoke to Doc Tilden about it, gave him a sample of the water. The doc used his equipment. His opinion is the water was tainted with arsenic. Sean also sent a telegram to a doctor in San Francisco."

"The friend of August Fielder's?" Maggie wrapped her arms around her waist, her appetite disappearing.

"Aye. Colin hired four men today and is looking for more. Sam and I are going to ride out early tomorrow morning, take a look around the pond. Maybe we'll spot something the lads missed." Brodie shook his head. "It's clear someone is targeting the family. We're needing to discover who."

Miranda looked down at her still full plate, her appetite vanishing, the same as Maggie's. "Are the men all right?"

"Aye. The lads moved the herd farther south. They'll be staying with the herd until we arrest whoever is doing this."

"Maybe they'll end up like the other six." Maggie didn't try to hide her disgust at those who'd tried to gun down the MacLarens.

"Maybe, but I'd rather be taking them alive. Someone is paying them to do this and I want to be knowing who." Cutting a piece of meat, he speared it. "The lads moved the cattle and men from the old Evanston ranch."

"No one is there guarding it?" Maggie asked.

"Nae. The cattle were the main concern and they've been moved." He put the food into his mouth, thinking through the events of the last week. "I should be with the family."

Standing, Maggie moved behind him, placing her hands on his shoulders. "You're the sheriff and you're needed here." She glanced over at Miranda, offering a grim smile. "Let's talk about this more once the danger has passed."

Miranda clasped her hands in her lap. "I never realized how dangerous living on a ranch could be."

"We've had troubles before," Brodie answered.

"Nothing like this, Brodie." Maggie moved back to her chair, exhaustion beginning to claim her.

"Nae, love. Nothing like this." Picking up his coffee, he took a sip. "I spoke with August today. Bay is investigating on his own. He has a theory who might be behind all this."

Miranda's breath caught, eyes widening. "Who?"

"Bay isn't saying, not until he's had a chance to explore his theory."

She leaned forward. "He must have told August something."

Brodie looked at Miranda, shaking his head. "If so, August isn't saying. I'm going to speak with Bay when Sam and I return tomorrow. Maybe the lad will learn something more by then."

Miranda picked up her fork, her appetite slowly returning. "I hope you have good news once you speak with him."

"Aye, lass." Brodie nodded. "So do I."

Chapter Eighteen

Sam and Brodie walked around the pond, looking for any tracks or signs leading them to the man, or men, who'd poisoned the water. They found nothing. No boot tracks, hoofprints, or empty vessels.

A telegram had been delivered to Brodie before he and Sam left for Circle M. A message for Sean from the doctor in San Francisco. He'd talked to his colleagues and they all agreed a small pond could be poisoned with enough arsenic to kill animals. And it could be accomplished quite easily by a single individual.

Sam lowered himself onto his haunches, looking over the pond. He'd worked for Pinkerton during and after the war, traveling to Conviction on a case. Brodie had persuaded him to stay on as a deputy. A couple months earlier, Brodie's sister, Jinny, had married Deputy Covington. The two couldn't be happier.

"Whoever did this knew where the herd would be, how much arsenic to use, when to get in and out, and left nothing to trace the action back to them. A group of men would've been sloppy, failing to cover their tracks."

"You're thinking it was one person, Sam?"

He nodded, then stood. "I am. There was a similar case back in 1863. Confederate raiders poisoned a pond where Union soldiers watered their mounts. Several horses died before it was discovered. The raiders were found and their confessions included how they poisoned the water. They were an arrogant bunch."

Brodie looked across the water. "Can the pond be used again?"

Sam shook his head, settling his hands on his waist. "I'm no expert, but seems to me you wouldn't want to risk it. I'd fill it in and keep the cattle as far away as you can. It would be safest to move them to Boundary River. There's little chance anyone would be successful poisoning the rushing water."

Colin, Sean, and Caleb stood several feet away, listening to the conversation. The rest of the MacLarens and their ranch hands watched the herd or guarded the other ponds. Leaning down, Colin picked up a rock, skipping it across the still water, then turned to face Brodie.

"Sam's right. We'll drive the cattle to the river. There are eddies where the water runs in a circular motion before returning to the main river. It runs right through Circle M land and there's good grazing on both sides. It will work for a while, but we'll be needing to find another solution before long."

Brodie nodded. "You're in charge out here, Colin. Do you need my help?"

"Nae. The lads and I can take care of it. Sean, what do you think about this pond?"

"I agree with Sam. We fill it in and hope whoever did this doesn't poison any others."

Quinn stepped up. "We've men guarding each one, but we'll not be able to do it for long."

Caleb stood off by himself, with little to add. Same as the others, he knew nothing of poisoning cattle or reversing the damage done to the pond. He could handle rustlers. This threat was beyond anything he'd ever experienced.

Moreover, he didn't want to explain to Brodie and Sam about the cuts and bruises on his face. He'd been the subject of merciless teasing since he and Quinn had joined the others. Worse, everyone knew the cause, and Heather wouldn't be pleased to know she'd been the subject of their bantering, no matter how friendly.

Something caught his attention. A sound, smell, gut feeling. Whatever alerted him, he turned around, spotting a cloud of black smoke in the distance. Not saying anything, he jumped on Jupiter's back, racing up the hill to get a better view. What he saw sent a shiver through him.

Reining around, he headed back down the hill, stopping in front of the others. "Fire. It appears to be south of the ranch. Maybe as far as Evanston's old house." Caleb looked at Colin. As the oldest cousin, and in the absence of Ewan or Ian, they all looked to him for direction. "Do you want me to ride out and see?"

Colin dragged a hand down his face. "We've no lads to spare."

"Sam and I will ride with Caleb," Brodie said. "We'll stop at the ranch and get Thane, and anyone else they can spare."

Colin nodded, his voice urgent. "The worry isn't the house and barn, lads. We don't want it spreading to the pastures. We'll be needing that land to graze the herd over the winter."

Brodie and Sam raced to their horses, following Caleb up and over the hill.

Colin watched them leave, turning to Quinn. "Could this be getting any worse?"

Quinn clasped his cousin on the back. "It could have nothing to do with what else is happening."

Colin stared at him. "Are you believing that's true?"

Letting out a breath, Quinn dropped his hand. "Right now, I've no idea what to believe."

Caleb couldn't push Jupiter any harder. Watching the smoke thicken, blocking out the sun, his chest tightened. Not for the house or the barn, but for the land surrounding them. The structures had been well located.

He knew a wide swath of dirt separated the structures from the lush pastures. Plus, there were two wells. They just needed to take enough people to man the buckets and pray the wind stayed calm, as it had since dawn. Racing down the last hill, they spotted the Circle M homestead, all three letting out a relieved sigh.

"You were right, lad. The fire is farther south." Brodie reined to a stop in front of Kyla's house, hurrying to dismount. "Let's get help and ride on out."

"We'll need buckets and shovels," Caleb called as he rode to Audrey's house.

"I'll get them." Sam raced to the barn, grabbing all he could.

Caleb raced up the steps, shoving the front door open. "Heather!"

Audrey rushed out of the kitchen, wiping her hands down her apron. "She's not here, Caleb. Ewan, Ian, Thane, and the older lasses left as soon as they saw the smoke."

"How long ago?"

"No more than thirty minutes. Will you be following them?"

"Yes. Brodie and Sam are with me."

Audrey followed him outside, waving at the other two as they rode past. Clasping her hands together, she turned to go back inside, stomach churning as she wondered what else could go wrong.

"More water over here, Emma." Heather stood as close as possible to the smoldering embers, an empty bucket in her hand. Heat seeped through the soles of her boots, the bottoms of her feet beginning to feel the burn. "Thane, are you needing more water over there?"

"Nae. We're good here. Maybe the barn." Her younger brother pointed to where Ewan and Ian used sledgehammers to knock down siding still hot from the flames they'd been able to douse. Geneen and Coral shoveled dirt onto low flames refusing to die, as Opal helped Emma haul water from the well.

Thane had spotted the smoke early, alerting his uncles. They'd wasted little time. Within minutes, they gathered tools and rode off.

They worked in unison from the moment they arrived. The fire had never taken hold, allowing them to squelch the flames quickly. The reason the flames seemed overwhelming from a distance became clear as they dismounted. Mildred loved her oil lamps and kept several gallons of kerosene in both the house and barn. These had ignited just before the MacLarens arrived. Focusing on those areas, they were able to stop the fire before it spread too far.

Stopping to take a breath, Heather swiped a sleeve across her brow, doing her best not to breathe in too much of the smoky air. Glancing behind her, she blinked into the hazy sun, surprised to see three riders approaching. Blinking again, her lips curled into a smile when she recognized Caleb. Dropping the bucket, she stepped carefully around the scattered debris, rushing toward him.

"Caleb!" Her voice echoed across the now still yard. Everyone stopped in their work to watch as he slid from his horse, wrapping his arms around her, both totally unmindful of those around them.

He was within an instant of kissing her when a loud cough jerked them apart. Looking behind him, Brodie stood next to Sam, neither bothering to hide their smiles. Heather recovered first, moving toward Brodie.

"Are you here to help or just stare?"

Brodie chuckled. "Aye, lass, we're here to help, although it appears you've got it taken care of." His gaze moved from the house to the barn, seeing his father. "Da," he yelled, then started toward him.

Grasping Caleb's arm, stopping him from following Brodie, Heather's gaze narrowed on him. "What happened to your face?"

Touching the cut on his lip, he shrugged. "I walked into an angry brother."

It took her a moment to catch his meaning. When she did, her eyes widened, then sparked with anger. "*Quinn* did this to you?"

"He saw us on the porch."

Crossing her arms, she stepped closer to him. "Ach. The lad spied on us."

Caleb choked out a laugh. "He heard us outside and looked out the window. You were on my lap, and we were—"

She placed fingers across his lips, stopping what he was about to say. "So the lad hit you."

"I'd have done the same." Reaching out, he touched her cheek. "He loves you, Heather." Dropping his hand, he rubbed his jaw. "I got the message."

She cocked a brow. "And what message did my brother give you?"

"Not to hurt you, which I have no intention of doing." He looked behind her, seeing Brodie with Ewan. He smiled at Heather. "We'll speak of this later. For now, we need to finish here." They followed Brodie, coming up behind him.

"What can we do to help, Da?" Brodie asked.

Ewan clasped his son's shoulder, gesturing behind him. "As long as the fire doesn't flare up, we've got it taken care of."

"Any idea how it started?" Brodie asked as Sam joined them.

Ewan raked a hand through his hair. "There were two separate fires. One in the house, the other in the barn."

Brodie looked between the now charred structures. "Intentional then."

"Aye."

Brodie looked down, kicking a piece of smoldering wood, mumbling a curse. "Whoever did this doesn't know we abandoned the property or they wouldn't be wasting their time."

"Maybe not."

Brodie's brows lifted at Sam. "What do you mean?"

"They must know you need everyone to guard the herd and family. By setting the fire, they've forced you to pull people from both, leaving them vulnerable."

A sudden chill gripped those standing around.

"Sonofabitch…" Brodie rushed to his horse, mounting in one smooth movement. "Caleb and Sam, come with me. Da, are you and the others going to be all right to get back to the house?"

Ewan nodded. "Aye. We'll be leaving right away."

"I'll be riding with Brodie." Heather ran to Shamrock, ignoring the protests from her uncles.

"Me, too." Emma dropped the bucket, going to her horse and grabbing the reins.

When he saw the other two young women starting to move, Ewan pointed a finger at Geneen and Coral. "You'll be staying with us, lasses. And I'll be hearing nothing more about it."

Before Caleb could protest, Heather and Emma were already ahead of him, pushing their horses into a gallop. They didn't slow, not even when he called to

Heather. After a while, they slacked the pace, giving him, Brodie, and Sam a chance to catch up.

Caleb rode alongside Heather for a good distance, saying nothing, watching as she glanced over at him every few minutes. Knowing Ewan and the others would be right behind them, they took the faster trail that wound behind the cluster of houses, barns, and corrals making up the MacLaren homestead. Everyone could feel the tension in the group, the need to reach the herd as soon as possible.

Another hour passed in almost complete silence before they heard the bawling of cattle along the edges of the Boundary River. The sun had begun its descent over the western hills, indicating the men would be building fires and cooking supper before long.

The size and scattered nature of the herd required more than one camp. Riding to the closest one, they spotted Colin and Quinn, who stood from where they'd been seated and waved them over. The instant Quinn saw Emma, his bland expression changed into a smile before he tensed. He didn't let her dismount before stalking up beside her horse. When she started to get down, he placed his hands on her waist, holding her in the saddle.

"You shouldn't be here, lass."

Caleb saw the anger flash in Emma's eyes. Wincing at what he knew was coming, he looked at Heather, nodding at a nearby trail.

"Let's give them some time to talk."

They took the trail toward the river before anyone could stop them. When they got near the edge, he slid off Jupiter. "This should do."

Heather dismounted, ground tying Shamrock before turning to stare at a solid wall of muscle. "This will do for what?" Her gaze slowly worked its way to his shoulders, up his neck to his jaw, then lingered on his full lips for a few seconds before settling on his eyes. Her breath caught at the intensity directed at her, the way his soft blue eyes had darkened to the color of a midnight storm.

"I've waited all day for this." Caleb snaked an arm around her waist, pulling her to him, taking her mouth without a thought as to anyone who might wander by. Wrapping both arms around her, he splayed his hands across her back, groaning in satisfaction when she slid her arms around his neck.

Caleb kissed her as if he'd never get enough, desperately devouring her mouth in a way that said he'd never let her go. Blood thrummed through her temples at the way he took charge, moving his mouth over hers, creating a heat so intense she thought she might explode.

She felt an unfamiliar yearning, a tightness deep in her belly. As he moved his mouth one way, then another in greedy abandon, she felt as if her body were on fire and knew of nothing to douse the flames. Feeling his hands move lower, resting on her hips, digging into her waist, she sighed, feeling a quiver of intense sensation.

Squirming closer, she writhed against him, unsure what she was asking. She knew she needed something from him, not understanding what.

"Caleb..." she breathed out, her voice thick. "I want...I..."

He pulled back, his eyes darkening at the undisguised need he saw in hers before they fluttered closed. "I know what you want, sweetheart." Lowering his mouth again, his arms tightened, drawing her against him until they seemed to fuse together.

His mouth teased hers, nudging deeper and deeper until she arched against him, his blood turning to liquid fire.

"Please, Caleb..."

Hearing her need, feeling his restraint slipping, his mouth shook as it slanted across hers once more. On a ragged breath, he drew away, resting his forehead against hers, his body groaning at the loss.

Looking down, he saw the confusion in her passion-filled eyes. Lifting her hand, he pressed a kiss to her palm, then cupped it to his cheek. A crooked, boyish smile twisted his lips. Using a forefinger, he lifted her chin, kissing her once more before stepping away.

He didn't take his eyes off her when she lowered her face, staring at the ground, her breath coming in ragged gasps.

Shaking her head, Heather couldn't look at him. Her feisty, proud nature dissolved as sugar in a glass of water. She wanted to blame Caleb, wanted to believe him responsible for her lack of understanding of what was happening between them.

If there was anything Heather hated, it was losing control. Not of her temper, but of a situation, and especially her feelings. With Caleb, she couldn't seem to keep them hidden. She wanted him, and he'd made it clear how much he wanted her. The things she felt when he held her, kissed her, were confusing and disturbing. She didn't know what to do, how to react. Put her in a saddle, a gun or rope in her hand, she knew exactly how to act. With Caleb, she felt lost, unsure of herself...and she never felt uncertain.

"Heather?"

Biting her lip, she slowly lifted her head, meeting his gaze.

"Are you all right?" His eyes warmed, although she saw concern as his brows furrowed.

Swallowing the knot in her throat, she nodded. "Aye."

Looking around, making certain they were still alone, he cupped her face in both his hands. "When this is over, we need to talk. There are things I have to say."

Her heart hammered in her chest as fear mingled with anticipation. When she nodded, he leaned down, placing a warm, soft kiss on her lips. Drawing back, he kissed the tip of her nose.

"Soon, sweetheart," he said, taking her hand, walking back to their horses.

Chapter Nineteen

Conviction

"I'm not sure what you're asking me." Philip glanced around, uncomfortable at meeting Bay near the docks so early in the morning.

"Then let me be quite clear." Reaching into his pocket, Bay pulled out the document someone had slid under his office door. Unfolding it, he held it out, seeing a flicker of recognition on Philip's face. "All you have to do is nod if you recognize it."

The banker's gaze darted around the docks. Even at this early hour, there were scores of people. Some he recognized, most he didn't. A scant number paid any attention to them, going about their business as if no one else existed.

Swallowing, he gave a brief nod.

Folding the paper, Bay slid it back into his pocket. "Walk with me." They strolled north along the waterfront, taking them away from the center of town and the San Francisco Merchant Bank building. Bay didn't look at Philip as he spoke. "You couldn't have had access to all this information at your bank. Who helped you?"

Philip shoved his hands into his pockets. "A friend of the MacLarens. Someone who sensed a problem, but couldn't be the one supplying the information."

"A friend with access to their accounts at the Bank of Conviction?"

"It's not Mr. Fielder, if that's what you're implying, Bay."

"I'm not implying anything. I want to understand the motive behind someone providing me information that should have never left the bank."

Philip glanced at him, then looked away. "I'd think the motive would be obvious."

Looking out at the Feather River, Bay's expression didn't change. "Why don't you enlighten me?"

Philip's lips curled over his teeth, his gaze searching the walkway ahead, as if it held the answers Bay would accept. "You're a friend of the MacLarens. Getting the information to you seemed a good way of warning them of their financial vulnerability. Any major problems, or several small ones, could have disastrous effects on their debt."

"Sorry, but your argument makes no sense. First, they'd wonder where I got the information. Second, don't you think they're astute enough to understand their situation already? We aren't talking about some illiterate vagabonds. These are ranchers who've built a few acres into a large, successful ranch." Bay shook his head. "You'll have to do better than that."

Coming upon the northern edge of the walkway, they stopped, shifting to face each other.

"Then we're at an impasse."

"I think not, Philip." Turning back toward the heart of town, Bay started to walk again. "Do you want to know what I think?"

An instant passed before Philip spoke. "I'm listening."

"There's this young and quite pretty employee at the Bank of Conviction—"

Philip gripped Bay's jacket with both hands before he could get another word out. "You'll leave her out of this." His voice was brittle and hard.

Nonplussed, Bay looked down at Philip's hands, making no move to pull away. Lifting a brow, he kept his tone level. "I'd suggest you let go of me."

Glancing around, seeing people beginning to notice, Philip dropped his hands.

Straightening his jacket, Bay looked back down the walkway. "Now, as I was saying...I understand a certain manager at another bank is courting this lovely young woman." He glanced at Philip, seeing the man's jaw stiffen. "The man's boss gets wind of this and requests, in the nicest way of course, that the young man ask the young woman for certain information. As would be expected, the suggestion is made that it would be a mistake for the young man to refuse. Possibly a career-ending mistake." Again, Bay glanced at Philip, seeing his back stiffen. Knowing he was on the right track, he continued. "Not wanting to end his career, and with no other options, he does as his boss asks, using his ways of persuasion to convince the young woman to provide what he needs."

Bay pauses when Philip stops walking. Clearing his throat, Philip starts to speak, then stops, motioning for Bay to continue.

"It takes a few days, but the woman comes through. The information is provided to the boss, but unbeknownst to him, the young man keeps a copy, maybe two, for himself. Why? Because the young man has a conscience that's keeping him up at night." Bay waves to a man on horseback, nods to another, then continues. "There's only one person he can think of to give the information to who might see it as more than mere numbers on a page. Someone who'd see it as a direct path to the person or people threatening the MacLarens."

Stopping, Bay turned to face Philip. "This is a theory, mind you, and I've had only a few days to piece it together. That being said, I'd be obliged to hear your opinion."

Circle M

Ewan looked at Ian, Colin, Quinn, Brodie, and Caleb standing on one side of the room, expectant faces staring back at him. It was a sparse group. Most of the family and ranch hands were needed to guard the herd. On the other side stood August, Bay, and Philip, a young man few of the MacLarens knew by name.

"I know you lads are anxious to get back to the herd. When August explained to me why they'd ridden out this morning, I knew this was a matter we needed to discuss right away." He looked at his son. "Brodie's already aware of what's going to be said and he'll explain what he's done." Ewan nodded at Bay. "Tell the lads what you told me."

An hour passed as Bay explained, Philip filled in the gaps, and August gave his thoughts. All the while, they fielded questions from an increasingly agitated group of MacLarens. Not because of who they believed was behind the actions, but that they hadn't figured it out and stopped the man sooner.

"It's not as easy as knowing who's behind it, lads." Brodie pushed away from where he stood against the wall. "We're guessing Delacroix is behind it all. We've no proof. It's why Sam and Seth are following him."

"Your new deputy?" Quinn asked.

Brodie nodded. "Aye. Seth Montero. He used to work for Juan Estrada before leaving to work for a ranch near Sacramento. He knows the land as well as any of us."

Colin shook his head. "The man can't be working alone."

"Aye." Ian stood, walking to the window. "We already know he hired six to rustle the cattle, hang our ranch hand, and burn the hacienda."

"And others to poison the pond and set fire to the Evanston place," Caleb added.

"There's a man..." Philip's voice trailed off as he pinched the bridge of his nose. "I'm trying to recall his name. It's quite unique."

"What about the man?" Bay asked.

"I saw Giles with him once. He came inside the bank, asking for him. When Giles came out of his office, he made it obvious he wasn't happy to see him. Ushered him outside and I never saw the man again. Very tall, slender, sinister looking." Drawing his brows together, he pursed his lips. "Black. Black Jolly. That was his name."

Caleb jumped up at the same time as Quinn.

"What is it, lads?"

Caleb spoke first. "That's the same man Heather and Emma encountered on the trail. He'd been to see the Pearces about buying their ranch."

"Stealing it, you mean," Quinn added.

"Heather told me something wasn't right about him."

Quinn nodded. "Emma said he seemed vile, almost evil."

"When I get back to town, I'll be checking on this Black Jolly and have my other new deputy, Alex Campbell, start looking for him."

Bay stood, glancing around the room. "I'm glad to help, Brodie. I want this stopped as much as the rest of you."

Philip spoke up. "I haven't seen him in town except for that one day. He might be staying outside of Conviction. An old cabin maybe. Or he might have left."

"It's doubtful, lad," Ewan said. "Not with the fire at the Evanston place. I don't think that's something Giles would do himself."

Philip nodded. "True. He's not the type to get his hands dirty. Believe me, you'll know Black Jolly when you see him."

Ewan couldn't miss the concern on everyone's face. He looked at Colin, Quinn, and Caleb. "You lads ride back to the herd. It's important to be keeping your guard up. At least we've a good idea who's behind this and who he's hired."

Caleb started for the door. "Whatever you need me to do, I'll do it. Just get word to us."

Once Philip mentioned Black Jolly, Caleb couldn't get out of there fast enough. He'd placed his bedroll next to Heather's the night before, waking to her restless whimpers about her encounter with what she termed the 'black devil'. She hadn't been able to explain exactly why he intimidated her so much, but the effect had been immediate and intense.

If so many MacLarens hadn't been around, Caleb would have climbed in with her. Instead, he lay on the ground next to her, wrapping his arms around her, ignoring the daggers in Quinn's stare, until she drifted back to sleep.

As Jupiter's hooves pounded on the trail, his mind focused on Heather and getting back to her as fast as possible. He'd wanted her to ride back to the house with them, but she'd refused, saying they needed her to watch the herd while he, Quinn, and Colin were gone. Quinn had no better luck with Emma. They'd both despaired over leaving them behind, acknowledging they needed their help as much as they needed any of the men.

Taking the trail east, he began to relax at the sound of the bawling cattle. Reining up at the crest of the last hill, he waited for Quinn and Colin to ride up beside him.

"You've been riding like a madman, Caleb." Quinn looked past him to the herd below. "You'll be wearing Jupiter out if you're not careful."

"I notice neither of you were far behind me."

"Nae, but I'm thinking Colin wanted to stay longer with Sarah." Quinn glanced at his cousin, who'd begun to show signs of the strain of being away from his wife and son. "I told the lad he should be staying a day or two."

"He's right, Colin. We can make do without you for a night or two. Sarah and Grant need you more than we do right now."

Colin leaned on the saddle horn, drawing in a breath. "Nae. I'll not be sleeping until I know the danger is past. Sarah understands, and I know she's safe with Ma and the family."

Caleb's gaze shifted from the herd near the river, moving west, landing on what appeared to be a dark spot on the horizon. "What's that?"

Quinn and Colin followed the direction of his gaze, leaning forward on their saddles for a better view.

"It's not moving..." Colin's voice faded as he continued to stare.

"Wait...it is moving." Caleb nudged Jupiter ahead. "Toward us."

"Look." Quinn cursed under his breath. "There are more."

They could now make out seven riders coming over the horizon, riding on a straight path toward the herd.

Caleb reached into his saddlebag, pulling out his field glasses. Looking through them, he cursed. "The one in front is dressed all in black."

"We have to warn the lads." Colin began to rein his horse around.

"There's no time. We have to cut off the rustlers before they get closer. They'll ride off if they know we've spotted them."

Caleb agreed with Quinn, hoping he was right.

"Three against seven." Colin grinned. "I like the odds."

Checking the guns around their waists, they holstered them, then pulled out their rifles, looking at each other.

"Ready, lads?" Quinn asked.

"We shoot to kill?" Caleb asked.

Quinn smiled. "Aye."

"Then I'm ready."

Holding the reins in one hand, their rifles in the other, they touched their spurs to their horses. Leaning low over the saddles, the three hurried down the hill, riding to intercept the rustlers. Before the outlaws spotted them, Colin nodded to Quinn and Caleb, bracing his rifle against his shoulder as they let loose with the MacLaren war cry.

"*Creag an Tuirc.*"

The ferocious roar alerted not only the outlaws but those guarding the herd. Rifles discharging, they downed two men in quick succession, a third falling an instant later before the man in front, the one dressed all in black, raised his gun and fired.

The bullet whizzed past Quinn's cheek, slamming into Colin, knocking him off his horse. Seeing him fall, Caleb took aim, hitting the man he believed to be Black in the shoulder, as Quinn clipped another in the leg. As fast as it started, it ended.

Reining up, Quinn and Caleb turned around and sprinted back to Colin, as the remaining outlaws raced over the hill and out of sight.

Not waiting for their horses to stop, each jumped to the ground, kneeling by Colin.

"Colin." Quinn slid a hand under his head, while Caleb pulled away the fabric around the wound in his chest. "Colin, lad..."

"He's out, Quinn."

"The bullet?"

"It went straight through his shoulder." Standing, Caleb peeled off his shirt, wadding it into a ball before pressing it onto the wound. "We need to get him back to the house. Someone needs to ride for a doctor."

Neither noticed Heather, Emma, Blaine, and Fletcher ride up. Blaine jumped from his horse and leaned over them, staring down at his brother. "Is he..." His voice wobbled, moisture beginning to pool in his eyes.

Quinn shook his head. "Nae. Passed out, lad."

Heather placed a hand on Caleb's shoulder as Emma knelt beside Quinn. "What can we do?"

A moan left Colin's lips, his eyes fluttering but not opening.

"Colin!" Blaine called down to him, his voice strained.

Another moan sounded, his eyes opening, then rolling back in his head before he passed out again.

Quinn looked at Caleb. "We don't have time to get a wagon. Fletch, get his horse. I'll ride back with him on Chieftain. Blaine, you'll be riding beside me. When we get to the house, we'll send Thane for the doctor." He looked at Emma. "You'll be coming with me, lass. I'll not be leaving you here." Sucking in a breath, Quinn sent a worried glance at Caleb. "You and the other lads will be handling things here."

Caleb settled a hand on Quinn's shoulder. "You take care of Colin and don't worry about us. We'll be fine."

Shooting a quick look at Heather, Quinn's gaze narrowed on Caleb. "You take care of Heather. You'll be answering to me if anything happens to her."

A grim smile curved the corners of Caleb's lips. "She's safe with me, Quinn. She'll always be safe with me."

Chapter Twenty

A Cabin Miles North of Conviction

"Black..." Rushing outside, she lifted her arms up. Her small stature made it difficult to provide much support as he slid off his horse, struggling to keep from collapsing. "You're bleeding."

"Looks worse...than...it is." They made it to the bottom of the porch steps where he braced a hand against a rail and rested.

Glancing up, she grimaced at the dark clouds and the sting of the cold wind. "You can't stop here. You have to get inside where I can tend your wound."

"Bleeding's stopped," he ground out, sucking in a breath before taking the steps to the front door.

"That doesn't mean it won't start up again if we don't get it bandaged." Kicking the door closed behind them, she waited as he lowered himself onto the bunk, feeling somewhat helpless at his much larger height and weight.

Shoving the thought aside, she dashed to the stove. Ladling more water from a bucket into a simmering pot, she added more wood to the fire, then grabbed towels off nearby hooks. Dipping one into the pot, she wrung it out, then moved back to the bed.

"Lie down, Black, and I'll clean you up."

"Whiskey..." he moaned as the damp cloth touched the wound.

Leaving the towel in place, she walked to the cupboard, pulling down an almost empty bottle and the full one next to it. Resting on the edge of the bed, she lifted his head.

"Drink this. I'll use the other bottle to cleanse the wound." Holding it to his lips, she gasped when he gripped her wrist, gulping down what was left. Lowering his head back onto the bed, he nodded.

"Go ahead," he breathed out.

Wiping away the blood, she poured a portion of whiskey on the open wound, hearing his quick intake of breath. "The bullet is still in there."

"I know," he panted. "You'll have to get it out."

Straightening, she shook her head. "Not me. I have no idea what I'm doing as it is. Removing a bullet? That takes a doctor."

His eyes flew open, a chill making her shiver at the cold emptiness staring up at her. "There'll be no doctor."

Looking down at him, the anger she'd held in check for days crept forward, taking control. Standing, she settled her fisted hands on her waist, hovering over him. "If I remove the bullet, and you live, we ride out and never come back."

His nostrils flared, gaze narrowing on her. "I've still got business here."

"Fine." Turning away, she stormed to the other side of the cabin, picked up her coat, and started for the door. "I'll come back in a few days. If you're dead, I'll see you're buried."

She saw the instant he realized she'd reached her limit. His eyes widened, jaw tightened, lips curling before he blew out a tired breath.

"Dammit, we don't have time to argue."

"I agree." She took a couple steps toward him. "If I take out the bullet and you live, we leave. No more deals, no more jobs, no more meetings with Giles." She reached out her hand. "Deal?"

Snorting, he tried to lift his arm, but it fell back onto the bed. "Deal."

"You're believing the man you shot is Black Jolly?" Heather sat next to Caleb, rifles resting on their laps. No one had returned with news on Colin and tempers were running thin.

"From your description and Emma's, yes. Of the seven we saw, four were shot, including Black."

"The lads brought back three bodies. We should be burying them, but after what they did to Colin..." She looked away, swiping away the moisture from her face.

Settling an arm over her shoulders, he tugged her close, kissing her cheek. "The bullet went clean

270

through his shoulder. The doctor will clean him up and he'll be fine. Besides, he's too ornery to die."

A shaky chuckle escaped as she let herself sink into his side. "Aye, the lad is ornery. I know Sarah must be terribly worried."

"She's strong, as are all the MacLarens."

Sitting up, Heather looked at him, her brows drawn together. "And would that include me?"

Caleb threw back his head and laughed. "Especially you."

Shoving him lightly, she smiled before standing. "I've a need to walk around a bit." She lifted a brow, her meaning clear.

His face sobering, he stood. "I'll go with you."

"Caleb—"

"I'm not letting you go out there alone, even it is only twenty or thirty feet. I'll keep back, but I'm going. Now, come on."

He caught Bram's attention, nodding toward the bushes several yards away. As they reached a thick grouping, she handed him her rifle, cutting a path through the branches. Standing with his back to her, his gaze cut to the cattle.

With this size of a herd, they'd stayed about as long as they could. The water was sufficient, but the grazing land was almost depleted. Another day, maybe two at most, and the cattle would have to be moved.

"Thank you." Holding out her hand, Heather took the rifle. "What are you thinking about?"

"Where to move the cattle next."

Heather looked toward the river. All the MacLarens knew they would run out of southern grazing land soon. "We've had lads guarding the ponds. Maybe we can go north."

Caleb nodded. "We'll wait for word on Colin, then talk about it with the others and make a decision."

Movement from the camp had them looking up to see Fletcher. Heather hurried toward him.

"You've word about Colin?"

Shaking his head, Fletcher settled a hand on her shoulder. "Sorry, lass. No word yet." He looked at Caleb. "We'll be burying the three men, unless you think we should be taking them to town."

With Colin hurt and Quinn at the ranch, the others knew Ewan and Ian would have them look to Caleb for direction.

"We have no men or time to take them to town, and we can't leave them to lay out. Dig shallow graves in case Brodie needs to dig them up for identification. What do you think about moving the herd tomorrow?"

"Along the river?" Fletcher asked.

"If there are places for them to drink, yes." Caleb looked at Heather. She knew the property as well as anyone.

"The river picks up speed a mile down. We can't be stopping them there. But three or four hours south, the river slows to a crawl for a good distance. What do you think, Fletch?"

"You've got a good idea, lass. If we start at dawn, we can drive the herd and be there well before the sun sets. We'll also be a wee bit closer to Colin."

Caleb didn't need to hear any more. "Tell Bram. The two of you let everyone else know and send men to get those guarding the water north of here. We'll need everyone to move the herd."

"What about guarding the ponds?"

"We'll have to take our chances, Fletch. Our first priority is watching out for the cattle right in front of us." Caleb nodded toward the river and the almost three thousand head grazing its banks. "If we must fill in a hundred ponds, that's what we'll do. We've got the Boundary River and two others, plus numerous springs running through our property. In six months, they'll be overflowing with runoff from the mountains."

He looked at the imposing mountains to the east, knowing within a month, the peaks would be blanketed with early snow. By Christmas, the entire range would be covered, making the trails impassable for several months. In the spring, the snow would melt, sending thousands of gallons of clean water into the rivers and underground springs located on Circle M land.

"I'd best get Bram and tell the lads what we're about. Tomorrow will be a long day, so we'd better be getting down early."

"Make sure enough men stay on watch, Fletch. I don't think the outlaws will be dumb enough to come back tonight. Still..."

Fletcher shook his head, his mouth twisting into a wry grin. "I'm not expecting much from eejits like them. They don't behave like normal lads. I'll make sure we've enough watching so they won't surprise us again."

Caleb nodded. "Thanks, Fletch." Shifting his gaze to Heather, he watched as she continued to stare out at the cattle. She'd been doing the same all day, her face clouded with worry. "I'm not going to let them hurt anyone else, Heather."

Turning abruptly, she stepped toward him. "It's not your battle, Caleb. It's a MacLaren fight."

His brows furrowed at her terse response, an odd burning sensation starting to flare in his gut. Resting his rifle butt on the ground, he let his other arm hang loose at his side. "I understand that."

She stared at him a moment, nodding once, then stalked past him. Walking up the hill toward their horses, she didn't stop until she reached the top, slipping the rifle into the scabbard on her saddle.

Caleb couldn't move. He knew if enough time passed, she'd break down and say what she felt about him and his place in the family. She might care for him, maybe think she loved him in some small way. Deep in her heart, though, he'd always be an outsider and she the princess of the MacLaren clan.

He knew loving her wouldn't be easy. Over the last few weeks, he'd gotten a glimpse of the woman he wanted to share a life with, the Heather he loved. She'd shown him what their future could be like. He'd envisioned a partnership with a strong woman possessing skills to match his own. Now he knew it was all a façade.

The passionate siren he'd held in his arms was an illusion, a fantasy he'd conjured up in a ridiculous dream of a life together. When life got hard, he'd never be the one she turned to for strength or comfort. She'd turn to her family...the true MacLarens. Not some stray they'd taken in, no matter how much he knew they cared about him. The hardest part for Caleb was he knew Quinn and the others saw him as part of the family, even if she didn't.

Watching her mount Shamrock, he picked up his rifle, walking the short distance to Jupiter. Never taking his gaze off her, he stowed the rifle and grabbed the reins.

"I'd like you to make a circle south. Look for strays and drive them north. I'll do the same in the other direction. Don't worry about taking watch tonight. We'll need you rested for tomorrow."

Swinging up into the saddle in one smooth motion, he took off, ignoring her when she called after him.

Caleb couldn't think about her now. Couldn't think about them. He had a job to do and that would be his focus. Until the men and cattle were safe, the threat to the MacLarens eliminated, he'd stay, giving every waking hour to his adopted family. When the danger had passed, he'd do what he originally intended.

Caleb would focus on his own future.

Conviction

"We have him, Brodie. Giles Delacroix is our man." Sam sat across from him in the sheriff's office early in the morning, Seth Montero next to him. It had been almost a week since they'd started following Giles, five days since Colin had been shot. He and Seth hadn't left Giles alone for a single moment. "He finally made a mistake. Rode out to a remote cabin north of town."

Brodie sat forward, resting his arms on the desk. "What did you find?"

Sam looked at Seth. "It was Montero's turn to follow the man."

Brodie nodded at Seth to explain.

"Delacroix met with a man he called Black."

"Black Jolly..." Brodie breathed out.

Seth nodded. "That's what I think. I couldn't hear all they said, but they were yelling about something Black did. When Black came to the door, his arm and chest were bandaged. He moved slowly, and was stooped over in pain. It didn't stop him from threatening Giles."

"Did you hear what they argued about?' Brodie asked.

"Black was hired to do whatever he could to hurt the MacLarens. Giles wants their land." Seth shook his head.

Sam looked at Brodie. "It wasn't complicated. Seems Black had been hired to do the same before. He's a gunfighter with no qualms about how he makes his money. The problem this time was he went up against a family who fought back and had the resources to stick it out."

"Did you try to bring them in, Seth?"

Seth started to speak, but Sam held up his hand, stopping him. "I told him not to get into a gunfight, Brodie. I thought it best to get you the information and figure out a way to bring them both in for trial."

"When did you see them, Seth?"

"Late yesterday. I followed Delacroix back and told Sam what I saw. By then, it was close to nine, so we decided to talk to you this morning."

Sam sat back, crossing his arms. "Delacroix is still in town, Brodie. I saw him eating breakfast at the

Gold Dust this morning. He doesn't suspect anything."

Brodie rubbed his fingers back and forth across his forehead, his gaze focused out the window. After a few moments, he stood. "We need to talk to Bay. He's been working with a contact to come up with more information on Giles. With what he has and what Seth heard, we should have enough to arrest both Delacroix and Black Jolly."

"There's one more thing, Sheriff."

"What's that, Seth?"

"There's a woman involved."

Brodie's brows drew together. "How do you know that, lad? Did you see her?"

Seth shook his head. "No, sir. I heard Black say he wasn't doing anything more without speaking with the woman. He and Delacroix argued about it. When Black pulled a gun, Delacroix closed his mouth."

"They didn't mention the lass' name?"

"No, sir, but I got the feeling she was Black's woman."

"We'll talk to Bay about her. Maybe he'll know something." Standing, he grabbed his hat. "Let's go, lads. If we're lucky, we'll have them behind bars by the end of the day."

Circle M

Heather groomed Shamrock, tossed the brush into a bucket, then set the mare loose in the corral behind the barn. A week had passed without any further problems—no fires, shootings, or raids on their cattle. They didn't know if the outlaws had given up and moved on or if the last attempt had killed off the majority of their number. The MacLarens hadn't let down their guard, though.

They kept the herd together, close to the river with men watching them day and night. It wasn't easy. That many head required huge amounts of acreage and water. They'd have to move them north soon.

None of that weighed on Heather's mind. All she could think about was Caleb and how he'd managed to avoid her for days, taking different shifts watching the cattle, eating when she slept, riding out when she came in. He wouldn't even look at her when they passed within feet of each other—and it was all her fault.

Heather knew the others noticed, but no one dared say a word, not even Quinn, who usually dared to say whatever popped into his head.

At least Colin had improved over the last three days. Sarah fussed over him until the wound healed enough for him to get out of bed and sit outside on the front porch. She'd seen Caleb sit with him a few times, sharing stories, laughing, making her feel worse than she already did. Not once did his gaze turn in her direction, as if he knew where she stood and purposely shunned her.

Why had it taken Colin getting shot and her anger to flare before she realized the extent of her love for Caleb? Seeing Colin almost lose his life had sent a gut-wrenching fear through Heather so powerful, it felt as if her heart were about to split in two. She'd thought of Sarah and the loss she'd suffer if her husband didn't survive. In that instant, Heather knew she'd feel the same if anything were to happen to Caleb.

She'd gone about the rest of day on edge, waiting for news on Colin's condition, dreading the appearance of a rider who might bring a report of his death. Instead of taking comfort in her feelings for Caleb, she'd pushed him away. Worse, she'd known exactly what to say, what would hurt him the most, and she'd used it to her advantage.

"I thought you might be out here."

She turned at the sound of Geneen's voice.

"Aye. I know Ma and the others are expecting me in the house to help with supper. It's just so bonny this time of evening."

They walked out of the barn to the corral on the side, resting their arms on the fencing. "This used to be my favorite time of day."

Heather looked at Geneen, her brows drawn together in a frown. "Used to be?"

Geneen continued to look straight ahead. "Before Nate left. We used to walk out here, watch the sun set. No one ever noticed us, you know. Everyone was so busy, Nate and I could slip off for a spell when he'd come for Sunday supper or ride out with Brodie during the week." Geneen looked at her, a sad smile barely lifting the corners of her mouth. "Then his visits became fewer and fewer until he hardly came at all."

Heather had known how much Geneen loved Nate Hollis, Brodie's deputy. Until now, she hadn't realized the pain she still suffered at his leaving, riding out without a word of explanation.

Nate had fought for the Union as an officer. During one horrific battle, he'd suffered an irreversible wound, losing his left arm below the elbow. Making his way west, he'd learned of an opening for a deputy in Conviction. It had taken one fight, the odds decidedly not in his favor, for Brodie to make the decision to hire him.

Placing a hand on Geneen's arm, she squeezed. "The lad had problems, lass. Ma and Audrey said he couldn't deal with them here."

"We all have problems, Heather. The difference is most of us don't run out on the ones who love us." A single tear escaped, running down Geneen's cheek before she could swipe it away.

"Ah, lass, I'm certain the lad will be back for you. It was plain to all of us how much he loved you."

Shaking her head, Geneen's shoulders slumped as she gripped the fence for support. "That was before the opium took control. There was too much pain, too many nightmares, too many memories."

"Audrey says they got the opium from his system."

Geneen nodded, her voice flat. "But not his mind." Drawing in a shaky breath, she glanced over her shoulder at the house, then down at the ground. "Doc Tilden saw a lot of opium addiction during his time working on soldiers during the war. He said Nate's problems are far beyond his physical pain." Stepping away, she wrapped her arms around her waist. "I've come to accept Nate won't be back, Heather." Licking her lips, she focused her gaze on her friend. "I don't know what happened between you and Caleb. All I do know is you still have a chance to make it work. Do you know what I'd do if I had one more chance with Nate?"

Heather shook her head, swallowing the tightness in her throat.

"I'd grab it with both hands and never let it go. I'd tell him how much I loved him, that no woman would ever love him as much as me. I'd let him know I'd do whatever it took to help him get over whatever evil gripped him and never leave...never give up...never let him down." Brushing away another tear, she cleared her throat. "Then I'd wrap my arms around his neck and show him how much I meant what I said. If you love Caleb as much as I think you do, maybe you should think about what a future without him would look like, and if it's a life you want to have." Her bottom lip trembled on the last before she turned and walked to the house, leaving Heather to stare after her.

Chapter Twenty-One

Heather glanced down and across the table at Caleb. She couldn't remember the last time he'd sat next to her or acknowledged her presence. Her heart ached at the chasm between them. If only she knew what to do to fix the damage caused by her senseless words.

Several days had passed since her enlightening conversation with Geneen. Heather sat on the porch each night, staring at the stars, thinking over how she'd feel if Caleb packed up and left the same way Nate had. The comparison seemed useless. She and Geneen were nothing alike. Calm and serene even under stress, Geneen could ride and shoot as well as any man, yet sew and cook along with the women. Little fazed her...except Nate leaving. The tears she'd shown the other night made Heather ache for Sarah's younger sister. Tonight, she sat next to Geneen, the young woman's ivory skin and rosy cheeks showing she'd recovered from their conversation.

Geneen leaned over, lowering her voice. "Did you know Blaine and Caleb rode out a couple days ago on business for the family?"

A brow lifting, Heather shook her head. "Nae. Do you know what it was about?"

"No idea at all. I asked Sarah and she doesn't know, either, but they were gone two days. Got back a few hours ago and went straight into a meeting with Ewan and Ian."

Heather knew how much her uncles trusted Caleb. In her mind, it boded well for his future at the ranch. They were a welcoming family, warm and caring. Still, they didn't easily allow people into their inner circle. The fact they'd known him since he was seventeen, their families traveling west in the same wagon train, helped.

"Just Ewan and Ian?"

Geneen nodded. "Odd, isn't it?"

Heather had to agree it was strange. A decision having to do with the family would normally include Colin, Quinn, and Brodie, as well as Blaine, Caleb, and Sean. Then a discussion would be opened up to the entire clan before a final decision was made. Everyone had a voice—at least those sixteen years and older.

"Did they bring in any of the other lads?"

"Not that I saw. I suppose we'll hear about it when they're ready." Shrugging, Geneen turned back to her meal while Heather shot a quick glance down the table at Caleb. Tonight, he sat between Blaine and Fletcher at Ewan's end of the table. The three spoke in hushed tones, their faces animated and eager. She couldn't help wondering what it all meant, feeling a stab of jealousy at being left out.

"Hope it isn't too late to join you."

Everyone looked up, smiles spreading across their faces as Sam walked in with Jinny on his arm, Brodie and Maggie following.

"Ach, it's never too late for you four to come home." Audrey hurried toward them, hugging each one, as those around the table adjusted their places to make room.

"You be looking very bonny, lass." Ewan hugged Maggie. "A few more months and we'll have another wee bairn in the family."

Maggie blushed, settling a hand on her protruding belly.

"And I suppose you'll be next, Jinny."

Jinny smiled, slapping her father's arm. "Da, we'll not be speaking of it around the table." She cast a warm look at Sam as he pulled out her chair.

"What brings you out here during the week?" Emma asked, taking hold of Quinn's hand under the table.

Brodie looked around, waiting until he got most everyone's attention. "We've got news." His announcement quieted the table.

"What news, lad?" Ewan set his fork down.

"We arrested Giles Delacroix as the leader of the gang committing crimes at Circle M."

He watched as eyes widened, jaws dropped, and chairs scooted back. Finally, Audrey spoke up.

"I knew he couldn't be trusted. Felt it right here the day he rode to the ranch when you lads were at the Estrada hacienda fire." She patted her stomach.

"Start from the beginning, son." Ewan pushed his plate away.

The room fell silent as Brodie explained Seth following Giles to the cabin and his meeting with Black. Afterward, Brodie, Seth, and Sam met with Bay and August, reviewed what they had, then brought in Philip Aunspach. In addition to what he'd already given Bay, the banker had agreed to provide information on withdrawals Giles had made for cash while in Conviction, money they were certain was used to pay Black Jolly and the other men.

"The best evidence, though, came from a journal Giles kept in a locked drawer in his desk. Now, I'll not be telling you how we got it, but once we did, there were no more questions to ask. We had the names of the men he hired, how much he paid, and the jobs."

"Including hanging our man, Brodie?" Ewan asked.

He nodded. "Aye, Da. Philip said he always was a meticulous man, believed in documenting everything." Brodie looked at Sam.

"It's a mystery how he never got suspicious of us watching him. When he came down for breakfast this morning, the five of us were waiting for him. All Bay had to do was set the journal on the table and

Delacroix crumbled." Sam shook his head, chuckling. "Never had an easier arrest in my entire life."

"What about Black Jolly?" Colin asked, his arm still bandaged from a bullet he'd taken from the man's gun.

Sam shook his head. "We rode out this morning to arrest him, but he'd cleared out. Seth also heard Black and Delacroix talking about a woman, but we don't know her name or anything about her. Anyway, he's gone."

Colin pinched the bridge of his nose. "For now."

Brodie held up his hand. "I'm not letting it go, lad. I've already sent word to all the towns around here and as far east as Denver, north to Seattle, and south to San Diego. Sam sent a telegram to Allan Pinkerton and the Texas Rangers. No one is giving up on finding that miscreant or the woman with him."

"Do you know anything at all about her?" Geneen sat forward, leaning around Heather to look at Brodie.

"Nothing. Giles doesn't know her, either. At least he says he doesn't. All he said was Black had a woman in town who helped him get information about us."

"Us?" Caleb's brow lifted.

"The MacLarens, lad." Brodie rubbed his chin. "Could've been anyone."

"So it could be a woman who's been in Conviction a long time and Black paid her to get information on us." Blaine leaned back in his chair, crossing his arms.

Fletcher nodded. "Or someone new he brought with him, someone who asked about the family. It's not as if people don't know us or as if we keep quiet about ourselves. Right, Quinn?" He grinned at his cousin, who tossed a napkin at him.

"We've little to hide." Colin rubbed the sore spot on his shoulder. "Everyone knew about the Estrada and Evanston properties. It would've been easy enough to learn where the cattle were grazing and men were located. Black could've used anyone."

The room quieted as they all thought of who the woman might be and where Black might've gone.

"Well, we won't be solving this tonight. It's grand news about Delacroix." Ewan looked around the table, a broad smile breaking across his face. "When supper is over, we'll break out the whiskey and sherry to celebrate."

Two days had passed since Brodie's announcement. The cattle had been split into smaller herds and moved to grazing lands up north. The ranch hands had returned after several days of scouting the ponds, providing excellent news. Deer and other animals had been drinking from the water, none showing any ill effects. It appeared Black poisoned just one pond—a miracle given the other losses they'd incurred.

Heather heard Caleb left the morning after they learned about Delacroix's arrest, returning late last night. Courtesy of Fletcher, she knew he'd been talking to Ewan and Ian since early this morning, so she'd asked to work with the horses, positioning herself to keep watch. Since she'd been the one to create the quarrel between them, she had to be the one to take the first step at healing it.

The longer Heather waited, the more her stomach churned and palms moistened. Ten minutes. That was all she needed to make her apology and set things right. Ten minutes, and they could be back to the way they were before she'd ruined things with a careless comment.

Hearing the front door open, she looked up, seeing Caleb walk out, followed by Ewan. As he stepped to the edge of the porch, her stomach lurched. Something wasn't right.

He wore his heavy winter coat. Underneath, she could see his thick leather vest. In one hand, he carried a satchel. Slung over a shoulder were his saddlebags. In his other hand, he held his rifle. Her mouth went dry at the sight. When Caleb set the satchel down, Ewan clasped him on the shoulder, then shook his hand. The sight made Heather want to lose her breakfast.

He was leaving and hadn't planned to say goodbye.

Heather stood frozen, watching as he bent to pick up his satchel and turned toward the barn. She knew the instant he spotted her watching. The smile on his face fell away and his step faltered as he made his way toward the barn.

Willing herself not to move, she watched as he walked inside, not bothering to spare her a glance. Shrugging out of his coat and vest, he walked to the back doors, whistling for Jupiter. When the horse trotted up, he slid a halter over him, then went to work grooming and saddling the gelding. She stood just inside, watching the muscles in his back expand and contract, his thighs flex against his pants, his rough hands smoothing over the horse, making her shiver.

Sucking in a ragged breath, she walked toward him, her throat constricting to a point she found it hard to breathe.

"Where are you going?"

He didn't stop what he was doing or turn to look at her. "I'm leaving."

Her first instinct was to pound him on the back, tell him he couldn't leave. Not when she'd finally figured out what she wanted.

"I don't understand. Where are you going?"

He blew out a breath. "Away, Heather. It's not important where."

Her entire body felt as if she'd been run over by a stampeding herd. Everything hurt, from her toes to her head. She hadn't expected to feel this broken at his pronouncement.

"But why, Caleb? I thought...I mean, you and I, Caleb..." She clenched her hands together, trying to stop them from shaking.

His shoulders sagged slightly before he straightened, tossing the brush aside. Turning, he almost weakened, seeing the pain in her face. But he couldn't. They both hurt, and hurting wasn't enough to make him stay.

"It's time to build a life for myself, Heather. You were right saying I'm not a MacLaren. I'm a Stewart. It's time I acted like one."

Stepping up to him, she placed a hand on his shoulder, but he shrugged it off.

"Caleb, I'm sorry. I didn't mean it. Please, don't go because I was an eejit and said something horrible."

Looking down at his boots, he shook his head. "It's more than that, Heather, and we both know it. You can do anything I can do. Seems there isn't a lot I have to offer. No land, no money. You're a woman who has it all and can take care of herself. I guess I finally came to realize it over the last few weeks, while all the troubles plagued the family. You don't need me, Heather—not for one damn thing."

"But..." she sputtered, unable to get any more out.

He turned toward the outside of the barn, extending his arm. "Look out there and tell me what you see."

Her bottom lip quivered as she followed his gaze. "The ranch, Caleb."

"Right. As far as you can see is MacLaren land. Circle M, the biggest spread for hundreds of miles. A few years ago, you were a big family with dreams. Now you're the envy of every rancher coming out west." He looked down at her, not a trace of jealousy on his face or in his voice. "This is where you belong, Heather. On Circle M, surrounded by your family." When he started to turn away, she grabbed his arm, stopping him.

"You could share it with me. There's no reason for you to leave, Caleb. Please, don't do this."

His eyes softened, as did his voice. Reaching up, he stroked a finger down her cheek, his will cracking a little at the sight of one lone tear.

"Ah, Heather, don't you understand? I love you, but I'm not a MacLaren and I don't think it's within you to ever really forget that." Dropping his arm, he stepped away. "I need to build a place of my own. Find a woman who loves me for what I can do for her, not for what I can do for her family. This may not make sense to you now, but one day it will."

Watching as he saddled Jupiter, her body shook, as if she were covered in ice. When he slid the bridle on and grabbed the reins, her heart cracked. With every movement, she prayed he'd stop, tell her it was a mistake, a jest he'd dreamed up with her brothers and cousins. It was a delusional thought. He was leaving—without her.

As he walked past, the full impact of the loss slammed into her. Rushing forward, she grabbed his arm, yanking him around.

"No. You cannot be leaving me, Caleb Stewart. I won't be letting you leave. I love you. I—I...love...you."

He closed his eyes, his throat working. He'd waited so long to hear her say those words. After all this time, they weren't enough. Placing a finger under her chin, Caleb lifted her face, his gaze meeting hers.

He shook his head, his voice thick and ragged. "I can't stay."

"There must be something I can say or do. I'll do anything, Caleb. Please. Tell me what I must do and I'll do it."

Dropping his hand, he settled his boot in the stirrup, swinging into the saddle. Glancing around, taking in the view one more time, he felt her hands clutch his thigh.

Looking down, he steeled his resolve. "You say you'll do anything?"

Her face brightened, eyes glassy.

"Then you've a choice to make. Stay or come with me."

Three nights had passed since he'd ridden off. Three nights Heather had cried for hours, hating herself for not saddling Shamrock and going with him.

Caleb offered her a choice and she'd made the safe decision, the coward's decision. He'd applied no pressure. It had been a simple choice. Stay with her family or take a chance on him.

Turning onto her stomach, she pounded a pillow already drenched with her tears. When had she gotten to be such an emotional, crying female?

The first two mornings, she'd woken red-eyed and weary, dragging herself through the day, doing minimal chores. The family knew to stay away, letting her bask in her grief. She doubted they'd let her get away with it a third day. Her time of wallowing in self-pity would be over as soon as the sun came up in the morning.

Sleep had claimed her not long after midnight, and even though it had been fitful, she climbed out of bed feeling better than she had since Caleb left. It was the time that had passed. It was the decision she'd made just before falling asleep.

Caleb had given her a choice, but not enough time to make the right decision. Sometime over the last eight hours, her pain had turned to anger. He had weeks to make his decision. He'd given her minutes to make hers.

The lad would hear about it for the rest of their lives—as soon as she found him.

Dressing, she pulled two satchels from under her bed, stuffing them with the essentials she'd need going into winter. Her coat and blanket would be tied behind the saddle, the saddlebags filled with other items, including food. She had some money and was almost certain she could beg some from her mother or Quinn. What she wasn't as sure about was if they'd let her ride off alone.

No one had said a word about where Caleb went, although she felt certain one specific MacLaren knew his destination. Pushing the satchels back under the bed, she hurried downstairs, cut off a slice of bread, then went in search of Blaine. Quinn and Caleb were like brothers, but lately, Blaine had been the one Caleb seemed to spend the most time with. And he'd been the one who'd disappeared with him for two days before Brodie came with the news about Delacroix.

Seeing him getting ready to mount and ride out, she waved. "Blaine. I must speak with you."

"I'm in a wee bit of a hurry, Heather. What is it?"

Looking around, making certain they were alone, she came close enough to grip his horse's reins. "Where did Caleb go?"

Blaine's eyes widened an instant. "Even if I knew, I wouldn't be saying."

"And why's that? Did Caleb tell you not to?"

He shook his head. "Nae."

"I know the two of you rode off for two days together, which is telling me you know where he is."

Blaine glanced around, seeing Quinn come out of the barn with his horse. "The lad needs some time before you go barging back into his life."

"Well, then, if you won't be telling me, I guess I'll be riding out on my own." She let go of the reins, turning to walk away.

"Wait a minute, lass. You can't just be riding off with no idea where the lad went."

"I'm a grown woman, Blaine. I can ride where I want."

"What are you harping at Blaine about, Heather?" Quinn swung up onto his horse.

"She's threatening to ride off to find Caleb."

Quinn glared at her. "You can't be doing that."

Turning, she stomped toward the house, glancing over her shoulder. "We'll be seeing about that."

"This may not be one of your best ideas, lass." Blaine rode on one side of her while Quinn rode on the other. "Maybe the lad's changed his mind."

Quinn nodded. "Aye. Maybe he's met another lass not as cantankerous as you."

"Or as stubborn." Blaine pulled up the collar of his jacket to ward off the chill.

"He's probably already married to some widow lady with three bairns. Right, Blaine?"

"Aye. You never know with a Stewart. They're an unpredictable clan, they are."

Ignoring their comments, Heather continued forward. At least she knew they were headed to Settlers Valley, a ranching town along the Feather River, eighty miles north of Conviction.

It had grown rapidly during the gold rush days, then slowed down when the ore thinned out. Its wealth now came from cattle, farming, and a few mines. Ewan knew several of the ranchers and businessmen. He predicted the town could grow as big as Conviction in ten years.

"Settlers Valley is over the next rise, Heather."

Her heart rate picked up at Quinn's words. For the first time, doubt crept in. What if the lads were right and he'd changed his mind, met someone else? Heather shook her head. She couldn't let fear stop her now.

It had taken hours of arguing, yelling, and bargaining with her family to get them to let her go.

When they were finally convinced she'd ride off with or without their help, they'd given in, dug into their savings, and made her promise to stay with Blaine and Quinn until they got to Settlers Valley. No one said a word about what would happen if Caleb changed his mind. Not one person believed he would.

Sitting at the top of the rise, they stared down at a town basking in the warm glow of the evening sun. Heather gripped the saddle horn, her chest squeezing, stomach churning. Her future lay spread out in front of her and she couldn't wait to grasp it.

Quinn looked at her, his eyes crinkling at the corners. "Last chance, lass. Are you certain?"

"Aye. I've never been more certain of anything."

Blaine let out a loud whoop. "Then let's be getting to it."

Caleb sat at the round table, cards in his hands, a glass of whiskey in front of him. A curly-haired redhead stood behind him, her hands massaging his shoulders, hoping her ministrations would result in more from the man who'd all but ignored her since arriving in town.

She leaned down, her warm breath brushing across his cheek. "Can I get you another drink, honey?"

"No, I'm good for now." Rolling his shoulders, he did what he could to shrug off her hands without being rude. He just wanted some time to himself, a couple drinks, and a few hands of cards before returning to the ranch he'd agreed to buy. His ranch. A slight smile curved the corners of his mouth.

Loud voices and the sound of boots pounding on the wood floor had heads turning to the door.

"I told you we'd find the lad in here, Quinn."

Caleb dropped his cards, jumping to his feet. "Blaine, Quinn. What the..." His words died when a third person walked inside. Even wearing men's clothes, he couldn't miss the luscious curves that kept him up at night.

Walking past his friends' outstretched hands, he stopped in front of Heather. Settling fisted hands on his hips, he glared at her. "What the hell are you doing here?"

She stepped back, her confidence faltering at his harsh words. Licking her lips, she lifted her chin. "I came to see you."

His lips twisted as he stared at her. "We said all we had to say, Heather MacLaren. You were given a choice. You made a decision. Enough said."

"I'm not remembering it that way, Caleb Stewart."

He leaned down, his face beginning to heat. "And just how do you remember it?"

From behind them, Quinn looked at the bartender, signaling for two whiskeys. "This is going to be good."

"I remember some miscreant implying I'm some type of pampered princess, then giving me *one minute* to be deciding whether to ride off with this eejit for the rest of my life or stay with my family." She sucked in a breath, her voice increasing in volume as her anger rose. "*One minute* to make a decision, then the eejit rode off and left me standing there." Reaching out, she poked him in the chest. "What kind of man would be doing that?" She poked him again. "What kind of man, Caleb Stewart?"

Blaine sipped his whiskey, nodding. "Aye. This was worth the ride."

Caleb gritted his teeth. "Stop it, Heather."

She crossed her arms. "Stop what, Caleb? Touching you, loving you, wanting a future with you? What should I stop? Because I've had a week to make my choice and I choose you."

He rocked back on his heels, his jaw going slack. "What?" he breathed out.

Dropping her arms to her sides, she clasped her hands together, too afraid to wrap them around his neck like she wanted. "You gave me a choice. You or my family. I choose you, Caleb Stewart. If you're still wanting me."

A second, then two, then three passed, the entire saloon quiet as a church on Sunday morning before

Caleb wrapped his arms around her, twirling her in a circle, whooping at the top of his lungs.

"Oh, darlin', I want you. I've always wanted you. I love you, Heather MacLaren, and I choose you."

Epilogue

Three days later...

"I now pronounce you man and wife. Caleb Stewart, you may now kiss your bride." The reverend stepped away, a smile spreading across his face as the groom swept Heather into his arms. Unmindful of the surprised faces on the few guests, he gave her a smoldering kiss, holding her longer than necessary, until he heard the unmistakable sound of Quinn clearing his throat.

Loosening his grip, Caleb set her aside, keeping his arm wrapped possessively around her. "I love you, Mrs. Stewart," he whispered against her ear, nipping at it once before straightening.

The reverend stepped up to them. "I now present Mr. and Mrs. Caleb Stewart."

A round of applause ensued, followed by whoops and hollers, as well as the familiar MacLaren war cry, which echoed within the almost empty church in Settlers Valley.

After Caleb made a surprise marriage proposal inside the saloon, Heather refused to return to Circle M, which meant Quinn and Blaine refused to leave Settlers Valley. A hasty telegram culminated in Audrey, Bram, Kyla, Ewan, Lorna, Emma, and

Geneen making the journey north for the ceremony performed by a reluctant preacher. When his wife not only insisted he marry the couple, but offered to make a cake and give them a reception, the soft-spoken man had no choice.

The reverend's wife stepped into the aisle, motioning toward a table in the front corner. "Everyone is welcome to refreshments." She walked past them, knowing they'd all follow.

Audrey slid her arm through her daughter's, tears of joy streaming down her face. "You'll be staying here then, lass?"

"Aye, Ma." Heather glanced behind her, seeing Caleb surrounded by MacLaren men.

"It's a lovely ranch Caleb is buying, Heather. The lad made a good decision." Lorna, Ewan's wife, stood on her other side.

"Uncle Ewan made it possible, Aunt Lorna."

"Aye, but the lad took the chance and moved away from a good life. As did you, lass. We're all happy for you."

Ewan had known Archibald Galloway, an elderly rancher, for many years, having met him through a buyer in San Francisco. A widower with no children or other family, Archie had several hundred acres on the Feather River, a large house, barn, bunkhouse, and small foreman's house.

With no heirs, he'd planned leave it to the man who'd helped him run the ranch for years.

Unfortunately, the foreman died of a sudden illness the year before, and none of the ranch hands had the commitment to take on such a large spread. At almost eighty, Archie needed a solution. He'd begun an exchange with Ewan, hoping the MacLarens would have an interest. His friend had been honest. They were stretched to their limit, but he had offered an idea.

The arrangement was simple. Allow a close MacLaren family friend to make a modest down payment, working off the rest of the agreed upon price out of the profits from the ranch. Archie would continue to live in the main house, while Caleb lived in the foreman's place.

After meeting Heather, Archie had insisted on one change—the couple must live in the main house after they married.

"It's a beautiful house, Heather. You'll have it fixed the way you want it in no time at all." Geneen stood beside her, looking better than she had in months.

She wore a beautiful green cotton dress, her deep red hair twisted into a complicated knot with tendrils softening her face, her green eyes sparkling. Heather found herself wishing Nate could see Geneen today, knowing the man would regret his decision to walk out of her life.

"You mean *we'll* be having it fixed up in no time, lass." She put an arm around Geneen's shoulders and squeezed. "I'm so glad you've decided to stay with us for a while."

Geneen looked out the door of the church, a wistful smile on her face. "It's time for a change. You and Caleb moving here is the perfect opportunity. Settlers Valley is such a beautiful place, and I know you'll need a friend in your new town—at least for a while."

Heather touched her arm. "You know, lass, you're welcome to stay as long as you want."

Geneen started to reply, stopping when the reverend's wife spoke up.

"Mr. and Mrs. Stewart." She motioned them to the table. "Are you ready to cut the cake?"

Taking Heather's hand, Caleb leaned close. "I'm ready for more than cake." Kissing her cheek, he chuckled when he saw her face flush.

"Caleb, you'll not be saying such things in church," she hissed, her mouth curving into a sweet smile.

"But I can be thinking about them, right?"

She groaned when he kissed her neck, then wrapped an arm around her, escorting her to the table.

Unable to hear the exchange, Audrey swiped a tear from her cheek. "They look so bonny together, Kyla. I'll be missing them both so much."

Taking Audrey's hand in hers, Kyla nodded. "I'll ride up here with you anytime you want, lass.

Quinn, Bram, and Blaine stood off to the side, quietly passing around a flagon of whiskey.

"What will we be doing about Black Jolly?" Bram asked, turning to the side so the reverend wouldn't see him take a sip, handing the flagon to Quinn.

"Brodie's doing all he can. I wish we knew who the woman was and if she left with him. I don't like the idea of someone spying on us." Watching as the reverend took a bite of cake while listening to Ewan, Quinn took a quick sip before passing the whiskey to Blaine.

"They'll be making a mistake and get caught. Outlaws like them always do." Blaine shook the flask, sneering at them before drinking the last of the whiskey.

Leaning against a doorway on the side of the church, a shadowed figure watched as people he knew, friends from his past, laughed and celebrated. His gut twisted, knowing how much he'd missed. A bitterness crept through him when he thought about the irony of seeing them so far north in a town where he'd escaped to forget his failures.

His breath caught, chest squeezing when his gaze landed on his biggest failure of all. She stood next to Emma, not thirty feet away, her stunning beauty reminding him of how weak a man he'd become. The steps he'd taken to regain the man he'd left behind now seemed insignificant when compared to what he'd need to do to win her back. Looking at her standing close to Emma, a smile lighting her glowing face, he realized he had little chance of winning her love a second time.

Without thought, he rubbed the rounded stump below his left elbow, wondering what his life would be like if he hadn't been standing in the exact path of the Confederate cannon blast. Shaking his head, he rid himself of the useless thought.

Looking at Caleb and Heather, Nate couldn't help smiling. They were good people. He was glad they'd finally found the courage to declare their love and come together. Nate wondered if he could ever do the same.

Straightening, he took one more look at the woman who owned his heart, pressed a hand to his aching chest, then turned away, leaving them to their celebration.

Thank you for taking the time to read Heather's Choice. If you enjoyed it, please consider telling your friends or posting a short review. Word of mouth is an author's best friend and much appreciated.

Watch for book six in the MacLarens of Boundary Mountain series, Nate's Destiny.

Please join my reader's group to be notified of my New Releases at:
https://www.shirleendavies.com/contact-me.html

I care about quality, so if you find something in error, please contact me via email at shirleen@shirleendavies.com

About the Author

Shirleen Davies writes romance—historical western romance, contemporary romance, and romantic suspense. She grew up in Southern California, attended Oregon State University, and has degrees from San Diego State University and the University of Maryland. Her passion is writing emotionally charged stories of flawed people who find redemption through love and acceptance. Shirleen has been on numerous bestseller lists and releases several books each year. She now lives with her husband in a beautiful town in northern Arizona.

I love to hear from my readers.

Send me an email: shirleen@shirleendavies.com
Visit my Website: www.shirleendavies.com
Sign up to be notified of New Releases:
www.shirleendavies.com
Check out all of my Books:
http://www.shirleendavies.com/books.html
Comment on my Blog:
http://www.shirleendavies.com/blog.html
Follow me on Amazon:
http://www.amazon.com/author/shirleendavies
Follow my on BookBub:
https://www.bookbub.com/authors/shirleen-davies

Other ways to connect with me:

Facebook Author Page:
http://www.facebook.com/shirleendaviesauthor
Twitter: www.twitter.com/shirleendavies
Pinterest: http://pinterest.com/shirleendavies
Instagram:
https://www.instagram.com/shirleendavies_author/
Google Plus:
https://plus.google.com/+ShirleenDaviesAuthor

Books by Shirleen Davies

Historical Western Romance Series

MacLarens of Fire Mountain

Tougher than the Rest, Book One
Faster than the Rest, Book Two
Harder than the Rest, Book Three
Stronger than the Rest, Book Four
Deadlier than the Rest, Book Five
Wilder than the Rest, Book Six

Redemption Mountain

Redemption's Edge, Book One
Wildfire Creek, Book Two
Sunrise Ridge, Book Three
Dixie Moon, Book Four
Survivor Pass, Book Five
Promise Trail, Book Six
Deep River, Book Seven
Courage Canyon, Book Eight
Forsaken Falls, Book Nine, Coming next in the series!

MacLarens of Boundary Mountain

Colin's Quest, Book One,
Brodie's Gamble, Book Two
Quinn's Honor, Book Three
Sam's Legacy, Book Four
Heather's Choice, Book Five
Nate's Destiny, Coming next in the series!

Contemporary Romance Series

MacLarens of Fire Mountain

Second Summer, Book One
Hard Landing, Book Two
One More Day, Book Three
All Your Nights, Book Four
Always Love You, Book Five
Hearts Don't Lie, Book Six
No Getting Over You, Book Seven
'Til the Sun Comes Up, Book Eight
Foolish Heart, Book Nine
Forever Love, Book Ten, Coming next in the series!

Peregrine Bay

Reclaiming Love, Book One, A Novella
Our Kind of Love, Book Two

Burnt River

Shane's Burden, Book One by Peggy Henderson
Thorn's Journey, Book Two by Shirleen Davies
Aqua's Achilles, Book Three by Kate Cambridge
Ashley's Hope, Book Four by Amelia Adams
Harpur's Secret, Book Five by Kay P. Dawson
Mason's Rescue, Book Six by Peggy L. Henderson
Del's Choice, Book Seven by Shirleen Davies
Watch for more books in this series!

Find all of my books at:
https://www.shirleendavies.com/books.html

The best way to stay in touch is to subscribe to my newsletter. Go to *www.shirleendavies.com* and subscribe in the box at the top of the right column that asks for your email. You'll be notified of new books before they are released, have chances to win great prizes, and receive other subscriber-only specials.

Avalanche Ranch Press, LLC
PO Box 12618
Prescott, AZ 86304